LAURI
KUBUITSILE

REVELATIONS

Revelations

First Published in Great Britain in 2020 by
LOVE AFRICA PRESS
103 Reaver House, 12 East Street, Epsom KT17 1HX
www.loveafricapress.com

LOVE AFRICA
PRESS
African Love Stories

ISBN: 9781916362864
Also available as ebook

ACKNOWLEDGEMENTS

I would like to thank the board of the El Gouna Writers' Residency (Egypt) who gave me space and time in 2010 to finish the rough draft for this novel. Such gifts are invaluable for a writer.

Revelations

CHAPTER ONE

She saw it right away.

The transparent blue scarf fluttered in the morning breeze trying to get free, stuck as it was on a branch at the bottom of the hedge.

When Elizabeth spotted it, she sucked in a sharp breath. Had Ditiro seen it on his way out that morning? Had her husband spotted the scarf; did he finally know? Know that everything they'd built was a lie; that she held awful secrets that ate at her without rest? Had the scarf finally revealed everything?

Imagining for a moment it had, she felt scared at first, and then, strangely, relief. She would be relieved if it all became known. She was not made for secrets; keeping this one was taking its toll on her. Though she knew once it was known everything would fall apart, she wondered if that might not be for the better.

A dry updraft of winter air flipped the end of the chiffon scarf up and caught the far edge of it on a higher branch. It flicked back and forth in an attempt to be let free, but to no avail. It was caught—completely now with no chance of freedom.

It came from him. He had taken to leaving markers, like a dog defining its territory. She was always on the lookout, ready to grab them up and hide them from her husband's eyes.

"What's your favourite colour?" he'd asked that night.

"Blue ... cerulean, actually. The colour of the Botswana sky. Why?"

"Just curious."

He'd obviously stored the information for later, to be used when standing in a shop trying to choose a scarf to leave for her at her gate, one she would see blowing in the cool morning air after her husband had passed it on his way to work. She shivered when she considered the forethought involved.

She walked to the hedge and unhooked the scarf from where it had been caught. She opened the lid of the rubbish bin and dropped it inside. It lay bright and welcoming among the curled orange peels and coffee grounds.

She didn't like leaving it like that. It shouldn't stay in there full of such jubilant colour; it didn't seem right. She reached in and grabbed the edge of a soggy newspaper deep down in the bin and flipped the lot over so that the scarf was lost in the rubbish, its colour soiled and ruined by what surrounded it.

It was gone. He was gone. At least, for now. But despite her desperate wishes for it all to stop, it wouldn't until he decided he was finished with her. She'd begged him so many times to leave her alone, but he continued—she was at his mercy.

In the meantime, she would have to remain on the lookout. She'd have to get to the phone first each time it rang. She'd have to look for his signs and remove them before her husband could somehow piece it all together. She had to be vigilant. She had to be thorough.

It was unlikely Ditiro had seen the scarf, though. No secrets would be revealed just yet. It had been placed for her eyes only. Ditiro's mind, full of his clients and cases, his busy schedule of court dates and high-profile meetings, made room for little else. A cerulean scarf caught in the bush had no place in his life. Her husband didn't notice such things.

She would not be caught out today; her secret was safe, at least for now. She stared down at the thin piece of soiled blue and dropped the dustbin's lid in place.

***

It had been a normal morning; a typical start to the day. Already, the summer heat spiced the morning air as she rushed to get herself and Lorato ready. Ironing Lorato's school uniform fresh from the clothesline, searching for a lost sock under the bed. They sat down to breakfast in their usual harried morning way.

"I'll be late today, I have a meeting with MmaDora," Ditiro said.

He sat down at the breakfast table in front of his laptop to read the online news. His clients included the president and many of the cabinet ministers, and news that happened overseas while he slept could often change the course of his day. He sipped his coffee and ate the croissant the Zimbabwean maid, Precious, had set down in front of him, without acknowledgment from him, as he raced through the day's headlines.

Elizabeth put Lorato into her tall chair and pushed it up to the table. Precious set a bowl of porridge in front of the small girl.

"Here, my baby," Precious said in the soft voice required of good domestic help.

"Ke a leboga, mma," Lorato said.

Elizabeth smiled. She would not let Lorato grow up thinking Precious was her servant, despite how Ditiro behaved. Precious was an employee of their household; it was her job. She was not anyone's aunty or anyone's slave. Elizabeth's working-class background balked at having domestic help, but Ditiro's insistence that they buy a five-bedroom house in the prestigious Phakalane suburb meant unless she gave up her own career to care for the mansion they now owned, a maid was mandatory.

Elizabeth sat down opposite Ditiro. "So, are you in court today?"

"No," he said without looking up.

"Don't forget Wednesday we have that thing at Lorato's school."

"Did you tell Lucilla like I told you to? If you tell Lucilla, then I'll be there, she'll put it in the diary. If you don't, I won't."

Elizabeth would not fight with him this morning, she reminded herself. "Yes, I told her."

"Then why are we discussing this now? If you told Lucilla, it's on my schedule. I'll be there." For the first time since she'd come into the kitchen, he looked up at her, but his eyes were full of impatience. "Is there anything else? I really want to read this before I have to leave."

She shook her head and blinked to try to stop the tears threatening to fall. She didn't want to upset Lorato. Besides, she'd cried enough. So many lonely days and even lonelier nights.

Ditiro was so far away from her, right there but so far. She sometimes thought if only they hadn't once been so close, if only she didn't love him so much. Then his distance wouldn't affect her as it did. She wouldn't feel it so deep. She would be able to take his curt replies. She'd never thought it would come to the point where she wished she loved Ditiro less.

That day at university when they first met, it was his eyes that had captured her. They flashed with such sharp intelligence. When he smiled, she said to herself, *this is the man I will marry*. She still remembered that, before he even spoke a word, she knew he was the man who would be her husband. She grew up a practical girl not pulled by fairies and stories about princesses, so she was the most surprised that such a thing happened to her. Love at first sight—what a silly notion. But it had happened; she had fallen in love with Ditiro as soon as she'd seen him. But she'd kept it a secret. She'd never told anybody. Not even him.

She hadn't known anything about him at the time. She hadn't known he was from a tiny country halfway across the world, and if she wanted to be his wife, she would have to follow him there. She hadn't yet realised his love for the law was his first wife and she'd have to take second seat. She hadn't known any of that, but in the crazy, wild clouds of first love, none of those practical hitches had meant anything.

At first, all they'd wanted was each other. He would accompany her through endless art galleries even though he knew nothing about art. She'd wait for him outside of the law firm where he clerked in the icy cold of a Midwest winter just so they could have those few extra minutes together walking back to his flat. When they could, they'd lie in bed for hours trying to learn every inch of the other one both inside and out. There had been nothing else but them.

When she got to know him, there had been even more to fall in love with in Ditiro. One thing was his way of thinking. It was so odd, Elizabeth sometimes listened to him like an anthropologist might listen to a member of a tribe only recently discovered. Despite its oddness and her belief that it was almost certainly flawed, she found his way of thinking and his approach to life comforting.

His beliefs were supported by his profession. Law was where Ditiro found the certainties his life's philosophy required. He didn't believe in grey. Grey issues were for people who hadn't worked hard enough, who'd given up along the way before the answer could be discovered. He believed if you looked long enough, through the laws and the case precedents, you would find the simple line that separated the correct answer from the incorrect one. There were no exceptions.

He applied this same reasoning to his life. Everything was rational in his world. Things operated by cause and effect. All problems had a solution. His thinking was the direct opposite to Elizabeth's.

For her, there was never a correct answer. The problem was always there lurking in the back like a hungry monster waiting for a passing, unsuspecting meal. Effects didn't always have causes. Shit just sometimes happened—it's how it was. She lived in a constant grey cloud where answers were fluid and situational and finding the way always problematic.

She fell in love with Ditiro's confident, just world. She suspected its fairy tale properties would fall away at some point, but she had hope it might hang on long enough, maybe very long, and on her best days, forever. She began to believe that Ditiro, just by his absolute faith in his life's philosophy, would keep her safe and on the right road, that things could be predictable and normal, as long as she kept by his side. She gave up her world and climbed into his because it was so much nicer there.

Once they were married and they moved to Botswana, she gave up everything. Elizabeth was wiped away; she was Mma Molosiwa, Ditiro's wife. The cost of her new life turned out to be very high.

Ditiro's job in the Attorney General's office kept him away for twelve to fifteen hours a day. Once he was home, there was no time for talking. If she was lucky, they'd have quick, frantic maintenance sex before he fell asleep. He'd often be awake and gone before she opened her eyes the next morning.

She was in a strange country where she knew no one. She was white and almost everyone else black, making her an obvious, identifiable outsider. She couldn't tolerate the arrogance of the expat community and their self-imposed isolation from Batswana, but couldn't seem to make any headway into the local, black community. Black Batswana were friendly to a point and then nothing more. Her whiteness stood like a brick wall between them. It defined her, nothing else. As if her entire self had been wiped away. No one could see her anymore.

She was making no friends and finding it impossible to understand her new home. Her husband was lost in his work, and she was so lonely.

When they'd first arrived, she'd set up the spare room in their two-bedroom flat to use as a studio for her painting. She'd spent the mornings walking around Gaborone sketching and learning the city. In the afternoons, she would paint. But her work was troubled; she couldn't get anything right. How could she put her thoughts and feelings on the canvas when she no longer existed?

She felt disconnected and distracted by the distance from Ditiro, which seemed to be growing, and the distance from her new home and the country that wouldn't let her in. She was like a ghost haunting no man's land.

Botswana was hot and dusty, so unlike her home of rolling cornfields growing high above her head. The trees were stingy with shade. She had thought such things didn't matter to her, but she missed the easily greened Midwest of America. Plants and people didn't need to fight for something free such as rain or shade.

Here, she could feel plants clamouring for the limited water, desperate for any moisture. Even a man urinating on its trunk would do. The neediness seeped off into the people. Most, always on the edge of disaster; poverty in a land floating on diamonds. It all looked lovely on paper, an African success story, but on the ground, something else spoke the truth.

Elizabeth was torn by what to do. How did you pass the suffering in Old Naledi, the glue-sniffing boys in the parking lot of The President's Hotel? You, on your way to the terrace for hundred-Pula-scones and tea. It all seemed so mean and bitter. She felt it pour over her, seep into her through her pores. She could not ignore it—it was taking up residence in her body, filling the vacuum there.

She found herself scrounging. Grabbing and holding tight. Looking for something she needed, but not quite being able to find it. Always hungry. She felt the tension build, the resentment. The old Elizabeth was not like this. This new one held everything tightly, jealously guarding and protecting even things she shouldn't. Angered by other people's needs, resentful of other people's successes. She seethed over nothing and blamed Ditiro for it all. He had brought her to this horrible place. He had wiped her away without a second thought. Nothing about her mattered; nothing was worth saving. She should fit in and shut up.

She'd complained to him that she needed a life, too. He was not around, and she needed to meet people and make friends. He'd listen but did nothing, changed nothing about his life to accommodate her.

Tiring of hearing her complaints, he'd suggested she open a gallery. She could paint as well as help Batswana artists with a place to sell their pieces, something very rare in the city. She liked the idea. It seemed like something that would get her out of the terrible place she'd found herself.

As soon as she started looking for a place to rent, she felt better. Action had always been her way of dealing with things. Ditiro knew exactly how to help her. He always knew the answer when it came to licenses and contracts for premises. They grew closer working on the project together, and Elizabeth was happy again. Maybe she could have a life of her own here. Maybe that would help with the problem between her and Ditiro.

The gallery was a great way to get connected with the local art scene. She discovered people with similar interests. She still wished she had more time with Ditiro, but he promised things would get better. His plan was to build up a reputation at the Attorney General's office as a hard worker who won complicated cases. He needed to put in the time now to get the benefits later. He wanted to eventually leave the government and set up his own practice.

Soon, he was given high-profile corruption cases and murder dockets. His name was commonplace in the newspapers and in the households around Botswana. If pushed to name a lawyer they respected, most Batswana named Ditiro Molosiwa. He was confident, never arrogant, honest, and completely committed to fair justice. Batswana respected him.

The gallery also grew. It was never profitable, but people began to view it as the place to get cutting edge artwork from Batswana artists. Elizabeth was pleased with this, but her own work was not progressing. She'd done a series of oils on Old Naledi that had raised some interest and were eventually bought by an art collector in South Africa, but since then, she couldn't seem to finish anything.

Her studios at home and at the gallery were full of half-finished canvases and books and books of sketches. She still couldn't get comfortable; something was missing. She felt neutered of feeling, insulated, and distanced from her home and the people around her. She sometimes felt scared for her sanity. She was sure she was suffering from some sort of depression. She'd sort herself out, though. She'd come right. She just needed to find the root cause of what was bothering her.

Many of the black artists still viewed her as their patron instead of their partner because of her skin colour. She couldn't push past the colour barrier to get to real connections. She wanted to engage with other artists, to discuss what the work meant, how they could do things together. They came to her for answers, when she only wanted to talk to them about questions.

Many of the white Batswana artists looked down on her for being married to a black man. Most were raised by Apartheid-era white South African parents or British neo-colonialists, and they couldn't let go of their inherited racist attitudes. She often wished everyone was colourless. She even wished sometimes she was black. If she were black, colour would disappear, at least for her black associates, and maybe they could become friends, finally.

Somehow, she found it more troubling that, with the gallery, she was surrounded by people all day, but still had no close friends and was perhaps lonelier than when she walked the streets of Gaborone and painted in their flat by herself. She couldn't see any way to break through, and it frustrated her.

In the end, the breakthrough would not be from her or Ditiro. It was a gift carried along with their daughter Lorato. She gave her a purpose and drive Elizabeth hadn't had since her days at university where she was once described as 'an exciting up and coming painter.' Lorato gave her the role of mother, and for a while, that was what she needed.

Elizabeth took a sip of her coffee and looked at her husband across the breakfast table. He was still handsome, his eyes still passionate and fierce, but she never felt the passion directed at her anymore. Though he was less than a metre away, he could have been on another planet, so far apart they'd grown.

"What time is the meeting with MmaDora?"

"We're meeting at the State House at seven." He didn't look up from the laptop.

"Seven? Don't you remember I'm going to Francistown to collect the pieces for Ludo's show? I won't be back until tomorrow."

She tried to hide her annoyance about his forgetfulness. The details of her life didn't interest him, even something as important as a new show at the gallery. Elizabeth was excited about Ludo's sculptures, and she had been speaking about them for weeks. Ditiro had obviously heard nothing.

He looked up from the computer. She'd finally gotten his attention.

"So I should cancel a scheduled meeting with the First Lady because you won't be home? Precious is here. She can take care of things."

Elizabeth wouldn't fight him, she reminded herself again, not in front of Lorato and the maid. They'd had the same discussion so many times before, so he knew how she felt. She didn't want her daughter raised by the maid like most of the children in their wealthy suburb of Phakalane.

"Well, there's nothing that can be done now," she said. "I'll get back as early tomorrow as I can. You'll send a car to collect her from school, then?"

Ditiro closed the laptop and stood up. He picked his jacket from the back of the chair and quickly slipped it on, then packed up the laptop and grabbed his briefcase. "Yes, I won't forget."

He kissed her on the lips. A dry, perfunctory kiss with no meaning, and then kissed Lorato on the cheek.

"See you later, Pumpkin-face. I'll have Rex bring you by the office before he takes you home. Maybe we can get an ice cream in town before my meeting."

"Okay, Daddy."

Lorato smiled up at her father, her god, her king. Elizabeth wished she could still feel that way about him and felt envious of her daughter's naiveté.

***

When she thought of it now, that day seemed dreamlike. Botswana was a land of huge blues skies and flat, dusty, brown landscapes, but the images of that day were red, dashed with violent, bold slashes of black in her memory. Red and black with sharp edges and a reckless, dangerous feel.

The morning and Ditiro's forgetting about her trip and the show had angered her. She knew everything about his life, which decided the course of hers. He treated the gallery as nothing more than a hobby for her to keep busy so he could get on with important things.

Sometimes, she wanted to shake him and shout, "Look at me! Look. See me. I am here." She felt so invisible, so insignificant.

When she left Gaborone, heading towards Francistown on the A1, she was furious. But she didn't know for certain at whom, but she was so angry, her knuckles had pulled white on the steering wheel she gripped so hard.

She was angry at Ditiro, of course. She was angry he wouldn't miss her when she slept away in a hotel bed in Francistown. She thought he might even be relieved since he could work through the night if he wanted to, not feeling guilty leaving her alone in their bed as she wouldn't be there.

She was angry that he spent the bare minimum of time with Lorato, but yet, he was the one Lorato preferred. Elizabeth was the task master. She was the one who had to make sure school work was done and baths were taken, teeth were brushed. He was the one who took her for ice cream.

She was angry she was living in this country where no one would ever see her as anything except white. She would be white first. Everything about her would first be described from the perspective of her colour. Colour was mandatory, pre-eminent in this part of the continent. The brutal history of colonialism precluded all else.

Botswana's neighbour's Apartheid system and the toxic thinking behind it spilled over the border freely. Batswana men who worked in South African mines knew how the system worked. The whites who crossed the border to take advantage of Botswana's varied natural resources also came tainted with the tenets of the system. White and black were colours of importance, definitions of a person. She could be Lorato's mother, but always described as Lorato's 'white' mother. She would forever, always, until she died or she fled for relief, be Ditiro's *white* wife.

When she stood before a canvas, what she painted there was not hers. She didn't understand it; it remained flat and two-dimensional, because she was not there. She'd been erased from her own life. Where she'd gone, she didn't know, but she was absent. Elizabeth was angry she'd let herself get to this point. She was Lorato's mother, Ditiro's wife. She was no longer Elizabeth; she'd left herself behind with all of the other baggage when she got on the plane to Botswana. Where was she? Where was Elizabeth?

Her anger distracted her as she drove, and the road disappeared behind her, the kilometres lost in her rage. Soon, she was leaving Palapye, nearly halfway. Over the railway tracks and she switched to fifth gear, preparing for the last long stretch to Francistown, but then, she braked. A young man stood on the side of the road, hitching. He was alone.

She never picked up hitchhikers. But that morning, she stopped.

In her memory, he stands, as if he'd been waiting for her all day. An air of entitlement surrounds him. Where had she been? Why did she keep him waiting for so long? He opens the passenger door and gets in without asking.

"I'm going to Francistown."

She doesn't know what she's doing. She can't understand why she has stopped, why this young man is getting in her car. He buckles himself in and looks at her expectantly. She's confused by what she's done, and now can't see what the next step might be. She's frozen.

He helps her. "We can go."

The reddish tinge persists as she pulls the car onto the empty road. Her anger subsides and she's not sure why— or at least that's what she tells herself.

CHAPTER TWO

"So what's your name?" Elizabeth asks him.

He wears a checked, flat-topped hat, old-fashioned for such a young man, but he wears it as a statement on his tidy dreadlocks. With his dress, he tells the world he is not like the others, the herds of young men Botswana seems full of. All eager to be successful. Beautiful in their youthfulness and energy. He wants to step away from them. He will make a new path, one that is his alone.

"I'm Tumelo. And you?"

He is not recognising their age difference in his language; she suspects he's about twenty-two or so, making a gap of nearly twenty years between them. If she were a black Motswana, there would be no "*and you?*" He would use respectful words. But there is no need here. She is an outsider; he will decide how he proceeds with no societal ropes reining him in.

"Elizabeth," she says.

He smiles at her, and the hard face he's cultivated during his rehearsals for being a man disappears and she can see that of a baby, the one his mother helped to walk on his bowed baby legs not that long before.

"Elizabeth. That's a nice name. What do you do, Elizabeth?"

"I'm a painter."

"A painter? In a car like this?"

"My husband is a lawyer. He's quite successful." She feels awkward talking about her husband to this stranger in her car. "So, Tumelo, I suppose you have a girlfriend?"

He laughs again. "Girlfriend? I'm only twenty-three. I don't have time for the stress of a girlfriend. They want time and money, and I've got things to do. I hang with a few girls, nothing serious." He looks at her. "What about you? Any boyfriends?"

She laughs though she doesn't intend to—it bursts from her pushed by the crazy thought that she might have a boyfriend. It would be like her keeping a camel or driving race cars. That's a life for someone else, not her.

"No. I told you I'm married."

"So, what does that matter?"

He's not being cheeky; he appears to truly not understand, but she keeps quiet. She's not interested in explaining anything to him.

"You're hot. Lots of guys must be after you."

She keeps quiet and drives. She thinks if she doesn't speak somehow, everything will not go wrong, although she feels the momentum building. It's gaining speed and will soon be past the point of no return. It will soon be too late to stop anything, but still, she makes no effort and instead watches as if she's not part of it.

He laughs, and she turns her eyes from the road to glance at him. He is looking down at himself, at his lap, between his legs.

"God, just thinking about you and how hot you are, and I've got a hard on. Look."

He's like a child with a toy. A dangerous toy he doesn't really understand how to use yet. She grips the wheel tighter and looks ahead, nervous. She doesn't know what to do. Everything is blurry and ill-defined. She can't see why things are moving so fast, and yet, her breath is slow and steady. The road ahead has gone narrow.

Tumelo reaches over and runs his hand from her knee to the top of her thigh, pushing her skirt up as he goes.

What is happening here?

She doesn't stop him. She knows everything is wrong. It feels good what he's doing, and she won't make him stop. Her anger surges again. Fuck them. Fuck everything. Everything outside of this car. Outside of this moment.

She can see he has unzipped his pants and has taken his penis out. He rubs it slowly with one hand, and his other moves softly up and down her inner thigh. She can't concentrate on the road. She struggles to breathe.

She's pulled off. She's driving in towards the bush away from the highway. It's a dirt road, and instead of stopping near the A1, she drives deeper, away from other cars. She doesn't know why she does it, at least that's what she tells herself. She's just doing, not thinking.

Tumelo has unbuckled his seat belt and is next to her. He has pushed her long hair back and is kissing her neck. He holds his hard penis in his hand, moving his grip up and down its length slowly. She parks the car under the shade of a straggly mophane tree, in a place not easily seen from the road nor from the fields on the other side.

She unbuckles her seatbelt and leans over, taking his penis into her mouth. Everything is suddenly sharp and certain. Everything is exactly what they are doing; nothing else exists. It is like she has burst from a fog and is suddenly wide, wide awake. She feels everything.

His penis is hard and smooth in her mouth. His hand on her breast is rough, her clit singing with each squeeze. He's pushed her skirt up, and she feels the leather under her bare bum, his breath on her neck, hears the birds out the window, the cars passing in the distance, her groans. She is there. She is finally right there.

After years of being in Botswana, now in this hot car on the side of the road, with this stranger, little more than a boy, she is feeling herself. Herself only. She is not wife. She is not mother. She is not white. Everything else about her falls to the background, the light dimmed so as not to attract attention. She is Elizabeth only now. Again. Nothing else. What she's doing, what she's feeling, is lit with a red laser spot. Defined and sharp. And it is only her. She was lost, and now? Now, she is found.

Everything is raw and rough and they can't seem to stop. They are out of the car. He pulls the buttons of her blouse open and pushes up her bra. He bites and sucks at her breasts, grabbing them in his fists. He pulls her to him with more strength than his tall, thin body might have indicated. He kisses her deeply, roughly, holding her by the hair, directing what he wants from her. He bites her tongue, and she tastes the metallic of her own blood.

He turns her over—she stands leaning over the car seat, her feet on the ground. He forces himself into her, ramming her. Her face pushes into the leather, and she screams out in pain. It's wonderful, and she feels fully alive.

She's desperate for the feelings, whatever they are, to continue. Pain is as good as pleasure. He stops and leans on her for a minute. She feels his wet, limp penis slip out of her, and she turns around to face him. He's no longer that boy playing at being a man. She's changed, but so has he. He opens the back door and pushes her inside. He's rough, but she's not fearful. Every push, every scratch, every tear is welcomed.

He pushes her back onto the seat, and her head knocks against the case of her laptop. As she notices one of Lorato's storybooks on the floor under the front seat, he bends down and starts licking her. He slowly builds up. He is wild; he sucks at her clitoris, and she can feel the orgasm building, all of her body focusing only on his actions. Just before she's about to come, he climbs on top of her and enters, knocking against the side of her vagina, his knee stepping on her inner thigh. His hand still rubs her, and she orgasms, one after another, as he rams himself deep into her.

They get back into the car, without speaking, and drive to Francistown. She checks into the hotel, and Tumelo follows her into the room. There is no discussion; it is assumed. She owes him, she guesses. New definitions live within the walls of the hotel room. She is woman, simple and clean. A sexual being with orifices to be filled and pleasure to be experienced. He is adept. She lets him lead her everywhere he wants. She is only thankful to be finally herself and finally feeling.

***

She wakes in the night and sees Tumelo sitting by the window in the dark, looking out onto the empty Francistown streets below. He turns to her when she sits up to pour water from a nearby pitcher into a glass.

"I like being here," he says like a boy, and she flinches, remembering suddenly that he is that nearly. She doesn't respond. "I've never slept in a hotel. It's nice." He looks back out the window. "One day, I'll sleep in hotels anytime I want. I'm going to be famous one day. Rich and famous."

She smiles at his dream, so limited, so naive.

He turns and looks at her lying back on the bed. His face is slashed with anger, and his words carry it outward.

"You don't believe me. No one does. But I'm different. I'm someone special."

"I never said anything," Elizabeth says. "How could I? I don't even know you. I know nothing about you. Perhaps you'll be rich and famous, who am I to say?"

"I'm at university, but it's bullshit. A waste of my time. I need to get going. None of us has unlimited time."

Elizabeth looks at his shadowed profile against the window. The residue of what they've done still lingers. In some way, she is thankful for him, this arrogant young man who knows nothing about life, who thinks wishes come true, who believes fame is a good thing, that sleeping in a hotel is happiness. Because she is grateful still, she does not dash his hopes. She keeps silent and lets him think what he wants without her truth squashing it to its correct proportions.

He talks more about how he is not like others, about how there is a destiny for him, a great one, already written. The vanilla-basted words, bland and of no real value, of so many self-help books and motivational gurus. Like muzak in an elevator, Tumelo drones on as Elizabeth lies back on the bed.

***

She's not sure when she fell asleep. The ringing phone wakes her.

"Hello?" she says into it, confused by where she is and what has happened.

Her mind is unable to reconcile the happenings of the day and night before with the sun streaming though the crack in the heavy hotel curtains. The warm, golden sun she'd always loved had turned to a harsh judge, shining light onto evidence that could not be denied. Then everything is made worse by the voice on the phone.

"Mommy?"

She looks at Tumelo spread naked across the bed, and bitter bile rises up in her throat. What has she done? Who she was yesterday cannot exist in the same world with her being Lorato's mother. She looks around the room. This is what she has done, she tells herself. It is finished. Permanent. A fatal mistake.

"Hi …baby," she says in a forced voice. "Are you off to school then?"

"Daddy bought me ice cream and we're late, so he took me for donuts this morning. I'm talking on his cellphone."

"That's nice." All she wants is to get off the phone. "You have a good day at school. I'll see you when I get home. I love you."

"Okay, Mommy. I love you, too. Daddy wants to talk to you."

She can hear the phone changing hands, and she takes a deep breath to steady herself. She can't do this. She can't talk to Ditiro, not now. She considers hanging up. Tumelo rolls over onto his stomach with a groan.

"Hi, Lizzie. How was the trip?" Ditiro asks in the same voice she knows, unchanged.

It's all confusing. How can that world, her world before yesterday, still carry on as if nothing has changed? She can't see how it will ever be right again, how she can fit back into that life after what she's done. She wants to cry out when she hears his familiar, comforting voice. She can't believe what she has done to him. She wants to confess everything. If she's punished, she thinks, punished harshly, mercilessly, she may come back cleansed enough to fit back into those roles: mother and wife.

"Fine ... I'll collect Ludo's pieces this morning. I should be back in time to pick up Lorato from school."

She can hear herself. Her voice is normal, and that frightens her. How can anything be normal now? Somewhere inside, there is an actor, a liar who can step up and run things while she is absent. She's listening in wonder.

"I missed you last night. I thought maybe after Ludo's show, we could go away. Just me and you. Leave Lorato with my mum. What do you think?"

She thinks how she could just say it. She could tell him what she's done. Let him know who she really is. But his voice is so kind, so loving. She can hear that he feels bad about how they left each other. She wants to tell him he needn't bother; he's paid the price many times over, only he doesn't know it yet.

She can feel the tears, but swallows them. God! What had she been thinking? Why had she done this to him?

"Yeah ... sure. That sounds nice. We'll talk when I get back."

She hangs up before he can say anything else. She can't bear it, not here with this man lying next to her. She can't hear the concern in her husband's voice and look at this naked young man lying across the hotel bed.

She shakes him. "Listen, Tumelo, you need to go. I've got work to do, and I need to get back to Gabs."

He sits up in the bed, makes no effort to cover his erection. "Okay, sure."

He walks to the toilet, then comes back and slowly picks up his clothes scattered around the room. When he's dressed, he turns to her. "So, can I get your number?"

"I don't think so." Elizabeth is sitting on the edge of the bed as she has since she hung up the phone. Will she be sick? She thinks she might. She wishes he would go.

"What? So you didn't enjoy yourself?" he asks. "You seemed like you did."

"I did, but ... It was wrong, okay. I'm married. I've got a daughter."

"I get that, but still, you might need company some time. I'll be back in Gabs next week." He sees her phone on the bedside table where she put it. He picks it up and dials. The phone in his pocket rings. He puts her phone back where it was. "I'll call you."

She watches him leave and tries to steady herself. It is over, and everything will go back to normal. *It never happened*, she tells herself, though she feels dirty and sick. She can't believe how she has violated Ditiro's trust in her. She hates herself for it. Did he do anything to justify this? She'd been angry and mixed-up, lost, lost for so long, but how did she get here? How had she let herself get to this place?

In the end, she finds pretending she's the person she no longer is is not as difficult as she imagined.

CHAPTER THREE

She thought about the scarf in the dust bin. She wondered how Tumelo got into the yard without their golden lab, Shumba, barking. Then she remembered they'd had Shumba in the house the night before for a few hours before Lorato had gone to bed. Tumelo must have put the scarf in the bushes then.

Was he watching them? Waiting for a chance to make a move? A chill ran through her at the thought. She knew him better now and knew he could do it. He could watch her every night out in the darkness, waiting for his chance. Nights and nights of sitting in the cold. One thing Tumelo had was close-minded allegiance to a cause. She'd learned that about him since that night in Francistown two months before. She was his current cause, and he was not going to be easily swayed away from her.

In the house, Precious was at the sink finishing breakfast dishes.

"I think I'll do some work in my studio before heading to the gallery," Elizabeth said.

"Okay, Madam."

Elizabeth had asked her not to call her madam, but Precious couldn't seem to get herself to call her employer by her first name, so she had given up on it.

In her studio, she closed the door and dialled Tumelo's number. He answered on the second ring.

"So did you like the scarf?"

"I put it in the dust bin, you fucker! Are you spying on me? Are you watching this house? I swear to God if you do anything … if you touch my daughter … or any of us, I will kill you," she hissed into the phone so Precious wouldn't hear.

"Chill, Lizzie-baby, I'm not into hurting anyone. I was just leaving you a present. A present only. I searched all over for the right colour. Cerulean is a tough colour to find in Gabs. Why don't we meet up today? I have a bit of free time in the afternoon."

He was impervious to her words, oblivious to the situation. No matter how many times she said no, he could not hear it.

"I told you it's over. Why can't you just fucking leave me alone?"

She'd been telling him this for two months nearly every day. He just couldn't get it.

She'd been living with the guilt and constant vigilance for only two months? She found that hard to believe. She was achingly tired from the constant stress of it.

"And don't call me Lizzie. I told you my name is Elizabeth."

He laughed. "But you like it when your hubby, Rre Molosiwa, calls you Lizzie. I thought I'd give it a try."

How did he know that? Where was he getting this information from? Was he following Ditiro, too?

"Don't ever call me that again. Stop phoning me, or I'll …" She struggled. She knew she was impotent. There was nothing she could do. Everywhere she turned was the chance of her adultery being revealed. She had no power to stop him. She couldn't tell anyone without her secret being exposed. She was trapped.

"You'll do what? Call the police? How about tell the President?" He laughed at her. "Bet it won't take long to get back to your dear Ditiro then. I wonder what he would think knowing his wife sucked my cock along the A1. She pulled off the road to give a useless young man like me a blow job. How do you think he'd take that information, Lizzie?"

She could see his arrogant smiling face through the phone.

"What do you want, Tumelo? Is it money? I could give you money if you'd just leave me alone." She sat at her desk, holding her head in her hand, weak from the struggle of it. She couldn't take it anymore. She wanted out.

"I don't want your money, Lizzie. Let's meet up. Just a few hours. So you can get a bit of relief. You know you like what I can do for you, baby."

"Fuck you!"

She hung up. She knew she shouldn't talk to him. It was no use. She wondered why he never thought to blackmail her. She remembered his dream of wanting to stay in hotels. That would have helped him achieve it, at least for a while. But a payoff didn't seem to be enough for Tumelo. He wanted more.

She sat down in the overstuffed chair near the window and lay back trying to get rid of it all. She breathed in and out the way she'd learned in a yoga class she'd once taken at university. She tried to visualise the stress caused by Tumelo leaving her body with each exhale. It wasn't working. The constant strain of what she'd done was affecting her. The guilt made her act crazy, one minute over-attentive to Ditiro and Lorato, the next minute snappy and sharp. She forever looked for the small signs in her that might reveal what she'd done. Did she move differently? Could he notice a change when they had sex? Did the guilt show on her face?

When she found something, like the scarf at the gate, then her mind scanned through all of the possibilities where her secret might have been revealed, over and over. Had Ditiro seen it? If he had, what would he do? Would he know what it meant? It was an insane roller-coaster that she could not get off of.

The familiar turpentine and oil paint smell of the studio calmed her eventually. She liked looking at her unfinished paintings even when struggling with her art as she was now. The potential of a painting excited her. A finished painting was nearly dead to her. Nothing more could be done. And maybe that was her entire problem, the reason why unfinished paintings were scattered everywhere.

She let her head drop back, and she looked out the big window at the wide expanse of lawn in her sunny backyard. Lawn in Botswana was a privilege for the wealthy. They had the right to guzzle more than their share of the limited resources, just like the rich everywhere. It sickened her, but hypocritically, she loved looking out over the greenness. It reminded her of a home left behind.

She knew Tumelo would never go to Ditiro and tell him what happened no matter how much posing he might do. He had nothing to gain by doing that. If he didn't tell him, and she never did, either, Ditiro would never find out.

There was nothing to worry about. Tumelo would eventually get tired of this game and move onto someone else, or something else, and Ditiro would never know. It was a mistake; it had been an accident. Wasn't she entitled to make a mistake? Over time, if she tried hard enough, she would forget all about it. Everything would all go back to normal.

She repeated these things often, in the hope they might be forced to become real, that all what she had done would be wiped away and she would go on with her life scot-free.

***

Though she felt like an outsider in Botswana, she never had any interest in going back to the United States. There was nothing there for her. If she were honest, she'd always felt like an outsider there, too, only the things that set her apart had not been as readily apparent as they were in Botswana.

It had always been only her and her mother. She'd adopted her mother's tagline, "It's us against the world." Though her mother repeated the line often, in the end, she'd never kept the promise it held. One day when the heavy burden of life had been too much, she'd slit her wrists.

Elizabeth had been at university, already dating Ditiro though her mother hadn't met him yet, when she got the call. Her mother's decision to end her life had taught her one thing: Don't count on people; they always let you down.

She was with Ditiro, but a wall of separation stood between them. She loved him, but she never quite trusted that love. Love was tricky and deceiving. People could change the terms in their own heads without informing you, leaving you out in the wind to stumble upon the truth long after it had been decided for you. You needed to make sure you were prepared, or it would tear your heart up. Her mother's suicide had done just that.

Even now with Ditiro and Lorato, she still felt it was her, alone, against the world. Her colour reaffirmed that every day. Ditiro with his smooth, brown skin, and Lorato with hers a few shades lighter, and then Elizabeth, the odd one out. She wondered sometimes if that was the true source of her loneliness and not the place she lived as she tried to tell herself. You can't be alone against the world and together with others. It couldn't work that way. Maybe where she lived played no role at all. Maybe, too, her colour was not the issue. Maybe it was just her. Maybe she was no longer able to let others in; maybe she was broken like that. Sometimes, she thought that was it.

And now, things were worse. Her secret kept her cordoned off even further from Ditiro and Lorato, behind a wall of impenetrable reinforced steel. She was alone in her battle against Tumelo. The walls were growing so tall now, she wondered if love would be able to scale them. She feared it wouldn't. Ditiro would never be able to reach her now, and it was all her fault. She'd made the mistake, and now, she needed to fight the battle, alone, until she won.

CHAPTER FOUR

Ditiro knocked on the thick oak door. He could hear muffled sounds behind, and then one of the President's bodyguards opened it, a tall block of flesh that smiled down at him.

"Dumela, Rre Modise," Ditiro said. "I'm here to see the President."

He knew all of the President's staff. He'd been the family's lawyer since the time the President was the Minister of Justice. When Ditiro left the Attorney General's office and started his own practice, the President became one of his first clients. Having the President of Botswana on your client list helped to ensure any practice's success, it had certainly helped Molosiwa and Associates, and Ditiro was grateful. But beyond that, he considered the President his friend.

"Oh, Ditiro, you're here," President Setlhoboko said from his desk. The Minister of Finance, Mrs. Dithebe, sat opposite him. "Let me finish with this, and I'll be with you just now. Take a seat. Katlego, bring Mr. Molosiwa some tea."

Ditiro sat down on the leather sofa, and the guard went off in search of tea. He wondered what the President needed now. Ditiro had just finished a plea bargain on his daughter's behalf. President Setlhoboko had two daughters, Dora, and Koko, the younger one.

Dora had been in trouble nearly continuously since she became a teenager.

Luckily in Botswana, gossip-mongering of the rich and famous was frowned upon, or else, the newspapers could have had a field day with her. She'd had more DUIs than Ditiro could remember. Once drunk, she liked to throw her weight around, telling anyone who wanted her to behave appropriately, "Do you know who I am?" Most backed off, and if they didn't, she had no problem using her fists to let them understand her point.

Despite Dora's behaviour or maybe because of it since they spent so much time together on her various cases, she and Ditiro had become friends. She had a quick wit and sharp eye for hypocrisy that he appreciated. She also had a serious problem with alcohol in a country where AA and rehabilitation centres were almost unheard of. Once she started drinking, she became the Mr. Hyde to her normal Dr. Jekyll. Dora alone offered Ditiro a lot of work for the firm. The family also had a wide collection of business interests from mining to tourism, and it was his job to keep everything legal.

His tea arrived. He spooned in sugar and thought about his wife. Lately, she'd been so distracted and behaving oddly. He was concerned. He knew mental illness ran in families, and he wondered if it might be time for Elizabeth to get some professional help. She struggled living in Botswana; she couldn't quite find her place, and he felt bad about that. He thought the gallery helped, but he wondered now if it was enough. She'd had a successful show with her latest find, a Francistown sculptor named Ludo Galani. The show had sold out, and for once, the gallery was in the black.

Despite the success, Elizabeth seemed more depressed than ever. He loved his wife and hated to see her suffer so much, but he didn't know what to do to make things better. All he wanted was for her to be happy; it was frustrating not being able to find a way to help her.

"Okay, that looks great," the Minister said, getting up to leave. She turned to Ditiro. "Ditiro, greet that beautiful wife of yours. I always think of her when I look at that painting I bought at her gallery. Who was that artist again?"

"Kolo. Kolo Ntshingane. It's the one of Makgadikgadi, right?"

"Yes, beautiful. I get so many compliments. I'd like to get one of your wife's paintings. When will she have her own show?"

"I'll let you know," he said.

The Minister left, and the President closed the door behind her and indicated Ditiro should take a chair at the desk. He smiled his trademark smile. He was a charismatic man, there was no doubt about that. His friendly, humble way with Batswana had earned him their respect and allegiance. Ditiro knew the smile and his "I'm one of you" attitude was part of the package that was President Setlhoboko.

The real man was far more complex, with a brilliant mind that caught every nick in an argument and, once found, he delved in until his opponent found nothing to hold on to and, left with no option, conceded. He knew the laws of Botswana word for word, hardly ever needing to consult his set of legal books. He was a faithful husband and a good father. He was a man Ditiro respected absolutely.

"So, how is everything going, Ditiro?" the President asked. President Setlhoboko was a big man both in height and weight, and the chair creaked as he sat down. "I wanted to thank you personally for the plea bargain for Dora's latest escapade."

"No problem at all," Ditiro said. "There was no need. It was an easy bit of work."

"I really don't know what to do with that girl. At twenty-four, she barely passed matric at that over-priced boarding school in South Africa, and now, no university will touch her. It's not even the grades as much as the behaviour. They don't want a foreign affairs issue when they eventually kick her out, which they'll undoubtedly be forced to do. MmaDora wants to take her to America to some expensive rehab centre for the movie stars there. I don't know. I was thinking we might be able to sort her out locally. Do you know about our new church?"

Ditiro had heard rumours that the President and his wife were attending The African Church of Spiritual Revelations. He didn't believe it, though, thinking the President had more sense than that.

Ditiro's father was a retired UCCSA minister so he had been raised with religion, but he had no use for it himself. He saw nothing good coming from organised religion except separation and wars. Rational thought could not operate where faith was the guide. It didn't make any sense to him. He operated from a position of rationality, and everything in religion flew in the face of that. To him, it was little more than a crutch for weak people. He didn't want to believe the President could fall for such things, a man with a mind like his. He didn't want to think less of the President, but couldn't help himself.

"No, I didn't know," he said, hoping the conversation would go no further.

"I like this church. That Reverend David Kissi makes some real sense. You should see that place on a Sunday. All the movers and shakers of this country. My gosh, we could hold a session of Parliament in there and we'd have a quorum." His laugh boomed. "But seriously, I brought you here to ask you a legal question. Reverend Kissi thinks the best thing is to get Dora to Ethiopia. This is where the head office of the church is. There they have specialists that can help her. I've mentioned it to Dora and she completely refused. Flat out. She thinks they're a bunch of crazies. Can you look into how we can have her declared mentally unfit so I can force her to go?"

Ditiro hesitated before answering. The President was a proponent of a person's right to run their own life, and now, he wanted to take over the running of his adult daughter's life? How little did he know about his daughter not to expect she would balk at such an idea? Ditiro felt sick at the prospect of having Dora declared unfit so some church person could take her to Ethiopia to pray over her. He couldn't believe the President was even considering such an option and that he was asking him to be part of it.

"Are you sure you want to go that route? Perhaps there's another way. Those rehabilitation centres in America are quite successful. I could look into things for you."

The President shook his head. "She won't even go to one of those, I'm sure of it. So either way, we need to have her declared unfit, legally. We need to take over things for a while. If we take her to America or Ethiopia, either way, it's going to be by force. But you've seen her, Ditiro, she needs help. She'll be dead if we don't do something. Besides, Reverend Kissi has assured me that the programme they have there is excellent. Are you up to it then? Do you think you can sort it out for us?"

Ditiro knew his obligation was to his client, in this case the President, but Dora was his friend. He felt he was betraying her having to agree to this, but he had little choice.

"Yes, I'll look into it," he mumbled. "But please, consider the rehabilitation centre option. I think MmaDora is right. If you'd like, I could fly over and check a few out for you."

"No, not just yet. We'll see."

The President got up, indicating that the meeting was over. Ditiro stood, and the President came around the desk. In an uncharacteristic manner, he put his arm around Ditiro's shoulder.

"Maybe you and your wife should come to church on Sunday. It really helps you to see things clearer. We need to all sort our ways before the time comes. I'd hate to see you and Elizabeth and your little Lorato left behind. According to the Reverend, the Second Coming is just around the corner. We must make sure we are among the ones to be saved."

Ditiro stopped and looked at the President. Yes, it was still the rational man he'd always known, but the words coming out of his mouth were nonsense. Left behind? The Second Coming? What was he talking about? Ditiro had read a lot in the newspapers about this church. Even journalists seemed to think it was the best thing to have ever come to Botswana. He couldn't understand the fascination. Were Batswana really this weak?

"But I thought that church preached black supremacy? Wouldn't Elizabeth feel unwelcome there?" He respected the President, but he certainly was not going to subject his family to that type of brain-washing. Never.

"Oh, no, it's not all about that. I don't think Elizabeth would feel uncomfortable at all." The

President dismissed the comment, but Ditiro had heard rumours.

"So are there other white people there?" he asked.

"Not really, but that's just because so many of these whites in Gaborone stick to themselves. They're all there at the Roman Catholic or UCCSA." The President took his arm off Ditiro's shoulder, and they walked to the office door. "Okay, well, let me know what you find out about Dora. We're in a bit of a hurry, so I hope you treat it as urgent."

Ditiro left the office unsettled. He had seen what happened to people in that church. The President was right—many of the ministers and permanent secretaries were members of the church. Many on his client list were fanatical about the Reverend David Kissi. They bought the preaching completely.

He didn't think it was a good idea if the President of Botswana believed that on an appointed day, decided by Reverend Kissi perhaps, the Second Coming would occur, and the sinners would be wiped from the face of the Earth and only the saved would survive. How could that affect his decisions? He wondered how the President had moved so quickly to believing such a fairy tale.

Reverend Kissi had been extensively covered by the local media. According to his story, he was born in Ethiopia, the true birth place of the black Nubian Jesus Christ. Kissi was a direct descendant of the royal family in Ethiopia. Why he had a Ghanaian name was never explained. Why he carried an Australian passport was another mystery. The journalists did not interrogate the questions vigorously. Everyone loved a good story, apparently, even if it was flawed and likely untrue.

Kissi preached that when the Second Coming occurred, all sinners would be killed by a wrathful God. He pulled quotes liberally from the Book of Revelation.

Sinners in Kissi's world were anyone not saved by his church and included fornicators, drinkers, drug users, adulterers, gays, and all white people. His church believed in the death sentence for homosexuals.

Ditiro was scared for Dora. He cared about her; he'd watched her grow up and thought of her as a little sister. Yes, she was an alcoholic and needed treatment, but going to Ethiopia with that church didn't seem like the help she needed. To him, the whole thing seemed to be nothing more than kidnapping.

He walked to his car and realised what he was feeling was sadness, loss. Had he lost Rre Setlhoboko to this crazy thinking, this dangerous church? He hoped not.

But perhaps Dora's parents knew better than him. They would never want to harm their daughter; they loved her. Ditiro knew that. He respected the President and knew he must have thought through the whole decision. He was not one for rash actions. It was true Dora was putting her life at risk. The last time she got the DUI, she had ploughed through a traffic circle on the Western Bypass and had been stopped by the massive streetlight pole in the middle. If it weren't for the airbags of her BMW, she would have been dead.

Ditiro would sort everything out for them. Though he didn't believe in religion, he knew it was a human right that must be respected. The right to believe as you wanted. He just hoped the President was doing the right thing for his daughter.

CHAPTER FIVE

Tumelo walked towards class getting increasingly annoyed. Elizabeth was starting to make him angry. Who did this woman think she was? So she was white— big deal. So she was married—so what? Marriage in Botswana was nothing but a social obligation; it wasn't about love. Most couples stopped having sex completely after a few years. Excitement had nothing to do with marriage, not in Botswana.

He knew that's what he and Elizabeth could have if she only gave it a chance. Why couldn't they be together? He liked the time they'd had in Francistown. He wanted her in his life. He was sure if she took some time to get to know him, she'd change her mind. Only, she wouldn't give him a chance.

His mind swirled from anger. He got to the door of the university lecture hall and realised the last thing he wanted to do was sit through an hour on the history of the media in Botswana. At this point, he was failing so badly, it was just a matter of time before he'd be asked to leave for good— fail and discontinue.

He didn't care about any of it, anyway. So many people worked hard getting their degrees and then they were back sitting at home in their villages, no job, and, worse than that, no prospects for a job and with parents and other relatives on their back about the fact that they went to university and should be popping out some money for them. What was the use of it all?

There was no way he was going back to his mother and his brothers in Mochudi, especially empty-handed. He couldn't do that to his mother; she had all of her hopes tied up in him. They'd lived in poverty ever since his drunk of a father got lost in Joburg and never returned. Though he had, at first, occasionally sent them money from his mining job in South Africa, in many ways, it had been better when he'd finally left for good. At least, there had been no more beatings for his mother and him and his two younger brothers.

But there was also no more money, no more food. It was a humiliation to queue with his mother at the general dealer, their wheelbarrow waiting to be filled with the destitute rations every month, having to deal with the rude owner who treated them as less than human because they were poor.

No, he would only return to Mochudi with the money to change his mother's life. He was wasting his time at UB just hoping something better would come along. He needed a better plan if he was intending to change things in any serious way. In any case, he knew this chump life wasn't for him. He was destined for something better; he'd always known that.

"Hey, what's up, Tumelo?" Mphoentle asked from behind him.

He looked back at his friend decked out in her mini-skirt and high heels, her typical 'come and get me' uniform.

He'd met Mphoentle shortly after arriving at UB. She'd helped him through some things, and they'd become friends. She had her own mission which also didn't work so well with the university plan, so they had failing as a common denominator to their friendship. She was too busy juggling her list of men. A lecturer and two married men from town were on her list of 'boyfriends' at the moment, so she had lots of money and little time for school.

"Let's blow this lecture. I've got Bobby's Jag. We can go for a spin if you want."

Bobby was one of Mphoentle's men. He was a big shot at Telecoms, drove a Jaguar to hook university girls, and gave his wife the Lexus to keep her quiet about his extramarital affairs. The wonderful married life of Gaborone big-wigs. Tumelo didn't judge them, but he had little sympathy for them, either. Everyone was grown up; if Mphoentle used them for money, they used her for sex. It was an arrangement, maybe not explicitly stated, but at least on some level, it was understood.

"Sure, why not? I've got nothing going," he said, turning away from the lecture hall just as the door closed.

Mphoentle drove them to a restaurant along the Western Bypass. She also had a credit card, courtesy of the UB lecturer, and bought them both lunch—big, thick steaks and a couple bottles of wine between them.

"Listen, I'm heading out to church after this," Mphoentle said, looking at the time on her cellphone.

Tumelo laughed, thinking she was joking, and then realised her silence meant she wasn't. "Church? You? Are you trying to get forgiveness for your wicked ways?"

"No, it's that African Church of Spiritual Revelations, that one out on the Western Bypass. I don't go there to find Jesus. For Christ's sake, do you think I'm a fool? I go there to meet men. For some reason, it's attracting all of the big fish of Gaborone. You must check out the parking lot on a Wednesday or Sunday. Mercs, Lexus, BMWs, Land Rovers by the dozen. All the ministers go there, even the President and his wife. I'm telling you, it is the place to be." She took a bite of her fillet steak and a sip of wine. "Great fishing place for people like me hoping to hook a big one."

She threw her head back and laughed.

"What? You think hanging out where the rich folk are will make you rich?" Tumelo asked.

"Hasn't hurt so far." Mphoentle finished her last bit of steak and glanced at her cellphone. "Listen, if I'm going to get to church on time, we need to get going now. So, can I drop you back at school?"

"No, it's okay. I can tagalong with you and you drop me afterwards. I'd like to see what you're up to."

***

Mphoentle was right about the parking lot. Tumelo could see no car cost less than half a million. What was up with this church? What were these rich people looking for? he wondered. From his seat, they had everything. Why waste time in church, on a Wednesday, even?

Mphoentle parked the Jag, and they made their way through the cars up to the massive warehouse which acted as the church. From the outside, it didn't look like much, a big yellow building, corrugated iron roof, but inside told a different story. Rows and rows of plush benches looked like they could accommodate thousands. There was a second-floor balcony where more benches looked down on the stage at the front where velvet curtains hung from ceiling to floor in drops that had to be over thirty metres long.

An organ as well as a complete band with keyboard, drums, lead guitar, and bass guitar sat to the side of the stage. The pulpit of intricately carved dark wood stood in the middle. At the back, an embroidered sign:

"Blessed is the one who reads and those who hear the words of this prophecy and keeps those things which are written in it."

Tumelo and Mphoentle were early and found seats near the front. He watched as the band members tuned their instruments. A man wearing a flowing white silk caftan walked back and forth between the pulpit and a room at the corner of the stage, carrying first a Bible and later some papers. He looked up occasionally and smiled out to people he knew in the crowd, nodding in acknowledgment. Tumelo couldn't keep his eyes off of the man.

He had light brown skin, high cheekbones, and eyes fringed in heavy lashes. He was beautiful, but it was more than that. He held power. It was like seeing the human form of a great tiger. Even sitting, the power of such an animal disturbed the calmness of the air around it and pulled all in to take notice. It was the same with this man. That energy drew all eyes to him.

"He's amazing, isn't he?" Mphoentle said, seeing Tumelo looking at the man on the stage.

"Yes ... Who is he?"

"He runs this church. He's called Kissi, Reverend Kissi."

The people filled up the converted warehouse, both downstairs and up in the balcony. Though the rich were in attendance, the warehouse was also full of normal, everyday people. Some even poor, wearing their worn suit jackets and Sunday dresses faded from their many washings. The band started to play, and the crowd quieted down to listen.

Reverend Kissi came to the pulpit, and the band stopped. The hall became silent.

"Welcome, my brothers and sisters," the Reverend said in a rich tenor that did not let Tumelo down.

It was the voice expected from this tiger-man. This man was special. This man was someone Tumelo wanted to learn from; he knew this man could teach him things, teach him ways to separate himself from the pack, to stand at the front and get noticed. In his heart, this was what he desired most. Money would come, but power was what he craved. The power of the man in front of him radiated out in waves as if he were a source of energy. Tumelo had never been in the presence of such a person before.

"Today, I will read from Revelation 7, verse 4, 'And I have heard the number of them which are sealed and there were sealed and hundred and forty and four thousand of all tribes of the children of Israel.'

"Who are these children of Israel that God will save after the final tribulation? Who are these people? Are they the Jews who walk the sacred land and claim it as their own? No. No, they are not the twelve by twelve thousand that will rise up to Heaven and occupy their rightful home. Edomites will not be among the chosen people, this God has told us. For the chosen people will only be like you and I, for the twelve tribes of Israel are the black people.

"The Bible tells us this. We, you and I, my brothers and sisters, are the chosen people, God's chosen people. When the Second Coming is upon us, the wickedness of the Edomites will be turned against them. All suffering that they have perpetuated will turn back on them ten-fold. The whoremongers and the liars and the homosexuals and the drunkards will be left outside the gates of Heaven on that day. On that blessed day. Amen."

The crowd answered back with Hallelujah and Amen. They were following Reverend Kissi's every word, hanging on each one that fell from his perfect lips as if they were words directly from God.

Tumelo sat fascinated by the way he manipulated the audience. Finding a scapegoat to lay your problems on had historically been a good way to gain favour. Hitler had used it effectively with the Jews, and Kissi looked to be using it with the whites. And it seemed to be working.

The music started, and people were on their feet, moving to the front of the church. The Reverend stood waiting, and as they came forward, he laid his hands on them, one on each side of their bowed heads. Mphoentle told Tumelo that he healed the people of their wounds, internal and external. Some fell to the floor after he touched them, and he bent down and picked them up, placing them back on their feet. They turned back, heading for their seats, their faces serene.

"Let's go up. I like this part," she said as if she were at the fun fair or the circus. For her, this was a form of entertainment. She got to her feet and attempted to pull Tumelo along, but he stayed put. He needed to watch. He wanted to understand everything about this man.

As the procession moved through Reverend Kissi's hands, Tumelo studied him. He got the impression that the Reverend was watching him, too. When the people went back to their seats, collection baskets were passed around, and the money was heaped in. Once full, ushers carried the baskets to the front of the church and dumped them into a large, clear plastic box. When they were finished, the box was nearly full, and the Reverend blessed the church.

The people streamed out of the front doors, and Tumelo lost Mphoentle in the crowd. When he exited the wide doors, he felt a hand on his shoulder. He looked around expecting to see Mphoentle, but instead, it was Reverend Kissi.

"My son, I saw you in the congregation. Are you new to the Church?" he asked.

"Yes ... I ... yes,' Tumelo said.

It was not common for him to be lost for words, but he wasn't sure if he could say he was new to the church. That would imply he had joined in some way while he hadn't. He'd only been visiting as a tag-along to witness The Mphoentle Show.

"I like to see young people active in my church. I wonder if you'd be interested in being an usher," the Reverend asked. "We're always in need of handsome, young ushers such as yourself."

Tumelo hesitated. He'd only accidentally gone to the church in the first place; now suddenly, he was about to be an usher? At the same time, he found it hard to refuse this man. Close-up, his charismatic powers proved exceedingly strong.

"Okay," Tumelo heard himself say. "What do I need to do?"

"Why don't you come around tomorrow at about ten and we can talk about it?"

The Reverend smiled. Tumelo smiled as he headed towards the parking lot. He felt happy; he felt chosen. His specialness was confirmed.

"Where were you?" Mphoentle said, annoyed, standing outside the car on the driver's side. "I need to meet up with Bob to give him his car back. He doesn't like me being late."

She got in and slammed the car door closed. She started the engine and moved towards the queue of cars leaving the parking lot before he could close the door.

He sat back with his head against the soft leather of the Jag's seats. Something significant had just happened. It felt like his life had taken a turn, a turn towards something important. He wasn't sure, but he thought so.

He was sure about one thing, though. He needed to spend as much time as he could with Reverend Kissi. He knew he had much to learn from him.

CHAPTER SIX

Elizabeth stood back from her painting to get a better look. It was nearly complete. When she looked at it from this distance, the inspiration was obvious. She hadn't realised it when she'd started—she'd just experienced an urgency to finish something, a feeling she hadn't felt for a long time.

The red and black abstract was the painting of her betrayal; she understood that now. The discovery had been frightening at first, but it felt good to get the feelings she'd been holding inside out, even if it was only on canvas. She wondered if anyone else would be able to see it in the painting. It vibrated with anger and guilt, fear and sexuality, with power, but she felt safe the source would be difficult to identify.

She could hear the bell at the door of the gallery. Since she was alone, she put down her brush and made her way to the front.

She checked the clock behind the reception desk when she saw Ditiro walking through the door. What was he doing here at two in the afternoon? She quickly made a run through everything. Where was her phone? Had there been a letter? Had she missed one of Tumelo's gifts? She hadn't heard from him for more than a month. She'd begun to relax her vigilance. Perhaps she had let something slip by in her complacency.

"Hey, baby," he said, grabbing her up in his arms.

Elizabeth didn't know how to act; she'd forgotten how to be comfortable in her husband's arms. Everything felt unnatural. She had to think before everything, as if she were an actor playing herself in her own life.

She and Ditiro hadn't been close for a long time, more so since her trip to Francistown. She feared closeness with her husband now. She feared when her guard was let down, everything would pour out in one big rush. He tried to kiss her, and she turned away so the kiss landed on her cheek.

"Why are you here at this time of day? I thought you'd be in court?"

"I got out early. Case dismissed. And thought I'd bring my wife some lunch." He held up two brown paper sacks that smelled of Mexican food, her favourite.

Ditiro got to work clearing a space at the reception desk and pulled the two high chairs opposite each other, then unpacked the bags.

"Will you join me?" he asked.

She smiled. She would try her best to play the part of Elizabeth, wife of Ditiro. But a scarf stuffed deep in a bin at home didn't mean the feelings had been tossed away, too. She was jittery, afraid Ditiro knew things he was not revealing.

Looking at him, she was suddenly certain he'd seen the scarf or read a message or heard a rumour, certain he knew everything. Why else would he be there with lunch in the middle of the day, suddenly with all sorts of time for his wife when before, she had to make appointments with Lucilla if she needed to see him? Something was wrong; she could feel it.

"I've made bookings at Mowana Lodge. We fly up on Friday, home Sunday evening. My mother is over the moon to have Lorato to herself this weekend. What do you think?"

Elizabeth dipped the quesadillas into the guacamole, delaying an answer. He'd been talking about getting away ever since she had come back from Francistown. She'd done her best to dodge any real commitment to the idea. Now, it was here. For her to say no would mean she'd need a reason. What could she say? She couldn't go with him because she couldn't bear the thought of him touching her after what she had done? No, she couldn't say that, so she said the only thing she could. "Sure, that sounds fabulous. Thanks for organising everything."

Ditiro's face changed, and the façade of jolly camper melted away. "What is it? What's wrong? Something has happened, I can see it."

"Nothing," she said too sharply, too quickly. "I'm fine, really. Just a bit tired. Ludo's show took a lot out of me. More than I thought. But I'm fine, really."

"No, you're not. Something's wrong. Are you depressed? Maybe you should see someone," he tried.

"See someone? You mean like a shrink?"

"Yes, why not?"

Elizabeth got to her feet and walked to the window. She'd lost her appetite.

"You know why not," she said into the glass.

"Things have changed. They take the mental health of women seriously, not like with your mother where they tried to write it off as female hormones and other nonsense. They understand women now. We can ask around, find someone good."

She turned back to him. "Do they take women seriously? I doubt it, and besides, I said I'm fine. I don't want to discuss this anymore. I said I'd go with you. What else do you want from me?"

She sat back down at the food, feeling bad about being so short with Ditiro. She could see he was concerned. He was trying his best. At least, he'd noticed something was wrong. That was something new, him actually seeing her.

She put her hand on his cheek. "I'm fine, really. Thanks for caring about me, though."

Ditiro took the hand in his. "I know I've been busy. Work just becomes so consuming, but I don't want it that way. You and Lorato are the most important things to me, and I've decided it's time my actions show that. I love you, Elizabeth. You need to believe that. I'm not like your mother. I'm not going anywhere, no matter what. I promise."

He still held her hand, but she turned towards the front door, away from him. Tears were running down her face. She wasn't sure she could hold up, not to gentleness, not to caring, not to love. She deserved none of it. He should have been shouting at her, punishing her, but instead, he was loving her, a person no longer worthy of it.

Before she knew it, he had taken her in his arms.

"Please ... don't ..." she tried, but he resisted.

In his arms, she was back to those early days where love had been all they needed. A place where love really did conquer everything. Back when she knew she was safe and everything would be fine. The tears finally flowed freely.

He held her tightly, and she almost believed his words. She almost accepted that if she told him everything, if she showed him how awful she was, how much she had disrespected everything between them, how ungrateful she had been for all that she had, that he wouldn't run and leave her alone. She almost believed it—but not completely. She knew him too well. She had broken his law. There was no grey area for such mistreatment in his world. He thought he would forgive her anything, but she knew him better.

She cried in his arms until she was weak and Ditiro's shoulder wet from her tears. She looked up at him. He was the same, the same man she'd fallen in love with, the one she still loved, maybe even more now than then.

"I'm sorry. I'm just not okay, I haven't been for a while. I don't know, maybe you're right. Maybe I should see someone."

Ditiro wiped the last stray tears away from her cheeks. "Yes, if it doesn't work, you find someone else. Just someone to talk to. To help you cope. I know it's been difficult for you here in Botswana."

"No, I'm fine now. With the gallery and Lorato ... I'm okay. This is my home now."

"Okay, maybe, but still, will you promise me you'll try to find someone? Even if it's in South Africa? It doesn't matter."

"Yeah ... sure, I'll ask around, to see who's good. Maybe it's time I get a bit of professional help, like you say. I certainly don't want to go the way of my mother."

The last bit was supposed to be a joke, but Ditiro didn't take it that way. She could tell by his reaction that he'd been thinking the same thing. That he would walk into the bathroom and find her dead in a bath of blood, the way she imagined her mother had been found.

"I'm kidding. I can't kill myself. I'm a chicken, remember?"

Ditiro smiled, and she kissed him. She loved him. She knew she did. And he loved her even when he was distracted and distant. That was what she needed to learn—everyone loved in their own way, and it needed to be enough.

She wanted things to go back to normal, whatever that was. Even if it meant the problematic, unsatisfied life she'd had before the trip to Francistown. She would take even that. She knew relationships needed to change. Through all of this with Tumelo, she was surprised at how quickly her expectations had lowered. What seemed the bottom that morning at breakfast now seemed the most wanted, most valuable thing. Now, she just wanted everything as it was. As if the mistake hadn't happened. As if she were still the honest, good wife Ditiro deserved. She hoped the trip to Chobe would sort everything out, put everything back to how it was.

***

She'd been so fearful of the trip up north, but in the end, she had been surprised at how quickly you could teach your mind to ignore, maybe even to forget. In Kasane, everything disappeared. There was no Tumelo, no Francistown; there was only her and Ditiro.

She sighed with contentment. They were alone on the boat, sitting next to each other as they watched the slowly moving shadows of elephants against the red sunset. She took his hand in hers and brought it to her lips.

"I love you so much. Thank you for this. It was just what I needed."

"I love you, too, baby. Don't ever forget that. I know I get so lost in my work, but always, you're with me."

"I know," she said, and she was almost sure she did.

She wished she had thought to bring her paints. The pinks and reds of the sunset begged to be recorded. She doubted such a spectacle would ever be put on again. There was nothing to be done except to sit back and enjoy it.

They left the boat and went back to the hotel where they had a suite. Ditiro closed the door and turned back to her. He led her to the wide bed and pushed the mosquito net to the side. He gently began removing her clothes, kissing each patch of skin revealed with quiet reverence.

Elizabeth closed her eyes and emptied her mind, wanting to feel each touch. By the time he entered her, she was tingling everywhere. For the first time in a long time, they were actually making love rather than getting sexual release. They took their time moving together and feeling the closeness they both needed. Time smoothed with them as they glided above excitement, holding them there until the pressure proved too much and they came together in a rush.

She lay quietly listening to the singing of her body, lying in the crook of his arm.

"That painting you were working on at the gallery was different," he said. "Is it some new direction you're taking?"

Her pulse quickened. He meant the red and black abstract. Her serenity vanished. Tumelo and the Francistown trip came crashing back into her life, rewriting the script of what had just happened. It was no longer her and Ditiro re-finding each other; it was now a lie, a disgusting charade. She sat up on the bed, pulling the sheet to her neck.

"No, I doubt it ... but you never know. Just something that came out." She wanted to move away from those feelings to get back to where they'd been somehow. "So what did the President want the other day?"

"That." Ditiro got up and went to the mini-bar and made each of them a drink. "If you can believe it, he wants me to get Dora declared mentally unfit so they can send her to some church in Ethiopia for treatment."

She took a sip of the gin and tonic he had handed her. As usual, she didn't see the situation clearly. There were always so many issues, so many different positions that could be taken. "She needs help. Maybe it will be okay?"

"A church, Lizzie? What can a church do for Dora? It's that crazy church for the rich guys on the Western Bypass, the one crowded with cars every Sunday. One of those that mix African traditional religion with Christianity and materialism, a bit of voodoo healing. It's nonsense. Nothing but nonsense. I don't see how they can help Dora. She needs a rehab centre, not a bunch of loonies praying over her." Ditiro sat down on the bed, visibly annoyed. "I'm scared for her. Yes, she has her problems, but this is not the way to find the solution."

"So did you advise the President that maybe he wasn't doing the best thing for his daughter?"

"Actually, that was what kind of scared me the most. I got the feeling speaking against that church, and in particular the minister of the church, might not be a good idea. In all the years I've known Setlhoboko, I never once thought a subject was off-bounds between us. But I could feel something. Something has changed. The President seems to have been sucked in by all of their nonsense. I don't think Botswana, or any country for that matter, needs a leader influenced by such religious people. Especially this guy. I've done a bit of research about him. He's some guy called David Kissi. There are quite a few patches of his past that are unaccounted for. The bit that's there shows that he was never that religious. At one point, he even owned a strip bar in Melbourne. It seems God only found him in Botswana."

Elizabeth sipped at her drink and watched Ditiro getting increasingly upset. She knew he hated religion of all sorts; he couldn't see how people could be so gullible when there were no facts to back anything up. She'd never discussed it with him, but she often wondered if her life wouldn't go a bit better if she were religious. Religion gave people like her, people who had trouble seeing the way clearly, a simple, easy path to follow. She didn't think that was such a bad thing. It might have kept her from getting to where she was. She had trouble believing in anything; perhaps religion would help her find faith. Faith in God, faith in Ditiro, faith in herself.

Ditiro set his drink on the side table and began massaging her shoulder. "I feel bad I'm helping him do this to Dora. She's my friend, I feel like I'm betraying her. She'll never forgive me, and to be honest, she shouldn't."

***

Before they left Kasane, they'd managed to get a bit of the closeness back. Elizabeth was getting better at erasing everything harmful from her memory, and she didn't know if that was a good or a bad thing. They arrived in Gaborone in the late evening and decided not to collect Lorato until the morning. They still wanted a bit more time alone. Ditiro parked the car in the driveway and then turned to her.

"I had such a great time this weekend. This is what we needed. We need to do this more often."

She held the side of his face gently and kissed him. "Yes, we do."

She got out of the car while he got their bags from the boot. She stopped when she saw them, froze on the spot. Everything came crashing back into place.

"What's that?" Ditiro asked as he came up behind her.

She bent down and picked up the new set of oil paints left on the stoop.

"I forgot," she said "Ludo said she'd drop them off for me. I should have told her we'd be away."

"That was nice of her, though," he said.

She picked up the paints and held them in her hand. They felt hot, and she feared they'd burn her; she wanted to drop them but didn't dare. She reminded herself she needed to act normal. She needed to remember her lie. They were paints from Ludo, nothing more.

Ditiro went around her and opened the house. He took the bags inside and came back to where she still stood.

"Are you coming in?"

She pulled herself back and forced a smile on her face. "Yes ... yes, of course."

She dropped the paints on the side table near the door. She'd dispose of them tomorrow and make sure Tumelo knew his gift was not wanted.

CHAPTER SEVEN

David Kissi liked beautiful things, and now that he had the money, he was becoming a collector. Beautiful paintings on the walls and beautiful women in his bed. He ran his hand down the firm buttocks of his latest conquest, a young woman he'd spotted in church. He had his wife, of course, but she didn't expect him to stick to her only. Nigerian girls were bred to be compliant wives who accepted most anything their husbands dished out, especially if he was able to provide well for them. Evelyn was more than happy finding interesting ways to spend the ample money his new business generated. As long as the cash flowed, she'd leave him to his beautiful collections.

"Okay, my dear, time for you to be off. I have an appointment."

The woman on the bed mocked a pout. David pulled her small body to him and laid her on top of his long, muscular one. He could feel himself harden again, but he didn't have time to attend to it. He kissed her thick, pouty lips.

"My never-pleased Tebby," he teased her. "I will search for you tomorrow when I'm free and make it up to you."

"Okay... you better," she said as she slipped off his body.

She dressed as he went to the bathroom for a quick shower. When he came back into his bedroom, she was gone, as well as the two-hundred Pula he'd left on the side table for her.

He checked himself in the mirror. Even at forty-nine, he was a handsome man. He liked seeing his reflection. He particularly liked his high cheekbones. He'd always known he would find success and power, but he had been as surprised as anyone that he had found his destiny in this tiny, hot country. Botswana. He'd only heard of it in passing before arriving here. When he'd stepped off the plane, he'd had no idea what a valuable country it would become to him, as precious as the diamonds it was known for.

One last look in the mirror, and he left for the church.

At the back of the church, in a separate block, were the church offices. Reverend Kissi's was a corner one on the third floor. It looked out over the Western Bypass. He often sat at his desk and watched out his big plate glass window as the airplanes headed off from Sir Seretse Khama International Airport.

He sat down at his desk to begin work on the sermon for Sunday, his Bible open in front of him, when he heard a knock at the door.

"Come in!"

Tumelo opened the door tentatively.

Reverend Kissi waved him to come in. "Come, my son. Come take a seat."

Tumelo closed the door behind him and took one of the heavy, cushioned chairs in front of the desk. Reverend Kissi remembered this young man from the day before. He had spotted him in the crowd. He was handsome, that was obvious, but that wasn't the reason he stood out. He had felt something from this young man, had sensed a hunger he could use to his favour.

"I'm so glad you could make it. So tell me young man, what's your name?"

"I'm Tumelo Gabadirwe."

"Tumelo, yes. Tumelo, are you a student?" Kissi sat back in his chair, his long fingers meeting under his chin.

"Yes, at UB. I'm a media studies student."

"Media studies. So how is that going?"

Tumelo smiled. "Not so great."

Reverend Kissi nodded. He knew boys like these. He was once a boy like this. He had spotted the impatient look in his eyes even when nearly lost in the crowd of the congregation. "A university degree is not the only way to succeed in life. Would you be surprised to hear that I don't have a university degree?"

"You don't?"

"No. Study is important, learning is important, but a degree is only a piece of paper."

Tumelo nodded. "That's what I've always thought, too. I feel like I'm wasting my time there at the university. Things are just passing me by. Opportunities."

The Reverend leaned forward, resting his elbows on his desk, and looked Tumelo in the eyes. "I see something in you. I think the church could use your talents. How about you become a collector? It's a full-time job. You collect money on Wednesdays and Sundays and then help with other church errands the rest of the time."

"Really?" Tumelo asked.

"My son, God lets me know things, things about people. I see what others can't. In you, I see a light that is being extinguished. I want to save that light. I'm only doing what God asks of me."

Tumelo hesitated. "Well ... okay ... when would I start?"

"Can you start now? The other ushers are busy at the back printing out the programme for Sunday's service. Maybe you can help them."

"Sure, great."

The Reverend got to his feet and came around the other side of the desk.

"You certainly are a handsome young man," he said when he stood next to Tumelo.

"Thanks."

Reverend Kissi put his arm around Tumelo's shoulders. He was not immune to the attraction of a young, virile man like this one, but he would leave that for now.

"Welcome to our family, Tumelo. I'm so delighted you've decided to join us."

***

Tumelo couldn't believe his luck. A new job with a man he admired, plus he was being paid five-hundred Pula a week, two-thousand Pula per month. He decided there and then he was done with university. He didn't care what his mother back in Mochudi had to say about it. He'd always known university was not going to get him where he wanted. He had a new plan.

He left the church after helping the other ushers with the programme and headed towards the room he rented in town. His cell phone rang, and he dug it out of his pocket. It was Elizabeth. With everything that had happened, she dwarfed to the background. What did he need her for now that he had Reverend Kissi and a new, exciting job?

"Hello?"

"Tumelo, what did I tell you about staying away from my house?"

"Chill, Elizabeth. It's okay. It's just paints. If you don't want me to leave you things, it's done. No more gifts. Actually, I've got some new stuff going on. Later, neh? Have a good life."

He hung up without listening to anything else she might want to say. It didn't matter anymore. He would excel in every way as Reverend Kissi's assistant. He would excel at everything in the church until Reverend Kissi realised he was special and taught him all he knew, until Reverend Kissi made him his understudy.

He wanted to be a tiger-man, too. He wanted that power. Reverend Kissi would teach him how to get it. Tumelo only needed to find a way in. He needed Reverend Kissi to trust him completely, to rely on him like no one else. He would watch and learn. He would see where the Reverend's weakness was, and he would step in and pull up the slack. He would make himself indispensable.

Lauri Kubuitsile

CHAPTER EIGHT

Ditiro didn't like having to do this. He'd told the President that there was no need to have a lawyer present. All the paperwork to have Dora declared mentally unfit had been filed. The President and MmaDora were once again their adult daughter's legal guardian. They could do with her as they wanted; they didn't need him around.

But the President had insisted he be there just in case. He wanted Ditiro there when Dora was told she was going to Ethiopia and had no say in the decision. When she was told that she no longer had a say over anything in her own life.

Ditiro sat on a sofa to the side, trying to stay out of the way, hoping not to be noticed. The President sat behind his desk, and the First Lady sat in one of the chairs at the desk while Reverend David Kissi filled the other chair.

Ditiro could definitely understand the attraction people felt for this man. He was tall and elegant, and well-spoken. When he'd taken Ditiro's hand to shake it, he had held it with both of his for some seconds longer, as if meeting Ditiro had been an honour he wanted to let last that few seconds more.

"I've so wanted to meet you. One of the few honourable men to walk this earth. A man so committed to justice is a man to respect. The President has told me much about you. You're one of his most trusted confidantes, I understand. And you've done such important work for the nation. Thank you for that."

Ditiro had not been sure how to respond to what seemed to be genuine praise. He'd found himself immediately liking the man, even with all that he knew about him, all of his misgivings about religion and the religious, about this man's effect on the President, about his dubious past. If he had nearly succumbed to it himself, Ditiro realised those with less biases than himself didn't stand a chance against the charisma of David Kissi.

"Nice to meet you, too," he'd said and then slunk into his corner, hoping that would be the extent of his interaction in what was about to happen.

They sat, waiting, the air heavy and tense. The President tried to keep conversation going, but each time, it fell flat. They knew Dora, and she was not going to react well when she found out she was no longer an adult, that people—Ditiro—had worked behind her back to take away her power.

The plan was that she would immediately board the presidential jet after being told the news. She would go to Ethiopia with Reverend Kissi and three of the President's bodyguards to ensure she made it safely the entire way.

Dora came into the office without knocking. She was a beautiful young woman, with a full, curvaceous figure and a handsome face, one that would grow more beautiful with age. She stopped just past the doorway when she looked around the room and began to put the pieces together, suddenly cautious. Ditiro hoped maybe she would be able to stand up against them now that she recognised that something was going on.

"Okay," she said at the door, her hands up in front of her defensively. "What the hell is going on here?"

Her mother jumped to her feet, already in tears. "Dora, we want to help you. We're afraid for you."

She tried to hug Dora, but her daughter pushed her away. Dora looked at her father, confused. They'd always had a close relationship, one that could be relied on.

"Daddy, what is this all about?"

The President chose a stern, hard position to avoid the tender parent's heart that beat in his chest.

"You're going to Ethiopia with Reverend Kissi. They have a programme there to deal with your alcoholism."

"Like hell I am! I told you I'm not. You and Mama might have become some fucking happy clappers, but I'm not part of that scene. I told you I'm going to get help. Didn't I promise you that?"

"How many times have you promised us that, Dora? How many times? Next time, you could kill someone or yourself. We can't wait any longer," the President said. "No. This is not up to you any more. We gave you your chance. Now, we are taking over."

Dora looked at Ditiro.

"Help me, Ditiro. Are you going to sit there and do nothing? You're his lawyer. Tell him he can't just force me to do shit like this. There are laws. I'm an adult."

Ditiro looked away and forced himself to stay quiet though everything inside wanted to shout that this was wrong. He wanted nothing more than to stop what he had started.

Dora turned to leave, but the bodyguards were there. They hesitated to grab her, but the President nodded, and they took control of her. She fought them, kicking and biting and shouting profanities at her parents and everyone else in the room. Ditiro couldn't watch.

"What the fuck do you think you're doing? I'm an adult! I have rights!"

The President held up a paper. "Not anymore. You've been declared unfit by the courts. We're your legal guardians, and we find it right to send you with Reverend Kissi to Ethiopia for treatment at his centre there."

"What? Legal guardians ... What the fuck is that about?" Dora was confused for only a moment. Then she looked at Ditiro. "You? Ditiro, you did this to me? I thought we were friends? I thought you cared about justice and human rights. How could you do this to me, you bastard!"

Ditiro kept his eyes on the floor when he spoke. "I'm sorry. They think it's best. They want to keep you alive. You're their daughter."

His words sounded as weak and feeble as he felt. He'd gone against his own morals to keep a client, it was as simple as that. He could have told the President he wouldn't do it, and in the past, that might have been fine. The President respected other people's positions, but Ditiro felt things had shifted. He felt this time, his refusal might have meant the President took his business elsewhere. So he'd ignored his own feelings and had done what he was told. He had obeyed.

"I'll die in that place! I'll die, and you'll be the one to blame!" she screamed at him.

The guards carried Dora to the car waiting outside the President's private exit.

Once she was out the door, the Reverend Kissi spoke. "Let us pray for our daughter Dora."

Ditiro stood looking out the window while the President and the First Lady bowed their heads. David Kissi opened his closed eyes for a moment when praying and saw Ditiro looking at him. When the prayer was over, the President, First Lady, and the Reverend headed out the door to the car that would take all of them to the airport. Ditiro turned in the opposite direction, wanting to be away from the entire situation as quickly as possible.

The Reverend turned to him just as he tried to leave and grabbed him by the arm. "I hope I get a chance to see you again when I return. In church, perhaps?"

"I don't think so," Ditiro said.

"Don't be worried by what the girl said. You've done the right thing today. God will bless you."

Ditiro said nothing. He looked at the Reverend's hand on his arm. The Reverend let loose, turned, and left the building.

CHAPTER NINE

Lorato loved learning to read. She'd always been a lover of stories, and now she realised that she could be in control of everything. She didn't have to wait until someone had the time to read to her. Once she knew how to read, all the books were hers for the taking. This made her more anxious than ever to improve her reading, and at every chance she could, she would sit with a book, often many grades above her level, asking Elizabeth, Precious, or Ditiro to sit with her and help her with the words she was not familiar with.

"Please, Mommy, just for a few minutes," she said to her mother who was hanging some of the paintings for the show about to open at the gallery in two days.

"Okay, let me do one more thing, and then I'll sit with you."

"You keep saying one more thing and one more thing," she complained.

Elizabeth smiled. Her daughter was right. She had made a promise. Besides, she still had all of tomorrow to hang the paintings when Lorato would be in school to work on the show. She plopped down on the floor next to her daughter. "Okay, you got me."

Lorato opened the colourful book about fairies and began reading. Elizabeth felt so good lately. It had been almost six months since Tumelo had last called, and he'd left no surprise gifts since the paints. She was beginning to accept that he might be truly out of her life and she might be able to forget the whole awful thing. She was doing a pretty good job of pretending it had never happened.

Since they'd got back from Chobe, Ditiro and she were closer than ever. Or maybe her shift in thought that made her see how lucky she was to have him. Whatever it was, it was working. He tried to get home at reasonable hours, and they managed to eat dinner together as a family most evenings. They were also able to have some time alone together as a couple after Lorato went off to bed. Things were getting back on track. Everything was going to be fine. She could finally exhale and relax.

She looked around the gallery at the water colour paintings of Batswana women done by a talented artist from Jwaneng. They were all so hopeful. Women at work, women with their men, women with their children. Elizabeth could have spent hours just lying on the floor taking the images in. She was excited about the show and knew it was going to be a fantastic success. Every thing felt so right.

"Mommy, I said, what's this word?"

"Let's see ... which one? Okay ... it's ugly."

Lorato dutifully repeated it, trying hard to get it to stick in her brain.

"Ugly," she said. "Ugly."

***

"She's finally asleep." Elizabeth sat down on the sofa next to Ditiro. "So how'd it go with Dora today?"

"It was just about as terrible as I expected it to be. Maybe worse."

"Really? Sorry." She rubbed her hand over Ditiro's head, massaging the stress away. "So did she go then?"

"She had no choice. The bodyguards carried her to the car. Kicking and screaming. It was pretty bad. Awful, actually."

"It sounds awful. Sorry you had to go through that. We can only hope it helps her. If it doesn't, I doubt she'll forgive her parents. I know Dora, she's not the forgiving type."

Ditiro turned to her, his eyes tired. "Dora didn't deserve what happened to her today. It was humiliating. I feel guilty because I was part of it. I just hope she comes out of this okay. She blames me, and rightly so. I shouldn't have done it."

Elizabeth took his hand in hers. "You were just doing your job. If anyone should feel guilty about what they've done, it's her parents. Besides, Dora could do with a bit of reining in of her wild ways. I'm sure she'll be fine. Religion can be good for some people. Maybe it will help her."

"I hope so." He ran his hand over his forehead trying to smooth out the stress wrinkles there, then reached forward for his beer on the table. "So what did the doctor say?"

"Oh, no. I knew there was something I forgot. This show is taking up my entire brain. I forgot all about the doctor. Completely. I'll do it next week, there's no hurry."

Elizabeth took a drink of her beer and curled up next to Ditiro. He put his arm around her.

"Lizzie, you've had that yeast infection for almost two weeks. I think you should go see Dr. Moleele tomorrow. It might be something serious."

"What could it be? I'm fine. I really have a lot to do with the show, it's on Saturday. The doctor can wait, it's nothing. I'll get something from the chemist."

Ditiro sat forward and turned so he could look at her. His face showed he wasn't going to give in. "Tomorrow, you go to the doctor. If you need help with the show, I'll stop by after work. Doctor first."

She laughed. "Okay, bossy-pants. But you better keep your end of the deal about helping or I'll be in trouble for the show."

He held out his hand to shake. "Deal?"

She smiled and shook it. "Okay, it's a deal."

***

Elizabeth was not a fan of doctors, especially when it meant them digging around in her vagina with her feet up in stirrups like some pig gone to slaughter. She liked her doctor, though, Dr. Moleele. She was a tall, lanky woman with a silly sense of humour, but an encyclopaedic knowledge of the human body, particularly the human female's body. Elizabeth trusted her.

"So how's Lorato?" Dr. Moleele asked, sitting down next to Elizabeth on the leather sofa in her office. She had delivered Lorato and always asked about her when Elizabeth visited.

"She's wonderful. She's reading now, if you can believe it. I can't get over how quickly it all goes."

Dr. Moleele's eyes clouded, or Elizabeth thought they had. Then in a flash, she was back to normal until she spoke.

Her sharp words stabbed the peaceful air in the office, pulling all fears and dark thoughts from the corners and crannies. "Elizabeth, I found something."

75

Elizabeth turned to look out the window behind the sofa. A woman passed with a box of mangoes on her head. A man on a black bike troubled the dust, racing along with a small girl sitting side-saddle on the rack at the back. A shiny car stopped, and a man with a laptop got out.

She didn't want to turn back to the doctor. She didn't want to know anything about what Dr. Moleele wanted to tell her. Things were going so well in her life, finally. She was happy. She didn't want anything to disturb that. She wanted life to go on just like everything went on out the window.

"Did you hear me, Elizabeth?"

"Yes ... yes. I ... what is it?" Having no choice; she wanted it quickly before she could stand up and dash away.

"Elizabeth, you remember we spoke about how I like to do a routine HIV test as part of all physicals and you agreed and said that was fine. Do you remember that?"

Elizabeth could hear the air con blowing behind her. It was a typical hot late January day; the coolness of the office had been welcome when she'd arrived. Now the cold blew on the back of her neck and sent shivers all around her body.

She'd been so happy. She'd been thinking about the new year, and the upcoming show. She'd been worried about Ditiro and how hard he was taking Dora's leaving. She'd been listening to her daughter reading her wonderful new words long after the book had been closed. She had been thinking of other things.

She had let down her guard, turned her back on the enemy, and like a seasoned warrior, the monster had pounced when she was most unprepared. When she had almost accepted happiness was something that she could have, too.

76

Dr. Moleele leaned forward and touched Elizabeth's arm, her fingers warm, a shock. "Elizabeth, are you listening? Are you okay?"

"Yes," she said too loudly and pulled her arm away from the other woman's touch. "I'm listening, go on."

"Elizabeth, your body is struggling to deal with the yeast infection because you're HIV-positive." Dr. Moleele said it in one quick phrase, like tearing off a bandage from a wound.

Elizabeth breathed in. Then she breathed out. She looked out the window, and everyone was gone. The man on the bike sped off to take the little girl where he needed to. The mango lady had transported her load and was likely sitting in the shade biting a long strip of skin from a sweet, juicy fruit. Where had the laptop man gone? Breathe in. Breathe out. Breathe in. Breathe out. Where had all of the people gone?

She turned away from the window and sat quietly looking at her hands resting on her lap. Of course in her altered state on her way to Francistown that day, in her absolute recklessness, she had never even considered that Tumelo should use a condom. It never entered her head despite the constant messages one heard in Botswana about HIV and the devastation of AIDS.

She felt sick by her behaviour. Of course it would mean she now had HIV. What had she expected? It was justice for all she had disrespected, for her ungratefulness. She needed to accept this; she'd brought this on herself. How silly she'd been to think Tumelo would disappear and she would be left happy with her little family, with her little life.

"To be honest, I was surprised. I thought you guys were one of the couples that were getting things right," Dr. Moleele said. Elizabeth could see the disappointment in her eyes, the sadness. "I know you were both negative before the pregnancy, and you were negative after. Something must have ... happened." She dodged saying it outright. Something must have happened. One of you had been foolish, and now you've been given a death sentence. "Maybe you need to speak to Ditiro."

It was clear that the doctor was trying to find a way to let Elizabeth know she thought Ditiro had cheated on her, that he had been the one who brought the virus to her. It was the common way in Botswana. The good, faithful wife gets HIV from the philandering husband. It would be the assumption.

But Elizabeth couldn't allow Ditiro to be maligned in such a way. He was the faithful one, the good one. She was the wicked one, the adulterer. She was the one who had brought the virus to him. Then the complete truth of this discovery came to her. She hadn't thought the diagnosis through to the logical conclusion. She could have infected Ditiro with HIV.

"Oh my God, no," she gasped.

Dr. Moleele moved closer to her and rubbed her back in an effort to calm her. "There is no need to see this as a terminal illness any more. You're still healthy. We need to take your CD4 count and your viral load, but I'm sure you won't have to go on ARV therapy for a long time, and even then, you can lead a healthy, productive life. I'll help you through it. There's nothing to be afraid of, Elizabeth."

She heard little of what Dr. Moleele said. She could not believe that she might have given Ditiro this terrible disease. He didn't deserve that. He was a good husband, a wonderful husband, and a great father. She deserved this, but Ditiro was innocent. Why did he need to be punished?

"... but Elizabeth, you need to speak to Ditiro, soon. He needs to know what he's done. He needs to get tested, and so does his... other partner."

Elizabeth pushed the doctor's comforting hands away. "No! No! God ... don't you see? It's not Ditiro? He's not the one who did this? It's me! I had a stupid, sick, one-night stand. I was so lost then, so lonely and lost, so stupid. God, I can't believe this is happening. It's me. I'm the one. Ditiro is innocent."

Dr. Moleele sat back on the sofa. Elizabeth could see she was reorganising her assumptions. "Okay, well ... still the same. You need to talk to Ditiro. And you need to talk to the man, if you can. Do you know how to find him?"

Elizabeth held her head and spoke to the floor. "Yes, I can find him."

"And you need to get Ditiro to go for a test. Does he know about the affair?"

Elizabeth spoke through her tears. "No. God ... no ... what am I going to do? You know him, Kagiso. He always does the right thing. He doesn't understand such ... mistakes. They would never happen to him. There's no way he'll forgive me ... he'll divorce me, I know it."

Dr. Moleele moved closer and took Elizabeth in her arms. "You don't know that. None of us know what we will do for love. It's a very strong glue. But you need to tell him. He might still be HIV-negative. It's not as easy for the man to contract it as it is for the woman. First, he must find out, then you two need to see what you're going to do. If you need anything, you let me know. I know of a very good couples' councillor who has worked with many discordant couples."

Elizabeth stood up. She needed to go. She needed to think. Picking her bag from the table, she turned and stumbled towards the door.

"Will you be okay?" Dr. Moleele asked.

"Yes ... I'll be fine."

She left and made her way to her car where fine had no place. Everything was a mess, a terrible, awful mess caused by her. Fine would not be a part of her life for a very, very long time ... if it ever had been.

CHAPTER TEN

The bell above the front door rang and woke Elizabeth from her trance. She'd been holding a small painting in her hand. It was of a little girl dragging a skipping rope behind her as she walked down a dirt path. It would be part of the show the next night.

She was not sure how long she'd been sitting with it, and though the bell rang, she couldn't quite leave the painting just yet. She'd invested too much in the little girl with her faded pink dress pulling too tight across her chest and torn on the edge. The girl walked as if her world would last forever. There would always be sunshine and skipping ropes and time to idle, zigzagging along a dusty road.

She wanted to live in that little girl's world. She wanted to escape there.

"Lizzie? Are you there?"

She only realised then, when Ditiro stood above her, that she had slipped from the desk chair and was sitting on the floor, her back leaning against the wall, her legs crossed in front of her. She realised, too, that it was dark. Dark outside the window, and dark in the office. She'd been looking at a painting that her eyes could no longer see. She got up.

"Sorry, I ... lost track of time ..."

"Are you okay? What's going on?"

She couldn't believe she was going to have to say words that would kill this man inside. An honourable man. A man who had held her through those dark months after her mother's suicide, when she had been sure she would die of grief. He had shown her hope, and she'd clung to it. It had pulled her through. She'd been grateful, would be grateful for her entire life for that. A man who had given her Lorato, who loved her and all of her flaws.

And yet, she'd been so disrespectful to him, so cavalier with the life they'd made together. She'd treated the love he had given her, a gift so precious and fragile and rare, as if it were rubbish, garbage of no value.

She'd never forgive herself. She was glad she had this disease. She deserved it. She only hoped she hadn't given it to him. She prayed to a god she was not sure was listening. Since she'd heard the news, she'd made deal after deal with Him.

Like a mantra, she'd been repeating: "Please let Ditiro not be HIV-positive, please God, you can have anything—you can kill me. You can take the gallery, my painting, let Ditiro divorce me, let him take my daughter, but please let him be healthy." She'd begged and pleaded, and she hoped someone, somewhere had heard.

Ditiro turned the office light on, and his face gave her an indication of what she must look like.

"What happened? Elizabeth, what's going on here?" He kneeled in front of her on the floor and took her in his arms. "Please, Lizzie, tell me what's happened? I'm scared now. Tell me, please."

She pulled away from him. She didn't deserve comfort. "I need to tell you something."

"What? Just tell me. You're scaring the shit out of me here. Whatever it is, it's fine, just tell me."

She stood up, and he stood with her, his face full of questions.

"Sit."

Elizabeth watched as her husband sat down at the desk, then she stood in front of him. Her emotionless voice spoke the words with purpose to get them out as quickly as possible, to be finished with the harm she was about to cause. "I have to tell you something. I ... I went to the doctor."

"Oh, no ..."

Ditiro tried to come to her, and she put her hand out to stop him.

"I'm HIV-positive. You need to go for a test to see if you are, too."

She stood with her arms at her side, waiting for his response. Bracing herself for anything.

"What? That can't be. We were both tested before we tried to get pregnant. We were negative. Both of us. How could you have gotten it? They've made a mistake. It must be a mistake. What did Dr. Moleele say?"

His rational mind found an answer, and he immediately felt better. They were not people who got HIV, so it had to be a mix-up. A laboratory mistake. It was the only answer for Ditiro in his sane, rational world.

"No, there's no mistake. You need to go get tested."

"No mistake? Then how? Baby, you can't think it was me? I would never ... I would never jeopardise us like that. I ... you've got to know that, I love you."

"No," she interrupted, still talking in an emotionless, mechanical voice. "No. I know it's not you. It's me. I had an affair, a one-night stand. I'm the one who did this to us."

Ditiro sat for a moment. The words that made no sense were being processed. He needed time to arrange his mind around this new image of his wife. He ran his hand over his head.

"You?" he said, confused. "You had an affair? You ... you ... cheated on me?"

"Yes."

Ditiro stood up. He looked at the ceiling for a moment. He breathed deeply, his hands on his hips. Elizabeth knew she would be given a defined sentence; no smudged edges, no places for manoeuvring, and she was not wrong.

When he finally looked at her, it was with a face she'd never seen before.

"I want you out of my house. I can't live with a whore. Stay away tonight. I'll tell Precious you're coming for your things tomorrow. I don't want to see you, so make sure you come when I'm not there, or you won't be let in. I want all of your keys to my house."

She went to her desk and fumbled in her handbag. She found the house keys and handed them to him.

"And what about Lorato?" Though she knew she had no right to ask, she needed to know.

Ditiro's voice was not raised. It held no evidence of anger in its tone. That was Ditiro; expressions of anger were for immature people. His speech was solid and decisive and unmoving.

"You stay away from her. She doesn't need someone like you in her life. We're done. You chose this, and now, we are done."

He left, and Elizabeth stood exactly where he'd left her. Until the room was cold and her arms stiff, she stood exactly where her husband had left her. She was alone again, just as she had always expected she would be.

CHAPTER ELEVEN

Precious didn't ask any questions when Elizabeth came by late the next morning.

"I've come to collect some things."

"I know, Madam. Mr. Ditiro told me you would come. He told me I must pack your bags for you, Madam. They're in the sitting room." Her eyes were brimming with tears. "Let me get them for you."

"No, it's all right. I can get them for myself." Elizabeth stepped through to the sitting room and saw two large suitcases waiting for her. She reached for them, but Precious was too quick.

"No, Madam, please, please, let me do it. Let me do this small thing."

Elizabeth relented when she saw Precious was near to crying.

She followed the maid to the car. Together, they lifted the heavy suitcases into the boot, and Elizabeth slammed it shut. "So that's it, then."

She'd felt nothing since Ditiro had left the gallery the night before. It was as if he had wiped her entire emotional brain clean like a teacher wiping a blackboard. She knew her life was over, and mourning for what she had brought on to herself seemed futile. She felt as if a cold wind blew through her middle, through an empty space there. She hadn't cried. The dead don't feel anything, and she was dead.

She turned to get in the car, and Precious grabbed her arm.

"Please, Madam, if you need anything, anything at all, call me. I can bring things to you...without Mr. Ditiro finding out. It is wrong this, you being chased from your home ... from your child. I can bring her to you when you call me."

"Thank you, Precious, but I won't need anything. And please don't think badly of Ditiro. I'm the one who caused all of this. You take care of my family for me, that's all I want. Can you do that for me?"

Precious was crying proper now and could only nod. Elizabeth had nothing inside to give this woman who cared so much for her. Emotions were things she had no use for. If she let in a little, the flood would drown her completely, overwhelm her, and leave her prostrate. So she had to try to feel nothing at all. She could do nothing for Precious and her misplaced sadness.

She got in the car and drove away.

***

For the meanwhile, Elizabeth stashed her suitcases in her office at the gallery. She couldn't let the collapse of her life interfere with the first show of a talented painter. The guests would be arriving in a few hours, and she still hadn't finished setting up.

She pulled out the folding tables from the storeroom and threw white linen cloths over them to make their chipboard tops more presentable. She divided the big bouquet of flowers she'd bought into four vases and distributed them around the tables. She laid out the snacks the caterer had brought earlier and put the wine glasses and wine out. She stacked the programmes by the door.

Lauri Kubuitsile

The artist would arrive soon. He was an art teacher
from Jwaneng, Kutlo Oaitse. He'd been painting in his
spare time for years, stacking the beautiful water colours
in his garage. He painted for himself, he'd told her. A
fellow artist had seen them once and told Elizabeth to
take a drive to Jwaneng and have a look. She had and,
with much effort, she'd convinced Mr. Oaitse to let his
paintings out of the garage.

His work revealed Mr. Oaitse had a deep love for the
women of the country. He was raised by a single mother
and had married another strong Motswana woman, and
they had five daughters together.

She looked around the gallery at his art on the walls.
His paintings resonated with the respect he held for
them, the joy he found in their everyday activities.
Women working in the fields chasing birds away, girls
playing with friends, teens talking together, city women
walking to work through the crowded Gaborone streets,
mothers holding their children in their arms, wives
cooking for their families.

Elizabeth looked around at the scenes of young girls
pushing wire cars, mothers nursing babies, old women
sewing in the shade. These were women who knew their
priorities. Family and community, respect and
responsibilities were where their priorities were found.
She, too, respected these women. She wished she had
learned the lessons they seemed to have been born
knowing; perhaps her life would not be so messed up.

She sat looking at the scenes, one after the other, and
got lost in their magic. She heard a knock at the door
and saw Mr. Oaitse, his wife, and his elderly mother at
the door. Elizabeth unlocked the door and checked the
time. Fifteen minutes, and the guests would be arriving.

"Rre Oaitse, Dumelang, welcome," she said.

Then she greeted his wife and mother as Mr. Oaitse moved around and looked at his paintings on the wall.

"I told this stubborn old man years ago to take those painting out of the darkness. It's good you came along, Elizabeth, to show him how talented he is," his wife said.

"They certainly are beautiful. I'm positive he'll sell everything tonight," Elizabeth said.

Mr. Oaitse came back from his tour of the room. "They look lovely. You've done a fine job, my dear, a very fine job indeed. But the prices? Can someone pay a thousand Pula for a painting?"

"Yes, definitely, and after this show and the press you're going to get, you will be selling them for quite a bit more than that, I can assure you," Elizabeth said.

She could see people starting to arrive, and she wanted to greet them and give them programmes. "Please excuse me, Rre Oaitse. Your future fans have arrived."

She surprised herself at how easy it was to forget the shambles of her personal life and take on the role of successful gallery owner. Many of Ditiro's clients were on the guest list and they asked about him, but she said he wouldn't be able to make it and they left it at that. She let the guests move around and get a good look at all of the paintings. It was a full house, and the room buzzed with excitement.

After about an hour, Mr. Oaitse gave a moving speech about the paintings and what they meant to him, and about how Elizabeth had worked hard to get him and his watercolours to the gallery. He thanked his mother and wife and his five grown daughters who had all shown up for the show.

Though there were prices on the paintings, the demand for each was so high, Elizabeth decided instead to auction them. They were twenty-five in all and. in the end, they sold on average for seven-thousand Pula each, well above the one-to-two-thousand Pula price tag. Money had never played a big factor in the gallery's operations, but now that she was homeless, the ten-percent gallery cut would go a long way in helping her find a place to live.

After the sale, the Oaitse family invited her to go with them for a celebration dinner, but she declined claiming she was tired and needed to get home to sleep. Lies on two counts.

After they left, the guests slowly trickled out too, many carrying their new paintings. Elizabeth sat down on the chair at the reception desk and looked at the empty walls. She was glad the show had gone so well, but sad the busy-ness involved with it, that had kept her sane for a few hours, was now over.

She didn't notice Dr. Moleele coming up behind her; she thought she was alone.

"Great show," she said.

"Oh, Kagiso, I thought everyone was gone. You're very quiet."

"Sorry if I startled you. Really great show. The paintings are gorgeous. You did a great job."

"Thanks. The paintings sold themselves really," she said. "I'm glad you managed to come. Sorry the Minister bid you out of that painting. I also loved that one. There was something so relaxing about the three girls sitting under the tree. I thought maybe they were telling secrets to friends they trusted. It was lovely, actually. I wouldn't have minded owning it myself."

"Yes, it made me think of me and my sisters when we were young. Rascals, the three of us, always scheming," Kagiso said and then changed the subject. "I stayed behind for a reason. I've been worried about you after you left the office. How are you doing?"

"I told him. He didn't take it well, as I expected. He kicked me out. He doesn't want to see me again." Elizabeth kept her emotions steady. She was not yet ready to break down. That, she would reserve for when she was alone, she hoped.

"Maybe with time, he'll calm down ..." Kagiso tried.

Elizabeth shook her head. "I doubt it. You know him. But anyway, I expected it. I'll make a plan."

"So where are you staying?" Kagiso asked.

"For now, here, actually. Between all of this and the show, I haven't had a chance to do anything. It's okay, though. I have a sofa in the office and a small bathroom. I'm fine. Really."

"Here? No. Listen, I have a small cottage at the back of my house. I built it for my mother. I wanted her to move to Gaborone, but she can't bear to leave her money-losing general dealer in Kanye. Apparently, her two customers would die without her." Elizabeth laughed at the doctor's joke and it felt good. "You could stay there for long as you need to. It has a kitchen, bathroom, everything you need."

"No, Kagiso, I couldn't put you out like that. I'll find something, don't worry."

"You'd actually be helping me. I need someone to feed my cats when I'm gone. Lately, I'm travelling all over with this chairperson position with Botswana Cancer Society. I always need to ask my sister, and she lives on the other side of town and complains about it the whole time. You'd be doing me a huge favour, actually."

"Really?" Elizabeth asked, unsure if Kagiso was just making it all up to be nice.

"Really. Now let's get your things. I'm exhausted."

Elizabeth got the suitcases from where she'd left them, locked in her office, and headed to her new home, one she tried not to hope might be temporary.

CHAPTER TWELVE

"Tumelo!" Reverend Kissi called from his desk. The young man came from around the corner.

"Rra?"

"Come, I want to show you something."

Tumelo went around the desk next to Reverend Kissi who had a paper in his hands. He held it out to Tumelo.

"I thought this Wednesday, you could read a few verses for the congregation. I see something special in you, my son. People like you. They want to be near you. I see them after the service. That's what we need in this church. I've wanted to bring a Motswana into the clergy with me for some time. I think you might be the right one for the job."

Tumelo smiled. He'd only been working for the church for seven months, and his plan was going perfectly. He'd made himself available night and day for Reverend Kissi, and it was paying off. The Reverend trusted him, even with errands regarding his 'beautiful collection' as he called his many girlfriends.

Tumelo took them home in the Reverend's BMW after he was finished with them, or took them shopping or dropped them at the airport if they were going on one of their many overseas trips, all done with complete discretion. He had become an important part of the Reverend's life. An indispensable part, just as he'd planned.

He took the paper. "Thank you for having such faith in me, Reverend. I'll not let you down. I promise."

"See you don't. And no papers, I prefer you memorise. It comes off better for the congregation if they think it's coming from your heart."

Tumelo already knew it was all about the show—the better the show, the more they came, and the more money the church got. It was not said explicitly, but he could see how it worked. He was slowly learning how to put on a good show by watching the Reverend in action.

One thing he'd discovered along the way was that the people came to church because they had problems. If the church was going to be a success, they needed to let the people know that first, God was watching out for them and them alone. The congregants were told that the evil ones were the cause of the problems, not themselves and their unwise decisions and actions. They didn't have to change anything about themselves. The church needed to identify the evil ones and ensure the congregation that, one way or another, they would be punished so there was no need for the church goers to worry. If the church succeeded, the parishioners felt their problems being alleviated and they were thankful.

Reverend Kissi used history and current affairs to his advantage whenever he could. For him, the evil ones were easy to see because the bulk of them were white. All the problems of black people came from the whites. Blacks were poorer than whites because the whites stole their wealth. Blacks were sicker than whites because the whites manufactured AIDS. Whites brought everything that was bad. They were the ones destroying the environment, the ones who created homosexuality, and the ones who brought drugs and alcohol to the blacks.

But on Judgement Day, all would be righted. The twelve tribes of Israel, the black people, would be saved and raptured to Heaven, and the Edomites, the white people, would be left behind to face the wrath of God.

It was the perfect story. That, combined with the Reverend's magical healing powers, made sure the hall was overflowing. Reverend Kissi was thinking of adding a Friday evening service, to the Wednesday afternoon and all-day Sunday ones that were so popular. And he was thinking of expanding. He was looking for land outside of Gaborone to build a massive complex where worshippers could stay to receive twenty-four-hour counselling and prayer. Reverend Kissi had big plans for the people of Gaborone. He wanted to expand his church around the country, farther even if he had the energy or the right people working for him. People like Tumelo.

Tumelo saw only growth and potential for himself within the church. His opportunities were unlimited, and, thanks to the church and Reverend Kissi, everything in his life was going perfectly.

***

The rainy season should have been finishing by the end of February, but the rain was pouring down when Elizabeth looked out the window of the cottage. It was a lovely place, the little cottage. The bedroom was in an open loft above. Downstairs was the sitting room, open-plan kitchen, and bathroom. She was thankful Kagiso had convinced her to take the place. Being there had helped her get through some terrible days and even worse nights.

Kagiso usually stopped by on Sunday mornings to make sure everything was okay, but mostly left her alone the rest of the time.

Elizabeth could do little else but lie in bed or stare out the window. Many times, she had stopped herself from calling Ditiro. She wanted to hear his voice, even if he had nothing good to say to her; she just wanted to know he was alive. And she wanted to talk to Lorato.

It was too soon, though. But she worried about Ditiro, about the HIV test. She wanted to know what had happened. If he was HIV-positive, too, they needed to make a plan for Lorato. Neither of them had made wills, and they would need to if they were both infected. They would need to designate a legal guardian. It had been more than two weeks since she'd told him, since he'd kicked her out. Elizabeth thought maybe he would have time to speak to her now, that his anger might have dissipated. She would not speak of them meeting to talk or about seeing Lorato, not yet.

She would not beg for forgiveness or to be allowed to come home. She only wanted to know if he had gone for a test. She needed to know that he would be okay. She hardly coped with the guilt that she might have infected him. Of everything, that was the worst.

She dialled his number, and it rang for a long time. He answered, finally, but said nothing.

"Ditiro?"

"Yes."

"Ditiro, I ... I just wanted to make sure you remembered to go for a test. The doctor ... I ... it's just that it is important."

"I know this, Elizabeth, I'm not a fool. I've already had the test."

"Oh. Okay, good. I ... can you tell me?"

"I'm negative, but of course, that can't be confirmed until another test after six months, but it looks like I'll be negative. It looks like you haven't infected me."

Short, clipped words of a stranger.

"Ditiro, I'm so sorry you must go through all of this. I'm just ... sorry. You don't deserve any of this. I'm thankful you're negative."

"Listen, I have an appointment. I've got to go."

He hung up before she could say good bye, but it was okay. She didn't mind at all. She was smiling. Maybe someone had listened to her pleas—maybe God, maybe her mother, maybe the spirits out there, she didn't know and didn't care really. If Ditiro could be healthy, she didn't mind if she lost everything. He would be okay, and that's all that mattered now.

***

Ditiro put his cellphone on the desk and looked out at the rain. He had nothing pressing for the day and couldn't concentrate anyway. He felt betrayed and sick by what Elizabeth had done, and, though days had passed, his feelings had not weakened. He was still as upset as he had been when she'd told him in the gallery.

He'd thought he knew her. He'd trusted her completely. One mistake, one lapse in judgement, and she had destroyed everything. He couldn't believe she had been so foolish, so reckless with his feelings and their family. So reckless with their love. He would never forgive her for what she had done. He knew that was not part of his nature, maybe not a good side, but we had to accept all of ourselves, both good and bad. He'd loved her and trusted her, and she'd betrayed him, so she needed to be cut out of their lives cleanly and completely. That was just how it worked.

He picked up the phone on his desk.

"Lucilla, cancel all of my appointments."

"Okay, Mr. Molosiwa."

He grabbed his jacket and headed out the door. He needed to get his mind off of his problems. He needed to be happy for a while, if that were possible.

***

Lorato was surprised to see her father walk through her classroom door. She ran to him. "Hi, Daddy. What are you here for?"

Ditiro winked at her so only she could see and not the teacher who seemed very suspicious of this father coming and taking his daughter out of school on a rainy Monday morning without any notice.

"You don't remember the dentist appointment I told you about?"

Lorato was quick to catch up with a game. "Okay … yes … I forgot."

"So will you have her back tomorrow? You know it's not good for children of this age to miss school. It disturbs their progress," the teacher said.

"Yes, Mrs. Peterson. She'll be back tomorrow. Promise," Ditiro said, picking up Lorato and dashing out of the classroom.

In the car after buckling her in, he spoke. "How about the book shop, lunch, and then the cinema?"

Lorato considered the proposal. "I don't know … How many books do I get to pick?"

"Two?" Ditiro tried, though he knew three had somehow become the norm on a book-buying trip.

"Three," Lorato said. "And you get to pick the movie."

He laughed at his daughter's excellent negotiating skills. "Okay, deal."

He pulled the car out of the school parking lot and headed towards the mall. Lorato looked out the window for a while and then turned to her father.

"This isn't the way to Mommy's gallery."

"We're going to the bookstore, did you forget?" Ditiro said.

He'd tried to explain as little as he could to Lorato about the situation between him and Elizabeth. He didn't want to upset her. He'd told her Elizabeth was busy at the gallery and had decided to sleep nearby at a friend's for a while. He wasn't sure what he'd tell her after that. He planned to make it up as he went along, but Lorato was a clever girl who could catch inconsistencies and lies so he had to be careful.

"But I thought Mommy would go with us. Mommy always goes to the bookstore with me."

"I told you Mommy's busy right now. She's going to stay somewhere else for now. I thought you liked being with me."

Ditiro didn't know how to tell his daughter that her mother would never be coming home. Never was such a big word with no options. He hadn't even found a place for it yet in his own life, in his own heart. He couldn't expect his five-year-old daughter to find a place for it in hers.

"Yeah, I like being with you. But Mommy always knows where to find the good books. I might buy the wrong ones." Lorato's face was screwed up with worry.

"But I know good books, too," he said. "I can try my best, and if I get lost, we can ask the bookstore lady. She's also helpful."

"Yeah. Okay."

Lorato went back to looking out the window. For now, he would leave it at that, and he hoped she would, too.

He knew he needed some help with this issue, how to get his daughter through the minefield her parents had created. He'd never in his life thought that divorce would be something he'd have to go through. When he'd got married, it had been for life. Now, he was here, and he didn't know how things worked.

He still loved Elizabeth, and maybe that made it worse. He didn't want to harm her, but he couldn't be with someone who'd cheated on him. It was not negotiable. It was wrong. Marriage was about love and respect and trust. If you didn't have that, you had nothing. She had destroyed everything. He tried not to think about the details of it, who the man was, what they did, because his anger rose to levels he wasn't sure he could contain. He kept his mind away from that and tried to think about the future, about how he and his daughter could get through it all and try to find a sensible, happy life on the other side.

He was thankful the test had been negative. Though he couldn't be sure yet, somehow, he knew in six months, it would still be negative. He needed to be alive and healthy for Lorato; she was all that mattered now. He needed to focus on her. When he thought that way, the pain subsided. Yes, he loved Elizabeth. Yes, he was upset the marriage was over. But he was Lorato's only reliable parent. He had to keep his priorities in check.

He pulled the car into the mall parking lot. "Okay, Pumpkin, let's find some books."

Lorato got out of the car and came to stand by her father as he locked the doors.

She looked up at him. "After the movie, can we pass by Mommy's gallery to show her my new books?"

Ditiro took his daughter's hand in his. "Not today, sweetheart."

CHAPTER THIRTEEN

MmaDora greeted them at the door. "Dumela, Ditiro.
I'm so pleased you and Lorato could make it."

She bent down to the little girl who was wearing her
favourite pink party dress. "Hello, dear, we have sweets
and a cake. We even have a merry-go-round, if you can
believe it?"

"A real one?" Lorato asked.

"Yes, a real one. Here, let me show you."

The First Lady took Lorato's hand and led her to the
back of the State House.

"The President is in the dining room with the other
guests," she told Ditiro as she walked away holding
Lorato's hand in hers. "Go on in."

President Setlhoboko had started an annual Family
Day at the State House when he took power. He
believed that the strength of a nation was built from the
strength of all of the families within the country's
borders.

It was something Ditiro believed, too. An invitation
to the annual Family Day was a coveted thing, and he,
Elizabeth, and Lorato had been honoured by being part
of every one held so far—except, of course, today. Now,
only he and Lorato were there. Even after two months,
Elizabeth's absence in their lives had not lessened. It sat
between them at dinner. It was there in Lorato's room
when he tucked her in at night, and it was heaviest as he

lay down to sleep in his bed that was too big and far too empty.

When the President had brought up the Family Day this year during a professional visit to his office, Ditiro had had to tell him that Elizabeth would not be coming. He'd told him they were separated, but hadn't gone into any details. Those were no one's business, even the President's.

"I'm so sorry to hear that," the President had said. "I know such things are very difficult, especially when there are children."

Ditiro didn't like his personal life mixed with his professional associations. He used to think of the President as a friend, but not anymore. The church had changed him, more and more during the time Dora had been away, almost seven months already. Now, the President was a client, little more.

"Yes, of course, but Lorato and I are fine. We'll be fine."

"I wonder if you might re-consider coming to church with us. It helps me get through difficulties. Reverend Kissi has a way of helping you see things more clearly. There is even a group for divorcees. You might meet someone new there."

"I'm sure the Reverend is helpful, but I'm not really a church-going type. I think I've mentioned that before." Ditiro was growing tired of this constant pressure from the President and some of his Ministers to join this church. "Actually, I think organised religion does more harm than good."

"I'm sorry you feel that way, Ditiro." The President hesitated; Ditiro could see he was trying to find a way to reconcile his respect for Ditiro and his belief in the church. "Yes, well, you know I care about you and

Lorato … and Elizabeth, too. Maybe you can get help somewhere else, then."

"Actually, I'm seeing someone for counselling, so it's all sorted." It was not true, but he had no interest in the President's church or his Reverend Kissi and wanted to get away from such personal subjects. "So here are the papers you need to sign."

Since that conversation, though, Ditiro could sense a distancing by the President. The church was important to him, growing more so each passing day, and Ditiro's strong opinions clashed against that. Even though that was the case, he actually wished he had said more. The issue had been opened, and he should have taken that opportunity to speak candidly to the President about the way the church and Reverend Kissi were beginning to influence the way the President ran the country. For Ditiro, this was a dangerous path, one he'd seen other leaders take, where sense and rational thought was replaced with the hocus-pocus of religion.

But he had left the topic that day. In his mind at the time, he'd thought it was to get away from the discussion about his problems with Elizabeth, but later, he was ashamed to realise it was also because he didn't want to alienate the President even more. He'd kept quiet because he didn't want to lose the President's business. It was cowardly, and he knew it. He told himself that if the opportunity arose again, he would not let it pass him by. He would warn the President, no matter what the consequences might be to the law firm. Someone needed to take a stand before it was too late.

Ditiro went through the double doors of the large dining room. He could see the merry-go-round out the window and children in a huge, red jumping castle. He looked to the back of the long galley dining room and was not happy to see Reverend Kissi holding court at the far end. Whatever he was saying had his audience captivated. No one even turned when Ditiro entered.

He went to the bar at the other end and ordered a beer. The bartender, who'd been working Family Fun Day for the last five years, shook his head.

"Sorry, Rre Molosiwa, no alcohol this year."

Ditiro wasn't sure he heard right. "No alcohol? How's this crowd going to function without alcohol?"

"It's him," the bartender whispered, indicating Reverend Kissi. "Everything's changing now."

Ditiro shook his head. "Okay. What's the strongest thing you got?"

"MmaDora made ginger beer. It's pretty heavy on the ginger," the bartender tried, laughing at how ridiculous it sounded. "Sorry, it's all I got."

Ditiro laughed, too, and accepted a tall glass of it. He stood away from the gathering at the back, but could clearly hear what was being said. The Reverend cut a striking figure in his long, black, silk caftan embroidered in gold with a tagiyah on his head to match. He was handsome and extremely charismatic.

"Imagine an Africa where the white man had never set foot. It would have been a glorious place. We had our ancient kingdoms and our strong cultures. If they hadn't come with their evil ways, Africa would be the richest and most powerful continent on Earth. Places such as England and the United States would be begging at our feet for handouts. The world order would be very different," Reverend Kissi said, and the group around him murmured agreement.

Ditiro thought something seemed odd about the gathering, and then suddenly, he saw it. Everyone was black. Family Fun Day had always been a multi-cultured affair with white Batswana, Batswana of Indian descent, coloured Batswana all in attendance.

But not today. Today, everyone was black. Ditiro realised it was by design, not accident. If he and Elizabeth were still together, she would have felt very uncomfortable in this gathering, more so having to listen to Reverend Kissi's speech.

The President noticed him standing away from the group and came up to him.

"Ditiro, so glad you could make it."

He held out his hand, and Ditiro shook it.

"You look good," the President said. "You must be finding a way to get through those problems you talked about. Maybe this divorce will be the best thing for you. We just never know what God's plan is for us."

Ditiro ignored the comment. "How is Dora? Have you heard from her?"

The President smiled. "Yes, actually. She's back, and it is a miracle. She's cured completely. No more drinking, no more bad behaviour. It really is a miracle. Reverend Kissi's friends in Ethiopia have done wonders. You'll see." A bell rang in the distance. "That must mean food is ready. Let's move to the garden. MmaDora has such wonderful news for everyone."

The President put his arm around Ditiro's shoulders and indicated to the others to follow him out to the garden. Reverend Kissi led his band of followers and walked up next to Ditiro.

"Nice to see you again, Mr. Molosiwa."

"Reverend."

"The President has told me about your problems. It's unfortunate such a powerful man like yourself had to be treated in such a way. But the morals of your wife's tribe are not like ours. I'm very sorry you had to go through such a humiliating experience."

Ditiro stopped, and the President walked on without him. The Reverend stopped, too. The men behind him passed around the two as they stood looking at each other. When the room was cleared, Ditiro spoke.

"I don't know what you think you know about me, but you're wrong. And it has nothing to do with you, it's none of your business. Listen, Reverend, con-show artists like you are a dime a dozen. I don't know what the President finds respectable about you. Perhaps you used the problems with his daughter to worm your way in, I don't know, but I find what you're doing to the people little more than theft. You grow rich and fat on their vulnerabilities. You have no shame using their faith to manipulate them into your racist beliefs, finding an easy scapegoat to lay the problems of this country on. There is nothing, nothing, you can ever do for me, Reverend Kissi, so please keep your misguided sympathies to yourself."

The Reverend stood for a moment, then slowly, a smile formed on his lips.

"Mr. Molosiwa, so secure of your place in the hierarchy." His face hardened for the next part he spoke. "Watch yourself. I wouldn't want anything to happen to a friend of the President."

Ditiro remained behind, waiting for his anger to subside as he watched the Reverend head for the garden.

***

Outside, Ditiro found Lorato, and they sat down at a table with some of his former workmates from the Attorney General's office. When everyone was seated, the President stood up at the front, and people became quiet.

"Friends, MmaDora and I are so happy you could be with us today for the Annual Family Day. As you all know, family is the most important thing, and I love this day most because it celebrates that. Strong families build a strong Botswana. Our family, like all families, has had its good times and its bad times. Today is a good time, one of the best. As some of you know, our eldest daughter was struggling with an addiction, an addiction to alcohol. Thanks to the Church of Spiritual Revelations and its Botswana founder, Reverend Kissi, our daughter is cured. She is home. She is healthy, and she is here today with us."

Heads looked around, and then Ditiro saw a young woman coming up the aisle between the rows of tables set out in the garden. She wore a shapeless white dress that fell to her feet and a white doek over her head. She looked down at the ground as she walked, her hands folded in front of her. When she looked up, Ditiro was shocked to see that it was Dora.

She looked forward to her father at the front and smiled as she walked to him. She had changed. She'd lost quite a bit of weight and her face was gaunt, but that was not it. Something was gone from the feisty woman Ditiro knew. He wondered what they'd done to her in Ethiopia. She lowered her eyes once in front of her father in an act of complete submission. The President took her hands in his and led her to the stage to stand beside him. The crowd applauded the change in the President's troublesome daughter. Ditiro clapped, too, but he was not happy. This was not Dora. This was someone else.

The President held up his hands to quiet the crowd. "This is not the only good news for this beautiful day God has given Botswana. No, today, I have something even more important to tell you. Reverend Kissi, can you join us on the stage?"

The crowd watched as the handsome Reverend stood up and made his way to the front. Once there, he stood tall in his richly embroidered black caftan in stark contract to the plain, white dress Dora wore. She stood now with her arms at her sides and her eyes lowered.

"Yes, yes. Just like that," the President said. "My people, today, I have the unique honour and privilege to announce to this gathering that my daughter, Dora, is to be married to Reverend David Kissi!"

There was a beat of silence, and then the crowd erupted into applause. Those who belonged to the church, the majority of the group, jumped to their feet in joy. People ululated and cheered.

Ditiro clapped, as was expected, but he felt unwell. Could no one see what was going on here? Was he alone, or had everyone else walked through the looking glass? And what about the fact that Reverend Kissi was already married? Did that not matter? Where had has wife gone to? Or was Dora to be some sort of second wife?

People rushed to the front to congratulate the couple. Ditiro stayed at the table with his former colleagues, among them Phetso Warona, one of the longest serving lawyers at the AG chambers. He shook his head watching the crowd.

"First no alcohol, now this," Phetso said, shaking his head.

Ditiro was still in shock by the news. "I can't believe it."

"Believe it, Ditiro. Before long, that fellow will be running this country. He already is by remote control. Mark my words, my brother, we are seriously screwed."

***

As soon as it was possible to leave without being rude, Ditiro found Lorato and slipped out of the State House and made for his car.

Lorato protested. "But MmaDora said I could have another ride on the merry-go-round, and this time, I would get the pink pony."

"I'm sorry about that, but we need to go home."

Ditiro was holding her firmly by the hand, nearly dragging her to the car. He felt awful about the role he had played in what had happened to Dora. He needed to get away. If he hadn't done the paperwork, she wouldn't have gone to Ethiopia; she wouldn't have been drugged or brainwashed into becoming the zombie that had been paraded in front of them so proudly. She wouldn't be married off to that shyster.

He was angry at the President. What had happened to the man he respected? The pragmatic leader who worked from a position of sense? Who could see dangers long before anyone else? Could he not see that Reverend Kissi was working a dangerous plan? A plan that had already destroyed Dora and was in the process of destroying the President and would likely take the country down, too? His head pounded, and he wanted to get far away from the place.

Lorato stopped walking. Ditiro looked down at her. She stood with her arms crossed across her tiny chest.

"Let's go," he said.

"No. I want to go back for my ride on the merry-go-round. MmaDora promised."

He didn't need this right now. He wanted to disappear quietly without having to congratulate the President on his daughter's engagement; he couldn't do that. If they stayed any longer, he might be forced to.

"I said we're going. Now let's walk to the car."

"No."

He could see Lorato was in no mood to be sensible. He picked her up and started towards the car. She kicked him and screamed about the missed merry-go-ride.

"I hate you! I want to go to Mommy! Take me to Mommy! I want to see Mommy!"

As he walked, he couldn't help but remember the kicking, screaming Dora that day. It had all seemed so frightening, the worst that it could ever be, but today, the subdued, quiet, accommodating Dora at the front had been far more frightening than anything he could have imagined.

CHAPTER FOURTEEN

Elizabeth poured herself another cup of coffee and spread out the Sunday papers on her small kitchen table. She watched the clock closely. On Tuesday, Ditiro had called her and said he would allow her to speak to Lorato on the phone. It was a gift she'd never expected. She didn't question his new decision. She could barely concentrate on the newspaper in front of her. In a few minutes, she would pick up the phone, dial the familiar number, and she would hear her daughter's voice.

She never fought Ditiro about anything, never asked for anything, either. She'd made her pact, and she intended to keep her end of the bargain. But she couldn't deny the pain she felt when she thought of her daughter. She had a folder where she kept everything she had that made her think of Lorato.

There were a few photos, some drawings, and one of the tiny bonnets she'd worn when she was just born. She'd found the things in her packed suitcase and was sure it had been Precious' work. Only a mother would know how much such inconsequential things might mean.

She took the folder out whenever the pain became too much. She'd spend hours going through each item in it, stretching her mind to remember every detail, each sound, each smell associated with that thing. One photo was of all of them on a boat in Cape Town going out to

Seal Island. Elizabeth tried to feel the wind blowing against her face and the terrible smell of all of those seals. In the photo, Ditiro holds her hand, and a three-year-old Lorato stands between them, smiling. If she tried hard enough, she could feel Ditiro's hand. And when she finally does, it's too much, and she closes the folder.

She checked the clock—quarter past eleven. Ditiro said she could call at half past noon and talk for fifteen minutes. She wouldn't call a second early or talk a second longer. She would follow his rules exactly.

She opened The Sunday Standard, anything to distract her. Never interested in politics, she skipped to the arts and leisure section. She started an article about a basket maker in the Delta, but then, her eye was distracted by a blurry photo in the bottom corner. She read the caption to be sure, but she knew already what her eyes were looking at. It was a photo of Tumelo.

He stood in front a massive crowd of people at some outdoor Christian revival in Palapye. The story called him Reverend Tumelo Gabadirwe. Elizabeth sat back in her chair, shocked. Tumelo, a minister? She couldn't believe it. She reread the article which was scanty on details. How on earth had Tumelo become a minister?

After finding out about her HIV results, she had called him to let him know about her status and to suggest he get tested, too. She knew he had given her the virus, it could be the only option, but she didn't know if he knew about his own status, and she'd felt obligated to call him.

"Tumelo, I'm calling because I got some news from the doctor that I thought you should know about."

"Elizabeth, I'm working now. I can't take time talking on the phone to you. I thought you said you

111

didn't want to ever hear from me again, and yet, you're the one calling me now."

"Okay, fine ... Listen, I found out I'm HIV-positive. I'm pretty sure I got it from you."

"Yeah, so?" he said, as if she'd told him she'd missed the bus or she wouldn't have a chance to collect the dry cleaning. As if her life was not a wreck because of him.

"So you knew you had HIV?" she asked.

"Yeah, so what's the big deal? Someone gave it to me. Why shouldn't I pass it around?"

Elizabeth couldn't believe what he was saying. At the time, she had just been chased from her house and had been unable to conjure up any emotions, even anger. All she could do was stop listening to him, so she'd hung up. That day, she'd sat with the phone in her shaking hands, not knowing how to respond to what he'd told her. Now, she mostly just wanted to forget it completely. She didn't want to have an out, to blame Tumelo. She was the one to be blamed. She'd had sex with him; she'd never stopped to think about anything, let alone using a condom.

She looked at the reinvented Reverend Tumelo Gabadirwe in the grainy newspaper photo and wondered what his flock of followers would think of their leader if they knew he was purposefully moving around giving HIV to people, that he even felt justified in doing it. She hoped someone would stop him. It couldn't be her; she was only just managing to get through her days. She couldn't deal with that kind of drama. She hoped someone would have the courage to take that battle on.

She looked at the clock. 12:29. She watched the seconds pass with her hand resting on the phone until finally, it was time. She dialled the number and waited for two rings.

"Mommy!"

Elizabeth heard her daughter's voice and thought she wouldn't get through it; she wouldn't be able to speak. She covered the phone and bent over, letting the tears fall on the linoleum tiles, trying to calm her aching heart.

"Mommy? Mommy, are you there?"

She wiped her face with the end of her T-shirt and did her best to control her voice.

"Yes, baby, I'm here."

"Daddy said you went to America for work. Why didn't you call us? You've been gone for a very long time."

Ditiro had already told her what he had told Lorato. They'd agreed they should take everything very slowly. He didn't think any of them were ready to tell Lorato the truth. He couldn't do it, so it would have to wait. She'd agreed to everything, as always.

"I'm sorry about that. I've been in a place where the phones didn't work. But at least, we can talk now. How's school?"

She looked at the clock—already, seven minutes were gone. She listened to every detail of Lorato's school stories. She wanted to remember everything. It would be her lifeline until the next time Ditiro let her call her daughter. Lorato talked about her new books and the party with the merry-go-round.

"Oh. yeah, Precious says hello."

Elizabeth looked at the clock. Thirty seconds left.

"Lorato, honey, I need to go. But listen, you be a good girl for Daddy and Precious. I love you so much. I don't know when I'll get to call you again, but please, baby, know I'm thinking of you every minute, every single minute, and I miss you so much."

"Okay, Mommy. Daddy says I need to go for lunch. Nkunku is here. Bye-bye, Mommy. I love you."

Elizabeth held the phone to her ear for a long time after the line went dead. She thought she could hear them sitting at Sunday lunch. She could hear Lorato swinging her legs dangling high above the floor. She could see Ditiro cutting Lorato's meat. She could hear and smell and see everything she had so easily discounted as unimportant details in another life so long ago.

After some time, she slumped to the floor where she rocked and wept, holding tightly to the phone, the thin, tenuous connection to her daughter.

CHAPTER FIFTEEN

It was surprising how easily Evelyn had made way for Dora. Reverend Kissi, now a bishop since he'd promoted himself, had explained to his wife the power he would gain by marrying the eldest daughter of the President of Botswana. She had been reluctant to disappear at first, but a permanent flat in London and a monthly allowance of ten-thousand Pounds had convinced her it was a good idea. Besides what did she want in this backward little country, anyway? She was on an airplane the same day. Problem solved with little fuss.

The wedding was in the church only. The Church of Spiritual Revelations only recognised marriages convened within its jurisdiction. The President thought it wise that Dora and Reverend Kissi also go through the District Commissioner so that a legal marriage certificate could be issued. He'd been told Reverend Kissi and his wife Evelyn had divorced, so there would be no problem. But that wasn't exactly the case.

He and Evelyn were married legally, but he'd had a different name at the time, a different life. A divorce might bring all of that to the surface, making things untidy for his new bride. As Bishop Kissi, he conveniently uncovered a rule in the Church's doctrine that banned marriages at the DC. The President had relented. Dora had no opinion one way or the other. She said very little nowadays.

The wedding was held in early June. Dora, a beautiful bride, and Kissi, the handsome groom, were married in front of a bursting hall of worshippers. Picture-perfect and camera-ready. Reverend Tumelo, Bishop Kissi's personal assistant, performed the ceremony. There was no honeymoon since Bishop Kissi had too much work with his new worship centre beginning construction.

The President had been so kind as to assist the Bishop to find land. A one-thousand-metre by one-thousand-metre plot along the road to the airport had been found and quickly purchased and converted into the church's name.

The planned centre had an amphitheatre that could seat ten-thousand and accommodation for a thousand. A restaurant, office complex, and shop finished the plan. Bishop Kissi hired a Chinese firm known for excellent workmanship in the fastest time possible to take on the project. He was very pleased with the progress, but still made sure to take daily trips to the site to keep an eye on things.

He heard a knock at the door. "Come in."

Reverend Tumelo opened the door.

"The car is ready," he said from the doorway.

"Good, good. Is Dora coming?" the Bishop asked.

"No, she's still at home in her rooms. She said she has a headache. It will only be you and me." Tumelo said.

"Okay, that's fine then."

It was a short drive from the church down the Western Bypass to the project along the airport road. The amphitheatre was at the front of the plot. It had a towering entrance that peaked to a golden shimmering cross three floors up that soared into the sky. The contractors had done an excellent job on it. Impressive was what he was looking for, and impressive was what he'd got.

Bishop Kissi and Tumelo walked to the back of the plot towards the hotel. Digging machines were excavating the swimming pool, and the air was filled with dust. Tumelo began to cough.

At first, Kissi thought it was only the dust that was causing the coughing, but then, he struggled to stop. Tumelo took a soiled handkerchief from his pocket and coughed into it. Kissi could see blood on it before Tumelo quickly shoved it into his pocket.

"Are you okay, Tumelo?" Kissi was concerned. He'd grown to like this boy very much. He had no children of his own, but he suspected his feelings for this young man were very similar to those of a father for a son. Most of the time.

"I'm fine."

Tumelo started coughing again, and Kissi led him to the nearby half-finished restaurant where the dust was less. He sat the younger man down on a stack of bricks and called to one of the labourers. "Go and get some water for him."

The labourer brought the glass of water. Tumelo drank it, and the coughing subsided.

"Thank you," Tumelo said, handing the glass back to the man.

"Tumelo, what's wrong? I can see something is wrong. Tell me the truth, I can help you." Kissi suspected there may be a problem. Tumelo seemed to have grown thinner. He was often sick.

Tumelo hesitated. "I'm HIV-positive. I'm sorry. I should have told you when I found out. I thought you might be angry."

"Angry? No, I'm not angry." Kissi remained calm. He knew the disease; of course, many of his parishioners had it. "For how long have you known?"

Tumelo hesitated before speaking. "Do you know that lawyer, the one the President likes so much, Molosiwa?"

Kissi knew the man, of course. He knew him and disliked him. A know-it-all-type, with all sorts of opinions about religion and church. Luckily, the President no longer listened to the lawyer's ideas with open ears. Kissi had directed him to a place where he could see clearly that Molosiwa was a misguided man.

"Yes, I do."

"He has a white wife, an Edomite. She gave it to me. Before I found the Church, before I found you, we had an affair, and she gave me AIDS. I think the husband found out about the affair. That's why they're separated."

Kissi was scared for Tumelo, but he knew he could find him the best doctors, the best hospitals. Tumelo would be back to healthy in no time. He would call his friend at Milpark Clinic in Johannesburg when they got back to the office. Tumelo would be fine. He'd get him to South Africa and get him the medicine he needed, no matter the cost.

But this information about Ditiro Molosiwa's wife, this was valuable information that could do much for the Church. He would wait, though. He would wait for the exact right time. Timing was important. He would let Tumelo get strong again, and then, the time would be right. As they say, information is power, and power was the thing Kissi craved most.

CHAPTER SIXTEEN

"How do I look?" Elizabeth asked.

"Awful. Scary, actually." Kagiso smiled. "Like I said the last two times, you look great. Sit down. Relax."

Elizabeth would never be able to repay Kagiso for her support over the last two months. She knew just when to disappear and when to pop up. She was never judgemental or prescriptive with her advice. She listened and tried to help Elizabeth to see things clearly and more sensibly instead of through her emotions. She left Elizabeth alone when she needed time to see her own way through.

Elizabeth sat down across from her at the table in the cottage.

"I'm scared I'll break down in front of Lorato. I don't want to do that. I don't want to upset her in any way. I want to behave perfectly. I want the visit to be a happy one."

She hadn't been able to believe it when Ditiro had called wanting to know if she could go out to brunch with him and Lorato the next Sunday. He had explained to Lorato that Mommy was back in Botswana, and, for now, she'd be living in her own house. She'd asked a few questions, but he said over all she'd seemed to accept the new situation.

Since the call, Elizabeth could do nothing but wait. That had been Wednesday, and though she went to the gallery and came home, that was all busy work, things to fill up the time in between. What she was really doing was waiting to see her daughter. Her daughter she hadn't seen for two months.

She couldn't get over how kind Ditiro was being. She stopped herself from reading anything into his decision. It did not mean that he was rethinking chasing her away. It did not mean that she would be able to move back to the house. It did not mean that there would be no divorce. All it meant was that on Sunday, she would have brunch with her husband and her daughter. That was enough for her, more than enough. She would not wish for anything else.

"You won't break down," Kagiso said. "You're going to do fine. If Ditiro has decided that you can see Lorato, it won't be the last time. It means he has decided she needs you in her life, which of course she does. It's a beginning. That should make you happy. You don't need to be scared."

Elizabeth reached across the table and held Kagiso's hands.

"Yes ... that's it, isn't it? He has told her I'm here. She will ask to see me. This will not be the only time. It's the first of many."

"Yes, you need to just take everything very slowly. Think about Lorato. She needs stability. Today, just keep thinking about Lorato."

Kagiso was right. In all of this, one wonderful thing had happened; Elizabeth had found her first friend in her adopted country. Kagiso was her doctor, her landlady, but much more than that, she was a friend, and Elizabeth was so thankful for that.

***

They'd agreed to meet at Bonita's, an outdoor tea garden at a plant nursery. It was a popular Sunday brunch spot especially for people with children as there was a jungle gym for the kids to play on while they waited for their food.

Elizabeth parked her car in the shady lot. She'd seen Ditiro's car as she drove in. She sat for a moment, her hands on the steering wheel, her stomach churning. This was the thing she'd been wishing for every hour over the last months, to see Lorato and to see Ditiro. Would they look the same? Would everything still feel the same? Would she be able to handle the new situation? She wasn't sure.

She hadn't seen Ditiro since that day at the gallery, that terrible day when she'd told him everything. She missed him though she knew she had no right to. Sometimes, something would happen and she'd think: "I must remember to tell Ditiro" and then the loneliness of no longer having him in her life set in even deeper. She didn't want to let him see any weakness today. She didn't want to burden him with anything else.

She missed him so much, though. It was as if she was half now, half of what she had been. It was hard to imagine the time when she'd wondered if she should have married him at all. She'd been confused, but now, everything was clear. He was the best thing that had ever happened in her life. That person, the one who hadn't understood the truth of her relationship, the importance of it, that was a different person. She knew if she ever got a chance to show him, he would see that no one could love him more. But she reminded herself not to think that. She knew Ditiro. He had made his decision, and it was not likely to change.

She got out of the car and walked slowly through the rows of garden furniture and trays of basil and marigolds, to the back where the tea garden was. As she neared it, she could hear children laughing, and, though she knew it couldn't be heard in the crowd of other children's voices, she thought she heard Lorato's laugh just above the others. Her eyes filled with tears, but she wiped them away with a flick of her hand. Today, she would be strong. She would show Ditiro she could be sensible and good, and he would let her see Lorato more often.

She saw him sitting under the shade of a wide fig tree at a table facing the jungle gym. She followed his line of vision, and there was her daughter, in a pink T-shirt and jeans, sliding down the slide until she reached the bottom when she stood up and spotted her.

"Mommy!"

Lorato ran to her, and Elizabeth grabbed her up in her arms. She breathed in her musty, sweaty smell as if it were expensive French perfume. She wanted to remember the feel of her daughter's sandy hands on her neck and the way she breathed hot air into her ear. These would be things she would remember over and over again when she was alone back in her cottage.

"Daddy says you have a cat," Lorato said.

"Well, not exactly. There are actually two cats, and they belong to Kagiso. But they spend a lot of time at my house, so in a way, I suppose they are mine. At least partly."

A little blond-haired boy shouted from the rope ladder. "Lorato! Come and help me!"

"I'll be right back, Mommy. I need to help Ian. He's still a baby."

Elizabeth watched her daughter rush to the rescue of her new friend. So unlike her mother, she made friends instantly wherever she was. Not like either one of her parents, actually.

Elizabeth made her way to Ditiro's table. Always the gentleman, though he didn't hug her or offer her a kiss, he stood and pulled out her chair for her.

"Ditiro," she started, though she had to wait to get control of her emotions before continuing. "Ditiro, thanks so much for this. You can't know how much this means to me."

They both sat down.

"You look thin. Are you okay?" he asked.

"Yeah, I'm okay."

Then, she knew what he meant. He was thinking about her status. Her HIV-positive status had fallen to the back of all of her problems; she hardly thought about it.

"No, I'm fine. It's not that. Kagiso has done all of the tests. My viral load is negligible, and my CD4 is in normal range. It's just ... you know ... things. And living alone, there's not much use of cooking."

"In any case, you should take care of yourself."

He felt like an old friend she'd lost contact with, one things had happened to in the intervening years. He looked older. He played with the cutlery and tried not to look at her. He chose his words carefully. She couldn't help but feel responsible for the changes.

The waitress came to the table. They ordered, then sat quietly watching Lorato playing with her new friend who was a few years younger than her. She liked it that way so she could teach him how to do things the right way—the Lorato way. One day, she'd be a very bossy big sister, and then Elizabeth sadly remembered, maybe not, at least not from her.

"So how's work?" she asked.

"We're busy. I have a big murder trial starting. Vehicular manslaughter. It'll take a lot of my time. It's likely to drag on for a while," he said. "Son of a bigwig. We'll see how it goes."

"I read in the papers about the President's daughter, Dora, marrying some minister. That was a bit of a surprise. Is it the same one who the President was friends with?"

She wanted to keep everything on the surface today. No digging into what mattered. Not today.

"Yes. A surprise to everyone ... and he's a bishop now. A father-in-law could not love his son-in-law more." Ditiro didn't try to hide his dislike.

"Well, that's a good thing, then," she said uncertainly.

"Maybe. There's just so much going on. It's as if everyone is behaving out of character and without rational thought ... without considering the consequences ..."

He stopped. She realised he'd stepped too near to important issues. Even he didn't want conflict today, and she was thankful for that.

"Sorry, I didn't mean us .... you. I mean what's happening in this church and with the President. I wouldn't be surprised if that bishop didn't become the next president of this country the way things are going. Actually, there's no need really. He's controlling the strings already." Ditiro looked around, lowered his voice slightly. "In any case, Dora is no longer drinking, so that got sorted out. A little bit like killing a mosquito with an AK47, but there it is."

Elizabeth could see he still felt guilty about his role in what had happened to Dora. She also could see that for once in his life, Ditiro was not certain and that scared him. She wanted to say something, but she couldn't since Lorato came up to the table. She sat down in her chair and drank some of the juice the waitress had brought.

"Mommy, when are we going to see your new house?"

Elizabeth hesitated, and Ditiro stepped in. "I think we can find some time next week if Mommy's free."

Elizabeth looked at her husband. She couldn't believe how giving he was being.

"Yes ... yes, of course, I'm always free. You let me know when you're coming, and I'll make sure the cats are ready and waiting."

The brunch turned out better than she could have ever imagined. They walked out to the car park together; Lorato swinging between Elizabeth's and Ditiro's hanging hands. Lorato was the connection that kept all of them from drifting apart and away from each other, a gift of love, just as her name suggested.

Ditiro opened the car. Elizabeth bent down and kissed Lorato, who put her arms around her neck.

"Bye, Mommy. I'll call you when we get home, okay?"

"Okay, sweetie. I'll be waiting to hear from you."

She watched her daughter climb into her car seat at the back, and she strapped her in place.

"Bye, honey. I love you."

She closed the door and turned to Ditiro, spoke softly so only he could hear.

"Thank you so much for this. You'll never know what you've done for me today."

"Lizzie ..."

He stopped. He looked across the parking lot, and when he turned back, his eyes glistened with tears.

"I don't know anything for sure anymore. Everything is off-kilter. I can't know what I really think ... I'm not used to this. I'm just trying ... trying to see what is right. I think that this was right ... today ... us being here. But no promises. I ... I don't know yet. I just don't know."

He got in the car quickly and didn't give her a chance to respond. It was probably better because she would have messed it all up. She stood stiff and rigid, waving as the car drove away with her husband and daughter inside—but without her.

Once the car was out of sight, she turned to the nearby tree. She put her arms out in front of her, her hands rested on the tree's sturdy trunk, and she wept, the tears falling into the purple begonias below her. People full from brunch veered around her, staring at the crazy woman. She didn't care. The tears drenching her dress were not tears of sadness, for once.

These were tears of hope. Tears of joy.

CHAPTER SEVENTEEN

"The President said you should wait in his office, Mr. Molosiwa," the secretary said, hanging up the phone. "He said he shouldn't be long."

Ditiro closed his laptop and stood up. He'd already been waiting thirty minutes, and he was supposed to be in court in two hours. He still needed to pass by his office before heading to the other side of town. But there was nothing to be done if the President was late. Ditiro couldn't leave; he'd have to wait for him.

"Okay, thanks, Boitumelo," he said.

He sat down at the small conference table in the President's office and opened his computer to work more on a brief he was preparing, but his mind was wandering.

The evening before, he and Lorato had gone to the cottage Elizabeth was renting at her doctor's place. He wasn't coping well with the in-between place they were in. He wanted things decided. Even so, he was sad when he saw how settled-in Elizabeth looked.

Her clothes were in the cottage's closet, her photos and paintings on its walls. To him, she looked like she had accepted the new situation of them being a family torn apart. He wasn't sure what he had expected. He guessed he'd wanted to see her more upset and confused, in a mess like he was. He knew he'd told her it was over, but he wasn't sure it was. He wasn't sure it would ever be.

He couldn't help but still have strong feelings for Elizabeth. They'd been together for more than fifteen years. She'd been his only proper relationship. They had been friends before becoming lovers, and that friendship had only grown stronger as the years passed. Not having her there as his steady place had him reeling off-course.

He still loved her; he likely always would, and the night before at her cottage, he'd felt lost. He'd wanted to grab her up in his arms and pretend nothing had ever happened, but pretending was something he was not good at. He worked with facts and obvious rational conclusions that flowed from those facts. Nowhere did Elizabeth's infidelity lead to them being together again. It didn't make sense. If it didn't make sense, it couldn't be. They had to be apart.

It was so hard to see her, though. He thought perhaps next time Lorato went to visit her, he would drop her off and come and collect her later. That would solve a lot of his problems. Not seeing Elizabeth would make it easier to begin seeing how his life worked without her in it, but for now, her absence was a solid, heavy figure, always with him.

His thoughts were interrupted by the door opening.

"Ditiro. Sorry. I was with the AG. We're trying to work out this new bill on homosexuality," the President said, shaking Ditiro's hand and sitting down at the table next to him.

"A new bill?" He was curious, though he knew it was none of his business.

"Yes, I'm quite excited. The AG is looking at the ways we can pass the bill and still stay true to the international conventions we've signed in the past. I think we've found a few loopholes. We want to institute a compulsory death sentence for serial homosexuals."

A death sentence for being gay? Had the President lost his mind? He was known internationally as a sensible man with integrity and a firm commitment to human rights. What was going on? Ditiro knew the answer to that question, so he treaded carefully.

"But don't you think that is a bit backward? We will be looked upon as pariahs by the international community."

The President's face hardened. "Botswana is a sovereign state, governed by its own constitution and the laws of this country—no one else's—only ours. It's time African states moved back to our traditional morality, and it's time we stopped being afraid of what the West might say. That's where Africa has gone wrong so many times, instituting policies that stem from foreign ideologies, ideologies we don't understand because they are not part of our culture. We might have all got our independence of government, on paper, in the sixties, but we failed to get our independence of mind."

Ditiro imagined he could hear echoes from the pulpit of The African Church of Spiritual Revelations. This was not the thoughts of the progressive thinker he knew when the President was Minister of Justice. This was someone else.

"Rre Setlhoboko, can I speak freely?"

"Of course, Ditiro. We're colleagues, but we're also friends. I respect your advice." The President signed the papers Ditiro had brought for him and then set them aside to listen. "What is it?"

Ditiro knew what he was about to say could be problematic, but he felt things were going wrong, and they were going very wrong very quickly. He needed to speak before it was too late.

"I think the Church is influencing you to act in ways that may not be in the best interest of the country."

The President considered his words for a moment.

"In what way?"

"Like this bill, for example. Where in our history were homosexuals given the dearth sentence? That is not part of our history, our culture. That is not traditional in any way. We believe in botho, respect for people. We have a long history of democracy. This kind of legislation is retrograde and actually anti-Setswana culture. It damages the image of the country, and, more importantly, it is a violation of the human rights of homosexuals. Even in a purely practical sense, how will it be enforced?"

Just then, the phone rang, and the President answered.

"Excuse me." He picked up the phone. "Sure, send him in."

The President ignored the question still hanging in the air and stood, heading towards the office door just as Bishop Kissi entered.

"David, I'm so glad you found time in your schedule to pass by."

"President," the Bishop said. He spotted Ditiro sitting at the conference table in the corner. Ditiro could see his disappointment, but he quickly hid it with a smile. "Mr. Molosiwa, how nice to see you again."

He walked towards Ditiro with his hand outstretched. Ditiro stood, shook his hand, and then immediately sat down again, saying nothing. If he couldn't speak the truth, he'd rather say nothing.

"Take a seat," the President said, indicating a chair at the conference table next to Ditiro. "I have good news."

For the moment, Bishop Kissi seemed more interested in Ditiro. "So how have you been keeping yourself, Mr. Molosiwa? I haven't seen you since the wedding."

Ditiro sat back and looked Kissi in the eyes. He was surprised to hear that Bishop Kissi knew he had been at Dora's wedding. He'd stood at the back of the massive hall packed full of people. He hadn't wanted to be seen at that church, but he'd needed to attend Dora's wedding. She was his friend, and he still felt guilt about everything. He'd tried to stay hidden in the crowd. How had the Kissi seen him? Had he been searching the crowd for him? That thought frightened him somehow. Was there nothing that got past this man?

"Yes, I was at the wedding. I've known Dora most of her life, since she was a little girl. I couldn't miss her wedding."

"But I didn't see you in the line afterwards ... the greeting line," Reverend Kissi said with a cold smile.

"No, I didn't feel I could congratulate Dora for something I felt was not in her best interests."

When the words were out, instead of feeling scared he'd offended the President, he felt relief. He hadn't said it to anyone except Elizabeth, and he felt his silence was a betrayal to Dora and a betrayal of his own beliefs.

A loud, booming laugh from Kissi rattled the trophies on the nearby shelf. "Well, you are nothing if not honest."

The President sat quietly watching the two men at the table.

Kissi continued. "And you? How are you now that your wife has left you? You seem to be such an expert on marriage, and yet, you seemed to have failed at your own."

Ditiro would not get emotional over this man, this shyster, this piece of trash. He stayed silent, and the President jumped in to his defence.

"Bishop, I'm sure Ditiro meant no offence about your marriage. He cares for Dora is all and wants the best for her."

Kissi looked at Ditiro and smiled. He assumed he had the upper hand. Ditiro left him to his assumptions. He never liked a man who let his temper control him, and he certainly wouldn't let Kissi force him to behave out of character.

"How I am is none of your concern, Bishop," Ditiro said calmly. He turned to the President. "We're finished with our business. I think I'll be off then."

"No, wait a minute. We were discussing the bill and your thoughts. I respect your opinions, Ditiro. I have ever since you were a young lawyer from university. You're right to some extent that I have changed since I joined the Bishop's church."

Ditiro had spoken privately to the President; he hadn't expected their discussion to be revealed to the very man who was causing the problems. He looked at Kissi who sat back in his chair, his hands crossed and resting on his growing stomach, as if nothing troubled him. Ditiro's gaze followed up the Bishop's body and met his eyes which revealed something else—they burned with hatred. And that hatred was directed at him.

The President continued, oblivious to the interactions between the two men. "Ditiro thinks it will be a bad idea to have Parliament pass the bill on homosexuality, that it will put Botswana in a difficult position. Perhaps you can explain it to him better than I, David."

As if talking to a child or a person of limited mental ability, Kissi turned to Ditiro.

"It's difficult to explain to a godless man such as yourself. People like you believe that homosexuality harms no one, so why can't the state just leave them alone? But us, those who have God in their lives, know better. Immorality harms everyone. The bill leaves room for those who have made a mistake. God knows humans are fallible. He forgives us our weaknesses. It is the repeat offenders who must be punished. We need to rid our beautiful country of all such immorality. Botswana is a land of God. Besides, these are western aberrations, nothing more. This is no behaviour for Africans. It was brought to the continent by foreigners. Let them take it back with them. We have no problem with them allowing homosexuals to practice in their countries. It is their sovereign right to allow what they think is appropriate. The same applies to us. When the Day of Reckoning arrives, we want to greet our saviour with a clean conscience."

Kissi sat back, satisfied he'd made his point.

"You see, Ditiro, we just want to make sure that when the Second Coming arrives, Batswana are among the saved. I think you can see our point now," the President said, as if such talk were reasonable.

Ditiro could have laughed if he didn't know the dangerous effect such actions could have.

He could see clearly that there was no point in arguing with either of these men. He could also see that Botswana was in serious trouble. He stood up to go.

"Well, you both seem to have thought it through. Not much I can say to that, since as Bishop Kissi has pointed out, I am godless." He towered above Kissi and looked down at him as he spoke. "I may be godless, but I am also patriotic. I love my country, and I will do everything in my power to ensure that it does not fall into the hands of charlatans, no matter which form they arrive in."

He said good-bye to the President. He was sure he could feel the heat boring through his suit jacket caused by the Bishop's hate-filled eyes on his back as he left.

***

Tumelo stood at the entrance greeting people as they arrived. Reverend Kissi was at the front. The service would start soon. It was Sunday, their busiest day, and the hall was full. He looked out the door and saw the black Bentley that brought the President and motioned to Bishop Kissi at the front. Bishop Kissi went to the microphone.

"Ladies and Gentlemen, please stand. The President has arrived."

The packed hall became quiet, and people turned towards the back as the President and the First Lady arrived followed by their four bodyguards. They greeted Tumelo who ushered them to the front where Dora, dressed in white cotton, head to toe, waited for them. She kissed her mother and then her father.

Once they were seated, the congregation sat down, and the Bishop moved to the podium.

"Welcome, children of God. Amen. Hallelujah. We are so blessed today. The President and his lovely wife, MmaDora, have graced us with their presence. Amen. Hallelujah. As you all know, the President is a man who takes his God with him wherever he goes. He walks the talk. He is currently in the process of ridding our beautiful, Godly land of yet another foreign imposed practice— the Edomites' immoral practice of homosexuality. Help our President make sure the bill is passed and our country becomes free of the scourge. We all need to work hard to prepare our land for The Rapture. Amen. Hallelujah."

The crowd responded. "Amen. Hallelujah."

Tumelo was on the stage now, standing behind Bishop Kissi. He was nervous, but they'd rehearsed everything. He knew what he was going to say. That was not what he feared. He feared what the effect might be. He was committed, though. He had made a promise to Bishop Kissi. He also knew today would be a turning point day for him. Everything would be different after today.

Earlier in the week, the bishop had come to Tumelo's office. He'd sat down without speaking, his hands holding his head, his eyes closed.

"I think the time has come," he'd said without opening his eyes.

"The time?" Tumelo had asked.

The Bishop had looked at him. "The time for you to tell the congregation."

He hadn't understood. "Tell them what?"

"About the Edomite and how she's spreading HIV to the young black men in our community, how she gave it to you."

The Bishop had been breathing hard, Tumelo hadn't known if he was upset or excited.

"About Mrs. Molosiwa, about me having HIV? Do you think that's a good idea? People might leave the church; you know how they can be around HIV-positive people. Stigma is still very strong in Botswana." He didn't like questioning the Bishop, but he'd seemed very emotional, Tumelo had wondered if he were drunk.

"No, people will believe and act the way that we want them to. If you tell the story correctly, you will be the hero. They don't know what they should believe; you must guide them to their own opinions. Don't worry. I'll show you."

And he had. They had worked on the script for the rest of the week. It had to be perfect if it was going to have the right impact.

"Today, I am going to ask Reverend Tumelo to come to the front and speak with you. As you know, this young man has become a pillar in the church and a valuable assistant to me. He is a child of God the Almighty. He wants to testify today. He wants to speak of something important. Welcome him."

The church band played as Tumelo made his way to the microphone. People in the crowd waved their arms in the air and sang with their eyes closed. Once he was at the microphone, the music slowly came to an end, and the congregation quieted in anticipation of his words. He looked out over the crowd, and his nerves subsided. He was powerful, at that moment the most powerful person in the room. He thought in that moment how quickly one's dreams really can come true.

"I greet you in the name of our saviour, the almighty Jesus Christ," he said.

The congregation responded, "Amen. Hallelujah."

"Today, I stand before you as evidence of the wickedness of those around us who have yet to find God. I was one of them before I found The African Church of Spiritual Revelation and the holy Bishop Kissi who pulled me to the path of righteousness. I was lost in the enticing world of Satan's soldiers, and I gave in. I gave in, Lord Jesus, I gave in—please forgive me," Tumelo begged from the pulpit, his voice catching with emotion, his arms raised above his head just as Bishop Kissi had instructed him to do. They'd practiced getting the catch in his voice just right.

"Amen. Hallelujah."

"I met a woman, an Edomite. She was beautiful and wealthy, but hidden behind her charms was the soul of

Satan. She was instructed by her ruler, and she was obedient to him. She took me in her expensive car to Francistown. There, we slept in a hotel together. She was a married woman, but that didn't matter to her. She was an adulterer, and I was a fornicator. She showed me many things that night, things I knew nothing of. I was still a child, easily swayed by money and beauty. She was a hardworking soldier of the Devil."

"Amen. Hallelujah."

The crowd was buzzing with excitement. They were being led by the words. Led to a place where they could hold the righteous position they so dearly coveted. The place where they would clearly identify the enemy. Simple with no ambiguities to confuse them. They came to church for such reasons, to untangle complicated lives, to classify the world into black and white, into right and wrong, into good and bad. To create fairy tales where they were always part of the happy ending and the bad ones were always punished. They would be the heroes, the victorious ones in the story.

"We spent only one night together, but it was enough for me to be punished for my wayward immorality. I accept God's punishment. He has shown me his love and mercy by bringing me into the arms of this church. But I stand here before you to confess, to confess that I am HIV-positive. I am HIV-positive because of that Edomite. She set out to lure young, black men like myself, and to pass on this disease created by her people to finish the Children of Israel. She was sent out to move among us and to destroy us. But she will not succeed."

"She will not succeed. Amen. Hallelujah." The crowd was getting riled. They could sniff the faint metallic, earthy blood scent in the air. Their pulse was racing; they were ready for the kill.

"I feel such pain in my heart. Not because I have HIV and I will someday die of AIDS. No, my brothers and sisters, I have no fear of death. I welcome it. To sit at the feet of my Lord will be a blessing I will accept with both hands. No, my heart aches for I know my words will harm some. My words will harm, but they must be spoken. The time has come. We must speak the names of Satan's soldiers. We cannot allow them to move in shadows and secrets among us." Tumelo raised his voice—he was nearly shouting. Sweat poured from his face as he pounded the pulpit.

"We must stand tall and fearless against the Devil. God requires that of us, and today, I will take God's challenge. I am here to take up arms against Satan. To battle him with all of my being."

"Amen. Hallelujah."

"Many of us know the celebrated lawyer Ditiro Molosiwa. He is a man who has served this country tirelessly in the name of justice. He is a trusted confidante to our President. He is a man we all respect. But he is also a man who has been lured from sense by the charms of the same woman. He has been manipulated and has veered from his chosen path to take up a path towards the side of evil. Why do I say this when I know this man is a friend to our President? Because I want to save him. I wish all of us to pray for the saving of our brother, Ditiro Molosiwa. I know, and I have been punished, but I want to save Mr. Molosiwa."

"Amen. Hallelujah."

"I will show no fear. I will show no fear! I stand here with Jesus and God, the Holy Father on my side, my brothers and sisters. I fear for Mr. Molosiwa because the Edomite who lured me that day, Satan's soldier who took me to the hotel in Francistown in her expensive car and laid me on the bed and infected me with this foreign disease meant to annihilate God's chosen people, is the wife to Mr. Molosiwa. Her name is Elizabeth Molosiwa. She came to Botswana on a mission from Satan. She is HIV-positive and is spreading it to all of us from the Tribes of Israel in an attempt to kill us before that glorious day arrives, before Our Saviour walks the Earth again and takes us in His arms to His garden in Heaven."

"Amen. Hallelujah."

"Please, today, I want us to pray for Ditiro Molosiwa. Pray his eyes are opened to the truth before it is too late. And pray for the President and his family. Let us pray."

Tumelo bowed his head and prayed in a loud emotional voice. It had gone better than he had ever imagined. There were no murmurs of disagreement. The congregation knew him and accepted his words, all of them. They were excited by the story. He knew Bishop Kissi would be very pleased. He prayed with his head bowed and his heart singing.

CHAPTER EIGHTEEN

It was difficult for Dora to leave the house without an escort. Bishop Kissi required she move with a bodyguard at all times. Besides being the President's daughter, Bishop Kissi was a very wealthy man; anyone with a bit of initiative could kidnap her and make a tidy sum in ransom, and he didn't want that. But today, she needed to get out of the house alone.

Since she'd realised she was pregnant, she'd stopped taking the pills Bishop Kissi gave her. He said they were to curb her craving for alcohol, and she had accepted that. She didn't want to go back to her alcoholic ways and had taken the pills faithfully, at least at first. They gave everything a softer edge and moved the world around her out, away at a distance where she was no longer a real part of it. It had calmed her to be cushioned from events. Still, she'd stopped taking the pills completely when she'd discovered she was pregnant. She knew she would never drink and harm her baby, so the pills were no longer needed.

As the days passed, and the medication slowly made its way out of her system, the world lost its fuzzy edges, and she no longer felt like sleeping all day.

Now, her mind was sharp, and she realised something had been going on. For months, ever since she'd left for Ethiopia, she'd felt as if her hands were tied. She'd had no interest in her life or anyone else's. She'd watched events happen. She was shuttled this way and that, and, in some manner, she was happy to have handed her life over to someone else to run; it was a relief in some ways.

She knew she'd had a problem with alcohol, and she knew once drunk, she behaved crazy and put her life and other people's lives at risk. She knew before she'd been taken to Ethiopia that something needed to change or she was going to be killed or be locked behind bars, even if she was the President's daughter. So she'd taken the pills, and suddenly, nothing mattered anymore.

At night, she would lie in her bedroom and hear the creak of the door that adjoined her rooms to that of Bishop Kissi. He would undress and climb on top of her, not speaking a word, not even checking if she was awake. He would insert his long, hard penis into her, and, even though it was sometimes painful, it was as if the pain was for someone else and not her. She was in her hazy, soft-edged world looking down on a woman spread-eagled under the large body of the Bishop, a woman who felt the sharp stab of the Bishop's penis tearing into her body. She was too drugged to feel the pain herself.

Now that her thoughts were her own again, she saw it all for what it was. Dora was clear now, and she knew she needed to escape.

She needed to get away before the Bishop found out she was pregnant. If he discovered the pregnancy, she and the baby would both be captive forever. A baby would give him the last bit of leverage he needed; a baby was a very valuable thing to a man like Bishop Kissi.

Now that her head was clear, she knew she had to make a move, and today would be the day.

She heard a knock on the door. "Come in."

It was Simane, her personal maid. "I've brought breakfast, Madam."

"Thanks. Leave it on the table. Please, tell Joel and Wandipa I will not be leaving the house today. I feel unwell. They can have the day off."

"Yes, Madam."

"And I don't want to be disturbed. By anyone."

"Yes, Madam."

Dora quickly ate her breakfast. The cup of pills sat on the tray as it always did. She dumped them in the toilet in her bathroom and flushed. She'd packed a light bag, filled more with the cash she'd collected over the last month, stealing when she could from the tithes, than with clothes. She needed enough money to get far away and still more to stay away for a long time. She opened her wardrobe to the line of white cotton dresses the Bishop demanded she wear, but not today.

At the back was a box of some of her old clothes. She dug out jeans, a T-shirt, a jacket, and a baseball cap. Once out of the house in those clothes, no one would recognise her. They'd all become too accustomed to the white-clad zombie the Bishop had created. They'd all forgotten Dora, the Dora she used to be, the Dora she really was.

She had a plan, one altered slightly after yesterday's service. She'd sat through the whole story from Tumelo, Bishop Kissi's lackey. The crowd had nodded and amen-ed and hallelujah-ed after everything he'd said as if he spoke direct words from God.

She had looked over at her father and mother nodding, and she'd felt ill. Here was this young kid none of them knew, speaking horribly about Ditiro and Elizabeth, friends of their family for years. With the words of this boy, all alliances switched, and they would follow this Tumelo to the ends of the earth—she could see it in their eyes.

She had wanted to shout and shake her parents, especially her father who always spoke of Ditiro as if he were the son he'd never had. What was this church doing to them? What was it doing to him?

After listening to that, she'd known she owed it to Ditiro to warn him about what was about to happen. She hadn't seen him or Elizabeth for a long time, but she still cared for them and couldn't allow this to happen without giving them some help. She was aware Ditiro had helped her father to get the legal right to send her to Ethiopia, but she didn't hold that against him. She had needed to get free from the alcohol, and though other things had happened, she was thankful she had things under control now. And even though the baby in her womb was half Bishop Kissi's, she felt a fierce protective love for it. Despite it all, she was happy she was pregnant.

She'd felt an energy in the church the day before. It had sizzled in the air. A fierce, vindictive hate had built slowly as Tumelo spoke. Bloodlust had filled the room. The congregation had been angry—they wanted justice. She was frightened for Ditiro, and especially for Elizabeth. She didn't trust the church members. They might do anything.

When everything in her wing of the house was quiet, she climbed out the back window. After a quick dash to the back garden, she unlocked the gate and found herself free.

Her heart pounded heavily in her chest. She hadn't expected it to be so easy. She stopped for a moment. The air filling her lungs felt so sweet and the sky seemed bluer than she'd ever remembered it though she'd seen a cloudless sky only the day before.

She smiled and rubbed her still-flat stomach. One phone call. A meeting. And she would be on a plane and gone, gone until Bishop Kissi disappeared from Botswana and her real father could be found again. Only then would she and her child return to the country she loved.

***

Ditiro sat with Professor Barnard in a booth in the far corner of the restaurant. He was representing the professor in a tricky divorce settlement. His soon to be ex-wife was unfortunately also his boss at the university. They were trying to do things amicably, but there were substantial assets and a child. To make things worse, Professor Barnard had had an affair with a former student, so there was likely to be a disciplinary hearing at the university instigated by his wife. All very complicated and all very ugly.

Ditiro was finding it difficult to keep any firm ground under their feet. Every passing day brought another problem, and his client was far from helpful. But nevertheless, he tried to keep a positive attitude since his client had sunk into a self-defeating depression. If Ditiro didn't keep upbeat, he feared the worst.

It had been a long, strenuous meeting. He paid the waitress and stood to go.

"So I'll meet with her lawyer tomorrow, and I'll let you know what happens."

Professor Barnard looked up from his plate of untouched food.

"Yeah ... okay ... Just see if she can let me keep the fish. She can take everything else, but I'd really like to at least keep those fish. She doesn't even like them."

Fish? They were seriously in trouble.

"Okay, I wrote it down. We'll get it all sorted out. Talk to you tomorrow."

Ditiro made his escape before Professor Barnard changed his mind and decided to give the fish away, too.

He rushed towards the entrance and nearly bumped into Elizabeth who was walking in with a tall, too-handsome man.

"Oh," Ditiro said, surprised. He was off-kilter seeing Lizzie with someone else and felt compelled to explain his presence for some reason. "Lizzie ... I was ... just meeting a client ... I'm ... leaving ..."

He listened to himself and felt worse as the seconds passed. He sounded so awkward, and she looked so beautiful. He could tell her hair had been freshly washed. It struggled to lay flat on her shoulders, the light bouncing off in all directions from its shiny surface. She wore a long, flowing Indian cotton skirt of which she had many and a purple tank top with layers of necklaces. She looked so much like the young hippy he'd met at university so long ago, the girl he'd fallen so desperately in love with, who'd grown into the woman he knew he'd likely never fall out of love with.

"Ditiro, how are you?" she asked, and he just barely heard her through his own cluttered thoughts. "You remember Peter. We're working on his show for next week."

Peter, who Ditiro apparently knew, but in a different time when he would have just been one of Elizabeth's artists instead of, perhaps, a man she found attractive and might start a relationship with. It made a world of difference. He struggled to be cordial.

"Dumela, rre," Peter said respectfully, reminding Ditiro that he was middle-aged and Peter, the artist he couldn't remember, was young and fit and virile.

"Yes, how are you?" Ditiro shook his hand but couldn't take his eyes off Elizabeth. "You look great."

His voice was low, almost low enough to make him think that maybe he hadn't said it but had only thought it.

"Thanks," she said, confirming that his thought had left his head, after all. "So are we still on for Sunday, then?"

"Sunday?" He couldn't remember at first in his confusion of thoughts, and then it came to him. They were performing Annie at Maitsong, and Lorato had asked if they could all go together, and he had agreed. "Yes ... of course. I'll see you then. I need to get going."

"Okay," Elizabeth said.

He left but glanced back when he was at the door and saw her speaking. Her hands flew back and forth as she spoke; they always did that. She spoke with her hands as much as her mouth. The young artist was listening intently, nodding, smiling. Ditiro wondered what she was telling him.

Before, she would have told him all about it in the evening when Lorato was in bed and they finally had time together. Then, before everything, he would have listened with half an ear, his mind busy with other things.

He wished tonight Elizabeth would be at home, in their home, sitting in her favourite chair, her legs tucked up under her. He wished she would tell him everything, every detail, every thought she had, every word she said, every dream.

If his wish came true, he would listen to every single word this time with complete attention because it came from her mouth, from her mind. He would cherish the conversation.

Then he thought clearly and knew she would not be there tonight, not any night. She was no longer in his life like that again. He turned and walked towards his car parked across the busy street.

He opened the door. Inside, he sat with his head resting on the steering wheel. What had he done? He'd thought Elizabeth's betrayal would finally sink in and his love would slowly seep away, but it wasn't working like that. Time did not heal his broken heart—whoever said that should be sued for false advertising, taken to prison for uttering a false statement. Time just made it worse. He seemed to love her more, not less. He wanted to go back into the restaurant and grab her hand and kneel in front of her and profess his eternal love. Forever and always. Nothing less.

She'd made a mistake. She'd made a mistake, that's all. She was human, and his stubborn, unforgiving nature had forced her out of his life. He knew it wasn't worth it. Pride up against love melted into the water it was made of. It just couldn't stand the heat of such a real thing. He'd made such an awful mistake.

He could hear his cellphone ringing somewhere in his briefcase where he had stashed it before the meeting. He sat up and sighed and then opened the briefcase and found the phone.

"Hello?"

"Ditiro? Is that you?"

He knew the voice but couldn't quite place it. "Yes, it's me. Who's this?"

"Dora. Listen ... we need to talk. We need to talk as soon as possible. You're in danger, and so is Elizabeth."

CHAPTER NINETEEN

Ditiro picked Dora up at a house in Old Naledi she'd directed him to. He suspected she'd gone there as it was the last place they would start looking for her. She had few friends left, but Jocko was a loyal and faithful one from when they were little kids growing up in Tonota. They'd always kept close, and he'd been happy to see her after the months she had been lost and locked up within the walls of Kissi's mansion in Phakalane.

"Okay, Jocko. I'm off. When everything is normal, I'll be back. Not sure how long, but I'll be back. Botswana is my home," Dora said.

Jocko was a tiny man in the baggy jeans and the hoody of a thug-wannabe. Ditiro doubted his criminality went much further than his clothes, though. The tears falling down his cheeks indicated a softness not conducive to any serious thuggery.

"Anything you need, you call. I'll be here waiting for you," he said.

Dora got in Ditiro's car, and they headed out. "My flight leaves at one-thirty so we don't have much time."

Ditiro wasn't sure how to start. "That day in your father's office, when they took you to Ethiopia—"

Dora interrupted.

"Forget it. You and my parents thought you were doing the best thing for me, and in a way, you were. I was lost, and the alcohol was going to kill me one way or another. You saved my life really. I would have liked things to have gone a bit differently, but it went the way it went. Done story. No hard feelings." She rubbed his shoulder. "Really."

"But I felt awful when I heard you were being married off to Kissi. I should have stepped up and said something ... I was a coward."

"Listen, Ditiro, you did what you had to do. Besides, have you seen my parents lately? Do you think anyone was going to listen to you? You didn't stand a chance. They've turned into some freaking zombies."

They both laughed at that, and the air cleared.

They drove past the massive complex the African Church of Spiritual Revelations was building. There was a large tree with a table in the shade about a kilometre farther down the airport road. Dora pointed at it.

"Ditiro, pull up there. We can talk in the car."

He slowed down and stopped under the tree. It was August, still winter, but the day was hot and sunny and the shade welcome, though they stayed in the car. There was no need to take chances. There were many church members, and any one of them could pass by and wonder what Dora and he were speaking about out on this road, though he doubted they would recognise her the way she was dressed.

"So what's going on, Dora?"

"I'm leaving. I'm not going to tell you where, not because I don't trust you, but because I don't want to put you in a difficult place. If you need to get anything to me, if you need to speak with me about anything, contact Jocko. He'll know where I am, and he can be trusted. Completely."

"What happened? What's going on?" Ditiro asked.

"I'm pregnant. I stopped taking the pills they've been giving me and, suddenly, my situation became much clearer. I can't let Kissi know about my child. I'll be trapped forever. A child would be the last thing he needs to trap my father forever. I need to leave before they all find out."

She glanced out the window, checking a passing car. She pulled her jacket up around her face and her cap further down.

Ditiro knew she was right. A child would link Kissi and the President through blood. He already held too much power over the President; a child would only make matters worse.

"If there's anything I can do to help ... money ... anything ... you must just say."

"You're one of the good ones, Ditiro. I always knew that." Dora smiled. "No, I'm fine for now. I have more than enough money, and where I'm going, I have many friends. Ditiro, listen, you and Elizabeth might be in danger."

"In danger? How?"

"Yesterday, a new minister at the church, a guy named Tumelo, gave a long sermon about how he had become infected with HIV. I think Kissi put him up to it. I know the Bishop doesn't like you. He doesn't like the influence you have over my father. I've heard him speak of it before. I think he forced Tumelo to say what he did yesterday. I'm sure it's not true. But the congregation was excited. I'm not sure how they'll respond, what they'll do."

Ditiro didn't understand what Dora was trying to say. "Why would something said at that church put Elizabeth and me in danger?"

Dora's face was full of concern. She hesitated to say the next words. She didn't want to hurt him, but she had to.

"He said Elizabeth gave him HIV. He was calling her the soldier of Satan, and though he tried to keep you out of it, he mentioned your name and insinuated that you were under her spell, under Satan's spell."

Ditiro sat back against the car seat. He took a deep breath, trying to level his mind. He'd never asked Elizabeth who she had slept with. He could only assume it was this man, this Tumelo. He gripped the steering wheel. He wanted to turn the car around and head to the Western Bypass, to the church's office, and find this man. How dare he say such lies when he was the one who gave Elizabeth HIV? He was the one who'd destroyed their life.

He took deep breaths trying to control his emotions.

"He's lying."

"Of course he is. I knew that." Dora rubbed his hand. "I know Elizabeth would never cheat on you. She loves you."

"No ... That's not it. Dora, Lizzie and I are separated."

"Oh, God ... I didn't know. I'm sorry. I was so away from everything, I don't know anything. Ditiro, really, I'm so sorry. I thought Elizabeth and you were fine, great actually."

He hadn't told anyone what had happened. He had only a few friends, none he was close enough to, to discuss such things. His parents knew they were separated, but didn't know any of the details.

"She had a one-night stand. I never asked who the person was. Maybe it was this Tumelo, I don't know. But she didn't give him HIV. He gave her HIV. We had tests when we decided to have a baby, and we were both negative. He gave her HIV. Do you think he did all of this on purpose? To make a point for the church? Do you think he purposefully infected Lizzie with AIDS?"

Ditiro could believe it; he could believe anything from this Kissi. The man wanted power, absolute power if he could get it. He was slowly sucking said power from the President. Ditiro stood in the way of that. Had Kissi organised for Tumelo to infect Elizabeth to get back at Ditiro so he would no longer be a block in his way? It made him sick to think it.

"To be honest, Ditiro, I would put nothing past Kissi. But that's not really important right now. Now, you need to think about Elizabeth. Whatever you're going through, she's Lorato's mother, and you need to protect her. These people are dangerous. They have a target now. To them, Elizabeth is Satan's worker, an Edomite out to annihilate the black Children of Israel. It's crazy talk, but that's what they think. The people on Sunday ... they were angry, they could be reckless. I don't know, I was scared, Ditiro."

He rubbed his hand over his head.

"But that's mad! Anyone who knows Elizabeth would know she could never harm people on purpose. This is seriously messed up. This Kissi needs to be punished for doing this. He can't just do as he likes. There are laws."

"Of course it's crazy, but I saw the way the people in that church responded, and I'm telling you, you need to be careful." Dora looked at her watch. "Listen, Ditiro, I know this is a lot for you to handle all at once, especially now when you and Elizabeth are having problems. It maybe wasn't right of me to just drop it on you, but I need to catch this flight. By this evening, they're going to know I'm gone. I need to be out of the country by then or I won't get another opportunity. I wanted to warn you, though, before I left."

"You're right."

He started the car and pulled back onto the airport road. The fury pulsed in his body like a living thing. He feared the strength of his emotions; he wasn't sure where they might push him.

As he drove, he tried to relax and think of something else. He was meant to protect his family, his wife. That was his job. Now, it looked as if the dangers that had entered their lives had been brought to them because of him, not Elizabeth, because of his close relationship with the President. Could Kissi be that evil, that calculating?

He pulled into the airport and parked the car. He started to get out to help Dora with her bags, but she stopped him when he tried to walk with her to Departures.

"No, I'll be okay from here. Someone might recognise me. You know Gaborone, far too small. If they see you, you'll be implicated in my escape. You have enough headaches. I don't want to be adding to them." She hugged him. "Thanks. Really."

She picked up her bags and started towards the airport entrance, then stopped and came back.

"Ditiro, I know it's none of my business, but people make mistakes, hey? I made more than my share. Elizabeth made a mistake. Please go to her. Help her. She needs you now."

She turned and walked away. He sat for a moment, unsure of where he needed to go. He wanted to go to Kissi and confront him, but he knew in the state he was in, things would get physical quickly; he wouldn't be able to control himself. He could kill him, he knew that. He wouldn't be able to stop. But there were more important things he needed to do.

He headed out of the parking lot and made his way to Elizabeth's gallery.

CHAPTER TWENTY

"I really like this one. The moon behind the clump of baobabs looks so eerie," Elizabeth said, holding up a black and white photograph.

"Yes, it's one of my favourites, too," Peter said. "How are you thinking of grouping them?"

The two of them were sitting on the floor with his photos spread out between them. She liked to have the artist involved in the process of the show. She felt they knew their thoughts behind their pieces more than any viewer might guess at, including her. Since she was also an artist, she knew how it felt when gallery owners excluded the artist once they had the work. She didn't like to walk into an exhibit of her work and feel like a stranger, and she didn't want any of the artists she worked with feeling like that, either.

"I really love these photos from Makgadikgadi. I think they make a nice trilogy. I see a theme of children, this photo of the girls walking to school holding hands, the primary kids singing at school assembly, the boy reading under the tree ... and that other one, where is it now ..."

She searched through the photos. "Okay, yeah, this one. I really love this one, Peter. I think this is so funny. What I love most about this is the boy's face. He's so very serious about what he's doing. I think it's a fabulous photo."

She held a picture in her hand of a boy in school uniform, a book bag on his back, and his school shoes in his hand, socks stuffed quickly inside, walking along a dirt path, between houses made of mud with tin roofs. He has stuck his feet into two drink tins, smashing them down in the middle to fit on his heels only and he was walking, as if on high heels, with a determined look, clomping down the road, his school pants hastily cuffed up to keep them clean, a very determined look on his face.

"I like that one, too. What do you think about the Joburg photos?" Peter asked, picking up a set of five portraits of women.

"I think they're great. I definitely want to use them."

Just then, the door opened. Elizabeth looked up, and Ditiro was standing in the doorway. From his face, she could see something had happened, something serious. She immediately thought of Lorato away at school and quickly stood up.

"What is it?" she asked without greeting him. "Is Lorato okay? What's happened?"

"Lorato's fine. We need to talk ... in private." He walked towards the back office, mumbling a greeting to Peter as he passed.

"I'll be right back, Peter. Just continue."

She followed Ditiro into the office and closed the door behind her. He was pacing back and forth. She knew something awful had happened. He was obviously upset.

"What? Tell me."

"What is the name of the man you slept with?" he asked.

Elizabeth stopped. She was confused why suddenly he wanted information that he'd refused her telling him when it had all happened.

"Why? What is this about, Ditiro?"

"Just tell me his name," he snapped.

"Tumelo ... Tumelo Gabadirwe."

Ditiro pounded his fist on the desk, and the glass vase tipped over and fell on the floor where it crashed into pieces. "I knew it!"

She bent down to pick up the pieces of the vase. "Hey, chill. You're breaking my things. What's going on, Ditiro?"

Peter burst through the door and rushed to her. "Are you okay?"

He'd been startled by the loud noise and the crash. Elizabeth was embarrassed one of her clients had been there to see and hear all of the drama.

"Yes ... I'm fine," she said. "It was an accident, a mistake."

Peter looked at Ditiro for explanation.

"She said everything's fine. Can we get some privacy? I'm her husband."

"Yes, she told me. She also told me you were separated." Peter stood where he was without moving.

Elizabeth was not going to allow the testosterone factor to lead to a fist fight.

"No, Peter ... really, everything is fine. Ditiro and I just need to talk about a few things ... alone. I'm fine. Really."

Peter left giving Ditiro a warning look before closing the door. Like a puppy trying to stand up to a grown dog. She might have laughed under different circumstances.

"Can we sit down?"

Ditiro sat on the sofa, and she pulled her desk chair from behind the desk and sat down in front of him.

"So what is this all about?"

"Okay. Apparently, this Tumelo is a minister in that church for the President, the African Church of Spiritual Revelations."

"I saw that in the paper. I couldn't believe it myself."

"Was he in that church then? When it happened?" Ditiro asked.

"No, I doubt it. He would have mentioned it."

"Yeah, well, yesterday, he did some big testifying in church. He told them that you gave him HIV."

"What? Who told you that?"

"Dora."

"I thought Dora was locked up in Phakalane. How did you talk to her?"

He explained how Dora had stopped taking the pills and managed to escape.

"Lizzie, I think this whole thing—this entire thing, the affair, the break-up, the HIV—all of it was organised by that bastard Kissi."

Ditiro never used foul language. He felt it showed that you were not a master of your mind; you could not control your emotions as an adult should be able to do. She knew if he was speaking like this, he was at breaking point.

"I doubt Kissi is that clever, or that organised. Besides, I only think Tumelo met him afterwards."

"Still, they're lying to get some political points with their church. They're using you, putting you in danger."

Though it was unfair of Tumelo to lie, she didn't see why Ditiro was so upset. Who cared about a few crazy church people? Let them think what they wanted.

"Okay, fine—they lied. It's done. Let's leave it."

She got up, and Ditiro rushed to her.

"No, Lizzie, you don't understand. Dora says these people are dangerous, very dangerous. They're making you out as some white Satan worshipper who came to

157

Botswana to spread HIV to all of the young, black men to kill them. They're sick. She said the people in the crowd were crazy. You know how mob psychology can work. You need to take this seriously."

Though she was angry about Tumelo's lie, she could see Ditiro was upset, and she didn't want to make things worse. So people knew she was HIV-positive; she would have to deal with it.

"But that's crazy. It's just all crazy. I'm sure it's nothing to worry about. Anyone who knows me will know it's all nonsense," she said.

Ditiro took her in his arms, and a surprised Elizabeth hugged him back. It must have been all of the emotion he was feeling because after a minute, he jumped away from her.

"I want you to move back home so I can keep you safe," he said.

She didn't understand what it all meant. She didn't want to read things into it that were not there. "Why?"

"I think these people might come after you. I want you at home. I'll get some security. You can move with a guard."

"But won't Lorato be confused? Won't she think things are going ... back to normal?"

She hoped so badly he would say yes—yes, they *are* going back to normal. That he would say, yes, I want you to move back home. I want us to sleep in the same bed again. I want us to be husband and wife again and forget all about this terrible nightmare we've been living through for the last year.

"No, we'll explain it to her," he said. "You can sleep in the guest bedroom. It's not safe to have you out there at the doctor's, most of the time alone. Anything could happen. At home, I can keep an eye on things. If Dora is exaggerating and everything seems okay, you can go back to your cottage. But for now, I think you should stay at home. At least for the next few weeks."

She couldn't have Ditiro, but she would have Lorato. She would be living with her daughter again. She tried hard to hide her excitement. She knew Ditiro was still very upset by the whole church thing, but for her, she saw it as a good thing. The church had brought her back home to her daughter.

CHAPTER TWENTY-ONE

Elizabeth lay on the bed looking out the window at the night sky. Her daughter was just a few feet away. She could get up and check her whenever she wanted. They'd eaten dinner together like they used to. She had sat at the kitchen table with Lorato as the girl slowly practiced writing her letter B across an entire page in her exercise book. Then, she'd listened as Lorato read her assigned passage for the night. Every little bit of it; she now knew was a precious gift she would never again take for granted.

Even Precious was happy. She'd sung throughout the meal even though Elizabeth had told her it was only temporary.

"That's okay, Madam, I'm just happy you're back."

Elizabeth could tell Ditiro was still not over the emotions he had been filled with during the afternoon. He'd drunk a few beers, and still, he spoke little and jumped at every noise. After Lorato went to bed, they watched some television, but he was distracted and nervous.

"I'll be fine. We'll be fine," she said, trying to reassure him.

"Lizzie, you don't know this man. He wants everything. You can see it in him. He's ruthless."

She tried but could not convince him. He'd called the security company, and the house and the gallery now had a twenty-four-hour guard. He'd told her tomorrow when she left for the gallery, another guard would be escorting her. She'd said nothing to all of this though she considered it overkill. If it made Ditiro calm down, then she would go along with it. She was just happy to be home.

She rolled on her side but then heard her cellphone ringing in her bag in the wardrobe. It was already very late; she wondered who would be calling her at this time. She got out of bed to get it.

"Oh, Elizabeth!" Kagiso burst out with relief when she heard Elizabeth's voice.

"What is it, Kagiso? What's wrong?"

"Where are you?" she asked.

"I'm at home, at Ditiro's. He asked me to stay here for a while. What's going on, Kagiso? You sound upset."

"It's the cottage. I'm at the hospital. I was on call and came in. While I was here, the police showed up telling me the cottage caught fire. It's gone."

"I'm so sorry, Kagiso. How? How did it happen?" Elizabeth asked.

"I'm here right now at the cottage. It reeks of paraffin. Somebody burned it down on purpose. It looks like it was arson."

"Kagiso, that's awful."

"I'm a bit frantic. I can't find the cats. I hope they weren't in there," she said.

"No, I'm sure they're not. They probably ran away, afraid of the fire. The windows were closed. They wouldn't have been able to get in," Elizabeth assured her.

"I hope so," Kagiso said.

Elizabeth looked out into the night that had a few minutes before appeared so welcoming. Now, the shadows behind the streetlight held menacing secrets.

The stars were cold. She slumped onto the nearby chair, her legs unable to hold her upright.

"Elizabeth? Elizabeth, are you there?" Kagiso asked.

"Yes ... I ... do you want me to come over?"

"No, my mother is here and my sister. I'll be okay. I'm so sorry about your things inside. I don't know who would want to do this to me. What would they gain by burning down an empty cottage?"

She ignored the question. "I'll come by and see you in the morning, first thing. Don't even think about my stuff, it's not important. I'll see you tomorrow."

She hung up the phone. *What would they gain by burning down an empty cottage?* They hadn't thought it was empty. They'd thought she was inside. They were trying to kill her.

***

In the morning, Ditiro seemed almost back to himself so she didn't tell him about the cottage. She'd tell him later. After thinking it over during the night, she didn't know for certain they'd meant to kill her. Who knew? It could be anything. She would wait to tell him after she'd passed by Kagiso's and spoken to her. There was no need to get him upset if she didn't have to.

"Okay, Pumpkin, go and get your school bag," he said.

"Can Mommy take me to school today?" Lorato asked.

Ditiro looked at Elizabeth. She knew what he was thinking; he was not going to have his daughter put in danger by riding with her in the car.

"You know what, Lorato," Elizabeth said. "I need to run by Kagiso's before I go to the gallery, so I won't have time today. Maybe another day."

"Okay." Lorato ran off to get her schoolbag, and Ditiro smiled a thank you.

She waited until Ditiro and Lorato were gone before collecting her new guard that stood with the house guard at the edge of the garden.

"Hi, I'm Elizabeth. I guess we're a team today."

"Ee, Mma Molisiwa. My name's Amantle."

Elizabeth noticed as Amantle got in the car that he had a gun. Guns were so uncommon in Botswana; it gave her a shock when she saw it. But then, she remembered the burned cottage, and she realised it was better this way.

When she got to Kagiso's house, a police car and another marked 'fire inspector' were parked in the driveway. She parked on the street and turned to Amantle.

"I just want to check my friend. Can you wait here?"

He shook his head and got out of the car and followed her up to the house. He stood to the side as she knocked on the door. Kagiso opened. Her hair was hastily pushed in a doek and she looked like she hadn't slept at all.

"Elizabeth, I'm glad you're here. The police are here. They want to know what was in the cottage. You came at the exact right time."

She spotted the cats behind her. "So they turned up?"

Kagiso smiled. "Yes, this morning. I think you were right. They got scared and ran off. I was so happy to see them."

She followed Kagiso into the house. She could smell the burnt organic scent of a paraffin fire and could see the charred remains of the cottage at the back of the house. A cold chill spread through her body. That might have been her death site.

"I'm so jumpy. I haven't slept at all," Kagiso said. "I just can't understand who would want to do this."

In the kitchen where they headed, there were two men. Elizabeth guessed they were the police officer and the fire official, and an older woman with Kagiso's smiling eyes.

"My mother," Kagiso said.

"Lovely to meet you. Too bad it's under such terrible circumstances."

Elizabeth shook her hand and then greeted the two men. She was right—the younger one was a police officer investigating the crime of arson, and the older, fatter one, was the fire inspector who would be assisting the police.

"I was renting the cottage from Dr. Moleele."

"Yes, she told us," the police officer said.

"There he is! The arsonist has come back!" Kagiso shouted from the window where she stood. She'd been putting the tea kettle on and spotted Amantle at the back of the house, apparently 'securing the perimeter.' The police officer and the fire inspector jumped to their feet and started for the door.

"No! Wait!" Everyone looked at Elizabeth. "He's with me. It's okay, he's my guard."

"Guard?" Kagiso asked. "Why do you need a guard?"

Everyone sat down, and she explained what Ditiro had told her. She felt terrible that because of her, this had happened to Kagiso. She took Kagiso's hands in hers.

"You have to believe me, I thought Ditiro was overreacting. I thought they were a bunch of overexcited church people. I thought they were harmless. I didn't think they would really do anything. I was just going along because Ditiro let me move back with him and Lorato. That's all I thought of it. I'm so sorry, Kagiso. I should have warned you."

"Elizabeth, it's not your fault. We don't even know if they're the ones, and if they are, they're guilty, not you."

"I feel terrible. I should have taken Ditiro seriously, and I could have warned you somehow."

Kagiso set a cup of tea down on the table in front of Elizabeth. "A warning wouldn't have helped. I was at the hospital. Please, don't blame yourself. How were you expected to anticipate such a thing?"

After giving tea to everyone, Kagiso sat down and spoke to the police officer. "So now you know the likely suspects, what are you going to do about it?"

"I've taken their names. From here, we'll pass by the church and speak to Bishop Kissi and hear what he has to say. We'll get back to you. In the meantime, Mma Molosiwa, if you could make a list of the items you had in the cottage, that would be helpful."

The police officer and fire inspector stood up.

"I think we have everything for now," the older man said. "We've got your numbers, and we'll call you if we need anything else."

Kagiso stood up and followed them to the front door. Her mother, a very youthful-looking seventy-year-old woman in jeans and a T-shirt, with a red doek on her head, grabbed Elizabeth's arm and whispered, "I know that church. They're very powerful. You must watch yourself, my dear. Watch yourself, they're very dangerous."

Elizabeth wondered if church people could be dangerous. Wasn't that against Christianity? Could they have done this? Could these people really want her dead just because of a lie told by Tumelo? More and more, it seemed the answer was yes.

CHAPTER TWENTY-TWO

Amantle took up his position near the gallery's front door while Elizabeth hung and re-hung Peter's photos, trying to get them in the exact position she wanted. The show was the next day, and they still had a lot of work to do.

She looked at the clock. Eleven-thirty. Peter had agreed to stop by at eleven, to see what he thought of her arrangement of his photos. He was late, which was not like him, but she was thankful for it. The early morning detour to Kagiso's house had taken more time than she had expected.

After seeing the remains of the cottage, she couldn't settle her mind. She tried to keep her thoughts away from the one thing that kept taking control of them— she could have died last night.

She kept seeing the cottage. She could have been dead because of the lies told by Tumelo. How long would that one indiscretion haunt her? Was it not enough that he gave her HIV? Now, he wanted to use her to earn points with his congregation? Once the church members realised she had not died in the fire, wouldn't they come after her again? Ditiro's guards had seemed such a waste of money, but she was thankful for them now.

She heard the door open and turned to see Amantle standing in Peter's way, stopping him from entering.

"Now this is not going to be too great for business if you don't let anyone in, Amantle," she joked, but his face stayed fixed. "He's okay. Really. He's one of my artists."

Peter rushed in when Amantle moved to the side.

"What's that all about?" he asked.

"Can I tell you later? First, what do you think?" She moved back so Peter could see his photos.

He walked around the gallery looking at his work from different angles.

"Feel free to move what you want. I want to make a quick phone call."

She left Peter with Amantle and went to the office to call Ditiro. She hadn't told him about the fire yet. She thought it would be better she told him about the cottage when Lorato was not around.

"Hi, Ditiro, can you talk for a minute?"

"Yeah, just a minute, though. I'm due back in court."

She explained what had happened. "I'm sorry I didn't take you seriously yesterday. I guess I didn't understand what was going on, how serious it all was. But I get it now."

"So what are the police doing? I hope they went and arrested that bastard Kissi."

He was more upset than he had been yesterday. The whole situation had moved from theoretical to deadly practice.

"They said they were going there. I'm sure they'll sort it all out. Ditiro, please, I'm fine, I have the guard here. At home, we have the guard, we'll be fine. We're all going to be fine. Please calm down. I hate when you get so upset. You remember I'm the emotional one—you're the stable, rational guy. We can't be changing roles now."

He laughed, and she felt better.

"Yeah ... okay. I'll see you later. I need to get back in court." His voice took on a tender edge. "Lizzie ... please be careful. I don't know what we'd do if we lost you."

"I will ... See you later at home."

She felt it was odd how amid all of this awfulness, she was also happy. They were back together as a family, at least for the time being, and that was a good thing.

She went back to the gallery and found Peter sitting on the floor looking up at his photos. He got up when he noticed her.

"They look beautiful just as you have them. I love the groupings. Really, really nice. Thanks, Elizabeth. It's so fantastic when people really get my work, and I can see you do. You found a theme where I didn't even know I had one."

"You knew the themes. Only your subconscious was hiding it from you." She smiled. "Do you want a cup of tea? I was just about to make some."

Peter suddenly looked nervous. "No ... Actually, Elizabeth ... I came by because I wanted to ask you something."

"Sure, shoot." She busied herself putting the kettle on, getting her cup from the desk.

"Some people have been talking. They said I should cancel the show."

She stopped what she was doing and turned to look at him. "Cancel the show? Why?"

Peter looked back at Amantle and then lowered his voice. "Apparently, there is some rumour about you ... that you're HIV-positive. Something happened at that big church on the Western Bypass last week. People are talking a lot of crap, but my friends think it might be a problem ... for my show, like to be associated with you."

She could tell Peter didn't want to be having this conversation; someone had forced him to do it.

"Does that matter if I'm HIV-positive?" she asked.

"No, not to me. Hell no, I have a lot of HIV-positive friends. Who doesn't in Botswana? But they say you're spreading it around, you want to kill black men. I know it's rubbish ... I know you, Elizabeth. It's complete rubbish. All of us artists know it's lies ... you're wonderful. You've done so much for so many of us. You're fantastic. It's just people, it's talk ... but it's my first show and all ... I just wanted to know what was going on."

"Peter, yes, I am HIV-positive. But I contracted HIV in Botswana. I have given it to no one. I would never want to pass the virus on. It looks like some people want to use me for a political plan they have. It's not true, but sometimes, truth is not all that important. All I can give you is my word. If you want to cancel the show, I have no problem. Really. I'll completely understand, and I will not think any less of you. It's totally up to you. I know it's difficult."

He shook his head. When he spoke, she could tell that his throat was choked with tears.

"I don't know why they want to do this to you. They call themselves Christians ... You're such a wonderful person ... so good. It's not fair."

"Not so good, but not so bad, either. Just a person trying my best to get through life, that's all."

He nodded. "We'll have the show. Damn them!"

"Yes, damn them," she said, trying to sound resolute and brave when she was neither.

If Peter's friends knew about what had happened at the church, it was likely many other people did, too. Though when comparing it with someone trying to kill her, it seemed inconsequential, still, she didn't like the idea of the whole country knowing she was HIV-positive and thinking she was on a mission to spread the disease. She felt helpless up against it all and was happy to have the show to keep her distracted.

CHAPTER TWENTY-THREE

Ditiro agreed to the appointment with the President, but only reluctantly. The papers the day before had printed front page headlines about Dora's disappearance. There was speculation she had been kidnapped or she'd run away with a church member. One of the tabloids suggested she may have been killed by the church as a human sacrifice.

He knew the President would mention Dora's disappearance at their meeting. He wondered if he would also speak about what had happened at the church the previous Sunday. He didn't leave the President guilt-free in what was happening to Elizabeth. He wouldn't bring it up unless the President did, but he knew he would struggle to contain his emotions and opinions on the subject.

Since Dora had told him everything, he'd been walking around in a red fury. Who did Kissi and his church members think they were? Where were the laws in this country? Though Elizabeth had given the police all of the information, they had made no arrests for the burning of the cottage. Were they waiting for someone to die before they acted? Arson was a crime in Botswana; at least it was the last time he'd checked. He suspected someone high up in the police was a member of the church, as so many of the highly placed civil servants were, and that person had stopped the investigation.

He pushed open the heavy door into the President's office and found Boitumelo on the telephone. She hung up and looked towards him.

"Good morning, Rre Molosiwa. The President is waiting for you, you can go through."

The President was sitting at his desk paging through the day's newspapers. Ditiro was not sure if it was the way the strong summer sun from the nearby window fell on his face or not, but the President looked like an old man; an old and very weary man. Many things had happened, but he still saw the President as a friend, and a surge of panic gripped him seeing the man so weak and fragile. He'd always seemed powerful, almost invincible, tall and commanding like a man that could withstand anything, one who would live forever. But like everyone, Ditiro could see in that moment that President Setlhoboko was an ordinary man, mortal like all of us.

"Ditiro ... take a seat. I'm glad you could find time to stop by, I know you're very busy," the President said, putting the newspapers to the side to give Ditiro his complete attention.

Ditiro noticed he'd been reading the stories about his daughter's disappearance. The President followed his sight line.

"I guess you know about Dora."

"Yes, I do." He waited.

"These newspapers don't know anything. They're just making up stories. MmaDora is sick with worry. We don't know if she's alive or dead ... where she could have gone."

The President shook his head, and Ditiro noticed his hands were shaking.

"Did you check the airport?" Ditiro didn't want to betray Dora, but he could imagine the pain her parents were going through. He'd be crazy with worry if it were

Lorato. At least if they knew she was alive, even if they didn't know where she was, they would feel better.

"No, David said her passport was there. We think she is likely still in the country, or dead."

"Dora is an intelligent woman. I would suspect she could get a hold of another passport."

He knew now why Dora had been wise to give him no details of where she was going. She'd envisioned this very meeting long before she'd left. She'd known Ditiro would not be able to watch her father suffer.

"Do you know something, Ditiro? Please, if you know anything, tell me," the President pleaded, and Ditiro could not bear to see him so compromised.

"Dora is fine."

"Have you heard from her?" The President came around the desk and sat next to him. "Ditiro, please, tell me. Where is she? Why did she leave? What do you know?"

Ditiro stood up and walked to the window. He looked out on to the mall in the distance. Everybody going somewhere, busy with their lives, their own problems. His situation which seemed of such monumental importance meant nothing to them. What was the right thing to do here? Where did his allegiance fall? He didn't like being confused. He turned back to the room, but facing away from the President.

"She was afraid of Kissi. She needed to get out of there to protect herself."

"Afraid of David? That's crazy. He loves her; he's been taking such good care of her. You've seen for yourself how she stopped drinking, how she has learned to control her temper. David has done miracles."

Ditiro turned to the President, barely containing his anger. "Miracles? Were you even paying attention? He was drugging her! Drugging her and then raping her when she was half-asleep. Is that a marriage? Was she in safe hands?"

He heard his voice raising and knew it was not wise, but he couldn't stop himself. He wanted to shake this stranger awake; he wanted the man he knew back.

"She left to protect herself. She's safe. Please don't try to find her. She will come home when she is sure she will be safe in this country."

The President sat back down quietly. His face was drawn, his shoulders stooped. Ditiro could see he was struggling with what he'd said. If he was to accept Ditiro's words, then he'd have to see that Kissi was dangerous. He would have to accept that he himself had put his daughter in danger because of believing in the Bishop.

These were difficult things for anyone to accept, especially a man like Rre Setlhoboko, President of Botswana, a man of insight and intelligence, a man who didn't get taken in by fancy words and conjurer tricks—but he had.

Ditiro sat back down next to the President. "Are you alright, sir? Should I get you some water? Maybe I can get tea for us?"

"Yes ... okay. Get Boitumelo—she can get tea."

Ditiro slipped out the office and helped Boitumelo get the tea things together. When everything was ready, she picked up the tray.

"No, it's okay, I can take it." He didn't want the secretary to see her boss the way he had left him.

When he went back in the office, he found the President on the telephone. He seemed to have completely recovered. Ditiro was surprised, but then realised who he was speaking to—Kissi, and where sympathy had been, disgust took its place.

"Of course. Yes, young women are like that, you are absolutely correct. ... Yes, I think it's a good idea to put out a press release, too. She's on holiday, there's nothing wrong, all speculation in the private press is just that, speculation. We might mention how such wild ideas can cause problems and that the press needs to control themselves or we may need to control them ourselves ... Yes ... no, you are right."

The President hung up the phone. Ditiro set a cup of tea in front of him saying nothing.

The President smiled up at him. "Thanks."

Ditiro sat down and waited. He didn't have to wait long.

"David has assured me I have nothing to worry about. He'd forgotten all about a small argument he'd had with Dora. He thinks now that may have been what caused her to say such things to you and to disappear without telling anyone. You know wives, Ditiro, always emotional."

What did Kissi have over people? How did they fall in line behind him like mice to the flute player? Ditiro felt like he'd been punched in the stomach.

"So what does Bishop Kissi suggest you do?" he asked.

"He says it's best we just wait. She'll come home when she's ready. It's only been forty-eight hours. I imagine if it was a lover's tiff, she'll be back by the end of the week."

"It's curious how the Bishop failed to remember the argument. Wasn't he the one who spoke to the media about her disappearance?" Ditiro asked.

"Yes, he was. He was worried. You know us men; we don't take these small arguments very seriously. For women, it's another story. He'd probably forgotten all about it, especially when he found she was missing. He really does love Dora. You can imagine how you would feel if Elizabeth suddenly was missing."

Ditiro could tell the President regretted he'd spoken the words as soon as they came out of his mouth.

"I mean, when things were better between the two of you. How is that going? Have you started divorce proceedings yet?"

"No, not yet."

"You should get on that. No need to drag it out, you must think of Lorato. Better things are sorted and you move on. Lorato needs a stable mother." The President looked at Ditiro over the tea cup.

"Elizabeth is a fantastic mother, and no matter what happens, she will always be in Lorato's life." Ditiro was struggling to stay calm—he needed to get out of the office. "I have another appointment. Maybe we can get on to the business you called me here for."

The President ignored the change in the direction of the conversation. "Sorry, Ditiro. I didn't mean any harm. I was trying to be practical. You know people are complicated. We never truly know each other, do we?"

"No ... you're right, we don't."

"You know how I feel about you, Ditiro. I just want to protect you."

He could take no more of their rounding of the issue that now sat before them.

"Protect me from whom? Are you talking about what Kissi's protégé said in your so-called church last Sunday? Is that it, Rre Setlhoboko?"

The President hesitated. He was not used to being spoken to in such a manner. "Yes, in fact, I am. I couldn't believe it. I didn't know Elizabeth was like that."

"Like what?" Pretences at protocol had fallen away. "That man is a liar! Elizabeth would never do anything like that! They have their agenda, and they will use anyone they can find to further it!"

"Ditiro, I can understand your anger, but it's not like that. Reverend Tumelo is a trusted assistant to Bishop Kissi. I don't think he can make something like that up. In the end, Ditiro, you don't know Elizabeth. She's a white American; you're a black Motswana—how could you ever get across the gulfs between you? You can't. Perhaps she's tricked you ... used you as part of this plan of hers. MmaDora and I were as surprised as anyone when we heard the truth. If we were duped, you shouldn't feel ashamed that you've been duped also. We really liked Elizabeth. You were in love. Love blinds us to such things."

Ditiro got to his feet, grabbing his briefcase from the floor.

"I can't listen to any more of this." He headed for the door and then stopped and turned around. "Do you know last night, your Bishop Kissi or one of his trusted assistants tried to kill Elizabeth? Are you aware of that? Is that how it is now in Botswana? If you don't like someone, maybe you don't like the colour of their skin, you can kill them? You tell your friend Kissi, I know what he's up to, and I will make sure he is punished for what he's done."

The President stood up from his desk, ignoring what Ditiro had said, and went to him. He put a fatherly hand on his shoulder.

"Ditiro, I know you're upset. When you calm down, you will be able to think clearly. In the meanwhile, please refrain from wild accusations and threats. They could come back to harm you."

Ditiro looked the President in the eyes, but the man he knew was gone. When he'd entered the office, he had felt pity for him and the pressures he was under, but now, he felt neither pity nor respect for the man before him, speaking in thinly veiled threats, believing a stranger over a trusted friend.

He had been thinking that the President needed to be saved, that he was really on their side, that he just needed to hear the truth, but he'd been wrong. It was too late for this man. He'd handed himself, his family, and the country over to Kissi and his church, putting everyone in danger in the process.

Ditiro could no longer count on him to behave logically. The President could not be trusted. He was now one of the enemies.

CHAPTER TWENTY-FOUR

Elizabeth put out the snacks and straightened the wine glasses. Peter was pacing up and down the gallery waiting for the guests to arrive. The guard, Amantle, was joined by Monthe tonight. Apparently, a photography show was a dangerous event. Ditiro didn't like the idea of a room full of strangers and had asked for an additional guard.

She looked out the door. It was five minutes past the start of the show, and the street was empty.

"They'll come," she told the worried face of Peter. "You know Batswana, always fashionably late."

Just then, she turned around to see a group of people arrive. At the front was Peter's girlfriend and behind her two of his friends. From behind them appeared Ditiro and Lorato.

"Hi, Mommy," Lorato said, jumping into Elizabeth's arms. Lorato spotted the tray of colourful tiny cakes. "Can I have a cupcake?"

Elizabeth set her back on the floor. "Sure."

"I thought we were late," Ditiro said as they watched Lorato at the snack table trying to decide on a cake. He checked his watch.

"You are," she said.

She was beginning to realise the rumours about her were more widespread than she had thought. She'd never considered herself naïve, but it was looking more and more as if she didn't quite understand the human capacity to always search for the bad story, to actively look for the worst in each other. It seemed they all believed she was the pariah. Anything they knew about her from before had been wiped away and replaced with a more exciting story.

Peter's friends tried to make the most of the situation, but after an hour, everyone's enthusiasm waned. Peter sat in the corner, his chin in his hand, looking at his beautiful photos. Elizabeth knew that an artist's ego was a fragile one. She hoped this wouldn't harm his very much. To have an exhibition of your work and no one showing up, no matter the reason, was a blow.

She sat down next to him.

"Maybe we should call it a day," she suggested.

"Yeah ... maybe," he said.

"You know this has nothing to do with you or your work. It's this whole situation with me. That's why they didn't come. Not your work, never your work. I guess we should have heeded the warnings."

Peter nodded. He stood up and went to his friends. They spoke a bit. His girlfriend hugged him. They made to leave.

"Thanks for everything, Elizabeth. You put so much work into this. I'm sorry it didn't work out," he said at the door.

"Don't even worry about that. Your photos are beautiful. Now you just need to find the right place to exhibit them. I know a few places in Joburg. I'll talk to them and let you know," she told him.

Peter waved goodbye to Lorato, who was busy making a necklace with the shiny metallic cupcake liners from the three cupcakes she'd eaten, and Ditiro, who was pacing in the corner, getting himself more worked-up with each passing minute as no one pitched up. "Bye, guys!"

Elizabeth watched the group leave and locked the door behind them. She turned to her little family.

"Well, you guys want to get home?"

"Look at my necklace. Isn't it beautiful?" Lorato asked.

"Of course." She turned to Ditiro. "Are you ready to leave?"

He said nothing, only picked up his jacket from the chair. "I think it's better Lorato rides with me."

She had accepted that was the way now. She was a target even with her guards. They needed to keep Lorato safe. "Okay, see you two at home."

She watched them leave. She turned back to Peter's photos and could feel the tears building. She had tried her best to make this country her home. That's how she felt about Botswana now—it was her home. She accepted that she had made a mistake. How would she ever be able to agree to host another artist's work knowing this could happen to them? It was over, over until people forgot the lies Tumelo had spread, and she knew that would not happen for a long time, maybe never. The gallery was what had held her together through all the awfulness, and now, it was gone.

She had a form of her family back, and that was good, but it was not permanent. Ditiro had told her as much. It was just to keep her safe. When the danger passed, she would be kicked out again. This time, it would be even worse since she would no longer have the gallery to keep her occupied. Even the cottage was gone, her little home she'd grown used to. Everywhere she looked was uncertainty. Everything she cared about was being taken away, one by one, as if by design.

Amantle and Monthe, the guards, waited for her. She would have liked a bit more time alone before facing Ditiro and Lorato again. She knew Ditiro was furious. He was taking the whole situation so personally. Already, he'd nearly had a fight with the President. She felt guilty about everything. Ditiro's anger, Peter's feeling of failure, the fire at Kagiso's cottage— everything was her fault. If she had just done the right thing, none of this would have happened.

She wiped the tears away with a flick of her hand and turned to her watchmen. "Okay Bo-rre, let's get going."

***

When she got home, Lorato was already in bed. Ditiro was in the dark sitting room drinking a beer which was clearly not his first.

"So she's off then?" Elizabeth asked into the shadows.

"Yeah, she fell asleep in the car. I carried her straight through."

She got a beer from the kitchen and came back into the sitting room. "Can I turn on a lamp?"

"Sure, whatever you want."

They sat quietly together, but the air was tense. She wanted to help him. She hated seeing him like this. She wanted to take the burden for him; it was hers to carry anyway.

She didn't know how to tell him, how to start the conversation. In the past months, she'd learned not to ask, not to initiate. She'd taught herself to wait for Ditiro, for whatever he wanted to give her. She didn't know how to speak to him anymore. In everything, she seemed to have forgotten.

"What I don't get is why you're not angry?" Ditiro said, a bitter edge to his voice.

She thought for a moment. She knew the answer, but she wasn't quite ready to say it out in words. At the same time, she wanted to be honest.

"I guess I think I don't have any right to be angry. I'm the one who started all of this."

"Started all of this? How? You are the victim here."

"No, Ditiro. I should have never had sex with Tumelo. That started this whole chain of events. I was feeling lost and angry, and I behaved like a child instead of an adult. I'm the one to blame for all of it."

She'd tried so hard not to let her emotions show. But when she spoke those words, when they were free from her mind and out there, they were suddenly so real. They were a solid confirmation of her culpability in everything. It was too much, and she began to cry. First only tears she couldn't stop falling, but then, the emotion built-up, and she had no strength to stop it.

She hadn't noticed Ditiro move to sit next to her on the sofa until she was in his arms. He held her to him, and her body shook with the strength of her feelings. The months of loneliness and fear poured out. The black sadness she'd hovered in since he'd told her to leave pushed to the surface and surrounded her. She let it wash over her, and she let herself feel the pain of it everywhere. The months of keeping things pushed into a tiny cage in her heart had come to an end. The door was open, and the emotions were free to do as they liked. And they filled every space in her.

Ditiro held her tightly. They rocked back and forth as she cried. Time passed without notice.

When Elizabeth calmed down, she looked up at his face and saw it, too, was wet with tears. He gently wiped his hand across her cheeks and bent down to kiss her.

First, a tentative, unsure kiss, but then one with purpose and meaning. She kissed him back.

He pulled her to his lap and kissed her neck, her ears. She lay back feeling each touch of his lips on her skin like something new. She was surprised her body was reacting, that there was feeling left inside for this. Ditiro slowly unbuttoned her blouse and laid his head between her breasts.

"I love you so much, Lizzie," he whispered like a prayer. "I've missed you."

She could feel the movement of his lips against her skin as he spoke the words she'd been begging to hear for so many months, the words she thought she'd never hear again.

She felt her heart catch on the edge of a star as her emotions, moments ago lost in a dungeon of solid black, soared into the heavens where angels flew, and wishes, held secret and deep for fear the knowledge that they existed and may not be fulfilled would kill her dead, were set gloriously free, and hope was reborn.

CHAPTER TWENTY-FIVE

The phone woke her up the next morning. When her eyes opened, she smiled to see she was lying in Ditiro's arms. It wasn't a dream from her sleep. It was real what had happened the night before. Smiling, she slipped away without waking him to get the phone in the kitchen.

"Hello?"

"Elizabeth?"

"Hi Kagiso, what's up?"

"Sorry I'm calling so early. I was at the hospital all night. Just got home now. Elizabeth, have you seen the Sunday paper?"

"The Sunday paper? No, why?"

"You need to get it. Those church people are at it again, the bastards. They're talking about your status, *in the paper*! Elizabeth, this isn't right. It's against the law. You need to do something. I can't believe they think they can just do this, that they have some sort of impunity!"

She found it hard to work up any anger in the morning after all her wishes had been granted, but she could hear that Kagiso was upset.

"Okay. I'll get the paper, but don't worry. You know how things go in this country. One day something is big news, the next everyone has forgotten about it. I'll talk to Ditiro. He'll know what to do."

Somehow, that seemed to make Kagiso feel better. "Yes, talk to Ditiro. You must fight these people. If you need me to testify in court, I can do it. Anything I can do, just ask. Who do these people think they are? This is Botswana, we have laws."

On this beautiful, fantastic sunny Sunday morning, she didn't think anything could get her down. Even the crazy church people.

"Okay, I'll call you later. You calm down, okay?" Elizabeth said.

"Yeah, you're right. I need some sleep. I'm tired and then I saw this ... Maybe I'll come around later. Would that be alright?"

"Sure, that would be great."

She hung up the phone and turned to find Precious behind her. She'd been great ever since Elizabeth had moved back home.

"What do you want for breakfast, Madam?"

"You know what, Precious, I'll take care of breakfast this morning. Is Lorato awake?"

"Not yet, but soon."

"Okay, can you keep an eye on her for a few minutes? I want to run to the shop and get a few things. Tell Ditiro I'll be back just now."

***

Elizabeth went to the supermarket down the road from their house. She shopped there often and knew many of the people. She greeted the manager near the door, but the woman seemed to be too busy on the phone to notice.

She wandered around the aisles picking things she knew Ditiro loved. Pork sausage, bacon, apple Danish. She got to the till and realised she'd forgotten to buy the newspaper even though that was the reason she'd come in the first place.

When she got to the magazine rack, she looked around and at first thought the newspapers were not there yet, but then looked down on the floor. Looking back up at her was a blown-up photo of herself, smiling. The headline read: "Is this woman on a mission to kill black men?"

She grabbed the paper and quickly folded it in half so no one could see her face. She knew it was futile since a whole stack with the same photo on the cover remained behind staring up at all who passed. When she turned around, she saw the customer at the till looking at her.

Elizabeth looked in the direction of the door, and the manager was off her phone staring at her, too. They were all wondering the same thing, she thought—they were wondering if the newspaper was right? Or perhaps that was what she hoped. It was more likely they believed the newspaper, as most people did. They were likely wondering who she was planning to infect that day, who she was planning to kill. She quickly paid for the paper, grabbed up her packages, and rushed out the door.

***

When she got home, she found Ditiro at the table with a cup of coffee, just starting his laptop and his daily perusal of the news. She was not exactly sure where they stood. She didn't want to assume the night before meant they were back together as a couple, but, still, she wanted him to know how wonderful it had been for her, how much she'd appreciated his tenderness when she'd been at her most vulnerable.

"You were up early," he said, searching for his glasses in his laptop bag.

"I wanted to buy some things for breakfast. I thought I'd make us something nice." She set the bags on the counter and started unpacking.

Ditiro got up and came to her. He turned her around and kissed her and took her in his arms.

"I know last night we were feeling a lot of things and maybe everything went fast and we didn't talk and work things through properly, but it felt right. I hope it did for you too," he whispered into her hair.

Elizabeth pushed back so she could look at him. "Yes. I want us to try. We can take it slow or fast whatever you want, but ... it feels wonderful being right where I am. Thanks for giving me another chance. I never thought you would. I'm so sorry for everything."

He kissed her again, and they held each other for a moment, then she moved away from him.

"I don't want to ruin this, but ... I wasn't just going out for food. Kagiso phoned. She said I needed to get the paper."

She dug it out from the plastic bag and handed it to him. He carried it over to the kitchen table and spread it out to read in the warm October sun coming in through the window. She started getting breakfast ready as he read quietly.

"Mommy, you're in the newspaper," Lorato said, coming up behind Ditiro.

Elizabeth looked at her husband who quickly closed the paper.

"Yes, I am. But you know, Lorato, sometimes, newspapers don't tell the truth. That newspaper is telling lies about Mommy, a bad story that is all lies. But it's okay. We don't care about any stupid newspaper, do we?" she said, picking Lorato up and giving her a kiss.

She didn't see any use in lying to her daughter. Lorato could read for herself. She might not understand it all, but the words were no problem for their precocious daughter. Elizabeth suspected, too, that the whole thing would soon be discussed at Lorato's school, so it wasn't fair to leave her in the dark.

"I bought sausages and donuts for breakfast. So why don't you go and find Precious and take a quick bath and come back and breakfast will be finished. Okay?"

"Okay." Lorato turned around and ran off towards Precious' room.

Ditiro opened the paper and finished reading.

"What kind of balanced reporting is this? They didn't even speak to you. They could easily have called you at the gallery or me at work to get our side. This is nothing more that sensationalism! Listen to Kissi—'These types of people need to be stopped. She is nothing more than a murderer. I personally believe she is one of Satan's workers.' Then it says, 'said the pastor of President Setlhoboko's church'—what is that supposed to do? Give this crap some sort of weight? So our President, who has seriously lost the plot, is a member of some whacked-out sect? Is that supposed to give this some credibility?"

"You know how these papers are. Don't get yourself so worked up. Please, Ditiro." She sat down across from him. "What do you think we can do?"

"First thing tomorrow, I'll be in the newspaper's office. I intend to make a complaint to MISA, as well. But we need to take legal action against Kissi and his church, even the paper if we don't get a front-page retraction. We need to fight these people at the source."

"Don't you think that'll make things worse? Maybe if we ignore them, it will go away. Maybe the police will get some evidence to link them to the fire. Maybe we should wait a bit."

Elizabeth wasn't sure she had the energy for this type of fight. She just wanted to be happy, back at her home with her husband and her daughter. She wanted all of this to disappear, and if they ignored it, maybe it would.

"Lizzie, they can't do this to you. They're ruining your reputation. They're ruining your business. And they are putting you and Lorato and me in danger. We can't sit by and let them do that. It's wrong. We need to stop Kissi."

When Ditiro said that he and Lorato were in danger, she felt sick. Would these people harm them? They'd tried to kill her. There were so many crazy people out there; maybe they would try to harm Lorato and Ditiro, too, to get at her. He was right; they needed to fight. Even though she didn't want to, she needed to protect her family.

"Okay, she said, finally. "With the gallery currently out of operation, I have a lot of time on my hands. Let's make a plan and we can get to work."

***

The sun had settled deep in the western sky, and the heat of the day was slowly disappearing. It had been a lovely Sunday even with the newspaper article. Ditiro eventually calmed down. They'd had a leisurely breakfast and then played board games with Lorato. It had felt almost like things were back to normal.

Elizabeth was at the back of the house pushing Lorato in the tyre swing when she heard someone coming out the door and looked up to see Kagiso's smiling face.

"Anyone home?" she said, coming towards them. Ditiro must have told her they were at the back.

"Hi, Kagiso," Lorato said from the swing. "How are Tom and Jerry?"

"They're fine. You must come and visit them sometime," Kagiso said.

"When?" Lorato liked things to be concrete.

"How does next Saturday sound?

"Stop the swing! I want to go and tell Daddy. He should write it down so we don't forget."

Elizabeth did as ordered, and Lorato jumped off and ran to the house followed by Shumba, their dog, who had been sleeping contently in the shade, but could not bear to be away from Lorato even if it meant picking his heavy body up and making his way to the house.

Kagiso looked at Elizabeth and smiled. "You look great. What's going on?"

Elizabeth wasn't sure she should tell, afraid she'd bewitch everything, but she couldn't stop herself. "Ditiro and I are going to give it another try."

"Oh, Elizabeth, I'm so happy. You two belong together." She hugged her. "Well, if nothing else, this dark cloud has a silver lining." They sat down on the chairs under the shade of a wide, old jacaranda near the swing. "Not to throw a wet blanket on everything, but I guess you saw the paper by now."

"Yeah, pretty bad. Anyway, Ditiro has a plan of attack."

"Good! I knew something needed to be done. These people can't get away with this. It just made me so angry. A person's HIV status is confidential. It can't be published in the newspaper."

"So did the police or fire marshal get back to you yet about the cottage?" Elizabeth asked.

"Yes, but it doesn't look hopeful. Apparently, they asked Bishop Kissi about it, but he has an alibi for the whole night. He was with his in-laws, the President.

Who can fight with that? And that Tumelo fellow was running some youth church camp in Serowe."

"But it's not like they would do it themselves. They'd send someone. Even I know that."

"That's what I said. Anyway, they said they were still looking into it, but from their voices, I don't have much hope."

"That's too bad. I was hoping if someone from the church got arrested, it would put an end to all of this. I guess we'll have to go the longer route."

CHAPTER TWENTY-SIX

Tumelo finished counting up the day's collection money and filled in the accounts book. He was trusted to count the money and enter it now, so it was easy for him to put a thousand or so Pula in his pocket without anyone noticing. He earned a good salary, but he was trying to raise funds to begin to live the lifestyle he knew he deserved.

For a Wednesday, the money was good. The Bishop would be happy. The newspaper story on Sunday had gotten people excited, and there had been plenty of new faces in the crowd today. He was happy since he knew it was because of him that the church was getting so many more converts. Bishop Kissi also knew it. He'd given Tumelo his own office and an assistant and a substantial salary increase. He was valuable to the church.

Tumelo liked the way his new life was progressing and the speed at which everything was happening. It seemed unimaginable it was only a year and half ago when he'd been a broke university student, and now, he had a second floor corner office and was earning a five-digit income each month, even without the cream off the top. He'd always known one day he'd be an important person, a great man, and it was happening. Who would have thought an inconsequential one-night stand would be the thing that turned his life to this direction?

His mother in Mochudi hadn't been happy when he'd told her he was leaving the university, but since he'd been able to send money home to help with his two younger brothers, she'd stopped talking about it. He hoped to build her a better house soon. They'd always lived in the two mud huts she'd inherited from her own mother; they had a pit toilet and a tap in the yard. He was an important man now, and his mother needed a cement house with electricity and plumbing.

He heard a knock on the door.

"Sorry to disturb you, Reverend Gabadirwe, but there's someone to see you," Joy, his assistant, said.

"That's fine. Send them through."

He put the money back ino the safe and when he stood back up, he was surprised to see Mphoentle. Soon after he'd started at the church, he'd stopped taking her calls and hoped that she might have got the message. Apparently, she hadn't. He didn't think being associated with her now that he was a prominent member of the church was such a good idea. Her ways might come out and church members would wonder about their association.

The door closed, and Mphoentle rushed to the window. "Wow! A corner office with a fantastic view. You are doing good for yourself, my brother. Very good."

"Mphoentle, how nice to see you. Can I get you a drink?"

She looked thinner than the last time he'd seen her, though still beautiful.

"Sure, what about a Coke?"

Tumelo ordered a Coke from Joy, and Mphoentle made herself comfortable on the sofa in the corner.

"So how's it going, Tumelo?"

He sat down across from her. "As you know, I've found God. I've been born again, and it is a wonderful feeling, being in God's loving light."

Mphoentle laughed. "Listen, Tumelo, you can cut the crap with me. I know you're not up here raking in the dough because you enjoy the warm light of your saviour. You found a sweet gig, and you're working it. Listen, you get all me respect, seriously. I wish I'd a thought of it first."

"No, Mphoentle, I've changed. Honestly, Bishop Kissi has shown me the truth of life; he's put me on the right path. Perhaps I can help you to find your way."

The Coke arrived, and Joy discretely left the office, closing the door behind her.

"Okay, whatever," Mphoentle said. She took a drink of her Coke and looked out the window. "Still, you're doing well for yourself."

"Bishop Kissi appreciates the good work I do for the church." Tumelo knew Mphoentle hadn't just come for a chat; he wished she'd get to it and get out of his office before Bishop Kissi passed by. He wouldn't want the Bishop to know he had such friends. "So what brings you here, Mphoentle?"

"Ao! Now you're too good to receive a friend. Did you forget I was the person who first brought you to this church, to your beloved Bishop Kissi? I'd think you'd be a bit thankful at least."

"Yes, of course I remember. I'm thankful, you must know that."

Mphoentle leaned back on the leather sofa crossing her long, bare legs in front of her. "I saw your big story in the Sunday papers."

"Yes ... well, you know journalists. Not always the most truthful people."

Suddenly, he understood why Mphoentle was here. Tumelo had forgotten about Mphoentle and what she knew. He'd tested for HIV the week before going to university and found he was positive. He'd been devastated, thinking his life was finished. At UB, there was a support group for HIV-positive students, but he hadn't been brave enough to attend. Someone had mentioned that Mphoentle was in the support group. They had a few classes together and became friends.

After some time, he'd told her he was HIV-positive. He'd needed the support at the time, but now, he realised it had been a mistake. He should have kept his status a secret as he had intended to from the beginning. He'd made a mistake confiding in someone, especially Mphoentle.

"So, you're trying to tell me you had no part in that news story?" Mphoentle threw her head back and laughed dramatically.

Tumelo feared someone would hear her.

"Is that what you're telling people?" she said. "Come on, I'm not that stupid. I know you're using this to up your gig here. I know your little secret, but I'm good at keeping secrets, you don't need to worry. But throwing that lady under the bus to up your status here … Ao! Tumelo, that's cruel, man! I'm bad, but you're on another level."

He didn't want to play this game with her. "Okay … so what … it doesn't matter really. Now she's out there passing it around, trying to infect all of us. Typical white behaviour. People should know. I was just making sure they did. Who got it when is not important. That's just not the point."

Mphoentle smiled. "Right. So you're just concerned about your fellow man. That's kind of you. But it does shine a different light on the whole thing if it comes out, that bit of information. The fact that you were already positive when you slept with her—don't you think? Don't you think people might get a different idea about the whole thing?"

He was losing his patience, and he wanted her finished and out of his office. He checked the door was closed, but still spoke in a low whisper anyway.

"Okay, fine. You got me. Clever Mphoentle, why don't you give yourself a fucking medal? What do you want? Why did you come here? Let's just cut to the chase so we can all be on our way."

Mphoentle put her hands up in front of her defensively. "Hey ... don't go all postal on me. I'm not here to mess up your gig. I'm your friend, remember?"

"So? What do you want? Why are you here?"

"I saw you in the paper and just thought I'd come around and do a little catching-up. Give you your kudos. Honestly, I'm your friend. I wanted to let you know I'm proud of you, that's all."

"Yeah, okay, you've done that ... Actually, I have a meeting, so ..." He stood up, looking at his watch.

"Oh, Tumelo, pushing me out so soon?" Ignoring him, she stood up and walked to the window, looking out at the traffic passing along the Western bypass, making no effort to leave. "I just thought you might be able to help your friend out with a few Pula is all ... you know us UB students are perpetually broke."

He'd expected as much. "How much?"

"I don't know ... a thousand?"

He went to his desk and counted out a thousand Pula from the money he'd taken from the collections. He handed it to her.

"Here. Take it, but I don't want you around here again."

Mphoentle quickly put the money in her leather handbag.

"Oh, Tumelo, your manners, they've really deteriorated." She walked to the door then turned back smiling. "See you around, my brother."

He watched her leave and then sat down at his desk. His hands shook. He knew what just happened was a close call; it could ruin everything for him. Mphoentle was a problem. There was no way she would not be back for more money. She had him good and tight in her trap, a fat cash cow she would milk until it was dry.

He had a problem and would need to think about how to solve it. He wouldn't risk his position; he had too much to lose. Mphoentle needed to be sorted out, and she needed to be sorted out soon.

CHAPTER TWENTY-SEVEN

Elizabeth loved her studio at the back of the house. It was nearly all windows and she liked keeping them open and letting the sun and the breeze in. Amidst all of the craziness, she was surprised to find she suddenly wanted to paint. Out of nowhere, she felt inspired. She hadn't done any of her own work for months, except for the angry red painting that had poured out of her like an animal released.

Now she felt the need to paint, and since she hadn't opened the gallery all week—there was no use since customers and artists didn't want to be associated with her right now—she had time to paint, too.

She'd started the painting thinking about the forgiveness Ditiro was offering her, and what a gift it was. She suspected true forgiveness had to come from a place of love. You needed to care about the other person enough to let it go and forgive. Ditiro had found that place for her.

But then, she thought about Tumelo. She'd never loved him, of course, so did that mean she'd never be able to forgive him? Would she have to carry this anger around for eternity? She suspected not. What was the use? It only harmed her. It made her into a person she didn't want to be, a hate-filled person.

She thought of these different sides of forgiveness when she painted. She'd start the abstract oil with blocks of orange and reds and yellows. The warmth of true forgiveness. She felt it. Ditiro had let her into the beauty of it. When he had made her leave, when he had chased her away in anger, she'd felt frozen out, cold, and isolated. Lost in a world of dark blues and black.

Now, she only felt warmth. But when she thought of Tumelo, she knew forgiveness for her would mean the lifting of a burden, not the warmth of yellow and orange. It would instead be an absence of colour, so in the end, her painting was full of airy spaces between the many-sided and shaded warm shapes. Forgiveness in its entirety.

She heard the phone ring somewhere deep in the house. Precious would answer it, but the ring pulled her from her painting, and she glanced at the clock. Already past two. She'd been painting since Lorato had left for school in the morning. She sat down and looked at her work so far. She'd made progress, and it felt good. Getting lost in her work was something she hadn't done for a long, long time.

Precious poked her head around the door. "I'm sorry, Madam. You have a phone call."

Elizabeth put her brush down and headed to the phone. "Hello?"

"Hi, is that Elizabeth Molosiwa?"

"Yes, it is. Who am I speaking to?"

"I'm a reporter from The Sunday Star, John Loeto. I wanted to see if you'd be willing to answer a few questions."

She considered it for a few minutes, not sure what to do. Ditiro had said it was unfair that the article in the paper didn't have her side of the story; this was her opportunity to put things straight. She would have liked to speak to Ditiro first, but she didn't want to lose the chance to get her story out there.

"Okay, sure."

He asked her what she thought of the allegations made by Tumelo Gabadirwe and Bishop David Kissi.

"I think they're crazy. Anyone who knows me would tell you the same."

"So are you denying the fact that you are HIV-positive?"

Elizabeth stopped. She couldn't lie. She would lose all credibility when the newspaper found out that, in fact, she was HIV-positive, and he would certainly find out; journalists seemed able to uncover even the most closely held secret and she hadn't kept her status a secret.

But at the same time, she thought of Lorato and Ditiro. There was still stigma around the disease. Once she came out with her status, once she confirmed it, the effect would not be hers alone to carry. The allegations made by Tumelo were still allegations—people could still choose to ignore them, but if she said that she was HIV-positive, then everyone would know the truth. Tumelo had pushed her to a place with no options.

"No, I'm not denying that. I am HIV-positive. I got it from Tumelo Gabadirwe. I was HIV-negative before I met Tumelo. I can prove it; I had an HIV-test before I got pregnant with my daughter."

"What were you doing with Tumelo to contract HIV? Aren't you a married woman?" the journalist asked.

"All marriages have their ups and downs. Mine is not immune. I had a very short, stupid affair with Tumelo, and he gave me the AIDS virus. I regret it, of course. Mostly, I regret the damage it caused to my family, but, thankfully, we're trying to find our way through, and I think eventually we'll be okay."

"And what about you spreading AIDS around and giving it to other black, Batswana men in some attempt to kill us, as the church has alleged?"

"Do you think that's believable?"

The reporter gave a nervous laugh. "No, not really. But what do they gain by spreading such kind of lies?"

"They gain members in their church. People are always ready to accept a scapegoat. Members in the church who drop Pula in the collection basket, they want an easy answer to their problems. I'm that easy answer."

"So you think they're using you as a scapegoat?"

"Of course they are. The members can now gather their energies around a common enemy —me. Already, someone in the church tried to kill me. I now need round the clock guards. This church is reckless and unsafe. It should be closed down."

Elizabeth was surprised to hear herself say such things. She had always played it safe looking at things from the sidelines, not taking a stand.

"Do you know our president, President Setlhoboko, is a member of that church? His daughter is even married to its founder."

"I know that, but where is Dora now? Why did she leave her husband?"

"Do you know something about that?"

"I ... no ... not really."

Elizabeth knew she'd said too much, but if the truth came out about Dora, it would help them to show the kind of person Kissi was.

"Do your job and you should be able to find out for yourself. This church is committing crimes. Is it legal to reveal someone's HIV status?"

"Well, I don't know ... I'm not a lawyer, but it might be. How old is your daughter, by the way?"

"She's five. Why?"

"Well, you say you had a test that can prove you were HIV-negative when you met Tumelo Gabadirwe.

Who's to say you didn't contract HIV after the birth of your daughter and then passed it on to him? Is that not a possibility?"

Elizabeth hesitated. She and Ditiro had spoken about lodging a case against Tumelo and the church for violating her constitutional right to privacy. The case would hinge on Tumelo having no right to reveal her HIV status to others. If he could show that she had given him the virus and was now spreading it around, he could plead that it was in the public's interest that he reveal Elizabeth's status to others.

When they'd discussed it, Ditiro had said that was not a problem since they had the results from the pregnancy, but the reporter had it right, she might have contracted HIV after she gave birth to Lorato. They needed some evidence that showed Tumelo had HIV before he met Elizabeth, and that evidence, they didn't have. Without it, that part of the case collapsed.

"Perhaps ... it's a possibility, but that is not the case here. Tumelo Gabadirwe gave me the virus."

She was annoyed. She hoped the reporter would not write the story from the wrong perspective and make her look even worse. She wanted to speak to Ditiro, so she quickly ended the interview.

"Listen, I need to go. Thanks for the interview."

She hung up the phone. She wasn't sure if she'd helped or harmed their case. She'd been feeling so positive after her productive morning of painting, but that was all gone now.

CHAPTER TWENTY-EIGHT

Elizabeth and Ditiro sat at the table reading the article written about her interview.

"It's okay. At least your side is out there," he said.

"But you see at the bottom, he brings out the problem with the HIV test. There was time when I could have become infected after Lorato's birth. We hadn't thought of that."

"But you didn't, and, besides that, you still have a constitutional right to privacy. If this Tumelo cared about public safety, why didn't he go to the police? Why rile up a bunch of impressionable church members who went out and started torching houses? Is that not inciting violence? As far as I'm concerned, these people have violated your rights and broken numerous laws."

"The police have no leads on that arson case. It would all be difficult to prove."

Ditiro put the paper down. "Tomorrow, I need to pass by the police. By now, they must have made some progress in the case. I want to see what they've got."

From what Kagiso had told her, the police hadn't accomplished much, but she didn't mention that. Ditiro should rather go to the police and find out for himself. He knew a lot of the police, and they might be more willing to help him since for a long time, he had been helping them put the bad guys in jail.

"Mommy, are you ready?"

Lorato came around the corner dressed in her lilac party dress, all ruffles and satin, and her shiny white shoes with short heels she called her "Mommy shoes." She'd been invited to a friend's birthday party.

"Let's go. I don't want to be late."

"Sure, sweetie. Let me get my handbag. You go and take Refilwe's present. It's on the table in the dining room."

"She's going to love the art set we bought her. I can't wait to see her open it," Lorato said, before rushing off to the dining room.

Elizabeth kissed Ditiro. "I'll be right back."

***

"Look, Mommy, a jumping castle! Bonolo and Patience are already inside. Stop the car!"

"Looks like some party."

And it did. There were balloons and decorations all across the front of the house. Children were already running around blowing plastic horns at each other and wearing golden crowns. The parents in Phakalane were getting more and more extravagant with birthday parties. Elizabeth found it a bit difficult, such over-indulgence. It hit up against her working-class ethics.

She pulled the car into the driveway and parked. Lorato rushed to get out.

"Wait, you're forgetting the present," Elizabeth said, stopping her.

She reached to the back seat to get the gift, and when she turned back, the mother of the birthday girl was at the car, standing next to the driver's window.

"Oh, hi, Lettie. Sorry we're a bit late. I lost track of time."

"No, don't worry. Actually, Elizabeth ... I ..."

Lettie was the marketing manager for one of the big diamond-cutting businesses. She was always on the radio and television giving interviews and yet, suddenly, she couldn't find her words to speak.

"What's wrong?" Elizabeth asked.

Still finding it difficult to begin, she said, "I'm sorry. I'd never do this, ever. You know Ditiro and I have known each other since school days. I know it is crazy and ignorant ..."

"What? What are you talking about?"

Elizabeth thought it had been the article only, that perhaps Lettie wanted to find a way to let her know she'd read it, but she could see now it was something more.

"It's the paper. Some parents called me this morning. This whole thing, actually. They're nervous about the kids playing together and if something can happen ... well, you know .... Things can happen, and I told them I'd make sure everything was okay, but some of them just wouldn't listen."

"What does that mean exactly? That you'd 'make sure everything was okay'?"

"Elizabeth, please don't take it like that. There's no reason to get angry about anything."

"Is that so? Lettie, why don't you just say what you mean? Don't be such a fucking coward! If you have something to say, say it."

Lettie took a deep breath and said it in rush as if vomiting the words onto Elizabeth. "I need you to take Lorato back home. We can't have her at the party."

Lorato was standing near the car still, looking longingly in the direction of her friends, waiting for the present so she could dash to the jumping castle and be with them. She had no interest in the adult conversation so hadn't been listening.

"Lorato, get in the car," Elizabeth said.

Lorato turned and looked at her mother. "Why? I'm going to Refilwe's party. I want to jump in the jumping castle. I can't get in the car now. You can come back for me later, after the party."

"Lorato, just get in the car." Lettie looked away.

"No! I want to go to the party. I have a card; I was invited. You said I could go. We're here already. It's not fair to change your mind now."

Elizabeth could see tears building up in Lorato's eyes, tears of frustration, and she could barely stop her own.

"I'm sorry, sweetie, but you can't go to the party today. Let's go home and get Daddy and we'll go to the jumping castle at Lion's Park. You can get ice cream and go on the water slide."

"But my friends won't be at Lion's Park. I want to go jump in the jumping castle here not at Lion's Park." She stepped away from the car defiantly, her hands at her side, her fists balled.

"I know. There's nothing we can do about that. There's a problem and we need to go. Please, sweetie, just get in the car," Elizabeth begged her.

Lorato reluctantly climbed into the passenger seat. The tears that had filled her eyes were now rolling down her cheeks and she began to sob, staring down at the floor of the car.

Elizabeth still held the birthday present. She turned to the driver's window and pushed it towards Lettie.

"Take this. We bought it for Refilwe."

Lettie shook her head and stepped back away from the car. She looked at the gift as if it held a bomb. She crossed her arms, refusing to take it.

Elizabeth opened her car door and walked to Lettie. In a whispered hiss, she said, "Take this present. We bought it for Refilwe. Don't humiliate us further by making us take it back home."

Lettie reluctantly held out her hands and took the present.

"I'm sorry," she said in a small voice. "I didn't know what to do. So many parents called ... I didn't know what to do ..."

Elizabeth got back in the car and buckled Lorato into her seat, then turned back to the driver window.

"How about having a little bit of compassion, just a tiny bit of humanity? Is that too much to ask from a friend? Is that just too much to ask?"

Elizabeth didn't wait for an answer. She backed down the driveway and headed home. Lorato sat next to her in the passenger seat, her lilac party dress slowly darkening from tears.

CHAPTER TWENTY-NINE

The police station was one of the new ones, three floors high made of face brick, and Superintendent Busang's office was at the top. When he found the correct office, Ditiro knocked on the side of the open door. "Koko!"

Without looking up from his paperwork, the police officer said gruffly, "Tsena."

"Dumela Rre Busang."

When Supt. Busang saw who it was, he stood up smiling and came around the desk to shake Ditiro's hand.

"Oh, Ditiro, I didn't know it was you. It's a surprise to see you here. Long time."

When Ditiro had been in the Attorney General's office, he'd gotten to know a lot of the police officers in Gaborone. Supt. Busang had been one of his favourites. He was conscientious and disciplined and had no time for any nonsense. He got things done the right way, the first time.

Supt. Busang offered him a seat. "So what can I do for you, Ditiro?"

"I think you know about the arson case at Dr. Moleele's house."

"Sure. It's under our jurisdiction."

"My wife was living in the cottage when it burned. We were having some problems, we were separated for a while, and she's friends with Dr. Moleele. Luckily, she was not in the cottage when the fire was started. As you know, it was arson, and your staff seem to be dragging their feet on the case. I wanted to see what the problem was so I decided to come over."

Supt. Busang said nothing but stood up and went around the desk to close the door. He sat back down and spoke in a lowered voice.

"Ditiro, you're a friend, and I'm telling you this in confidence, we've been told to stop the investigation."

"Stop the investigation? Why?"

"You know how it is. These things just come and we don't know the origin. But it's from the top offices."

"The President?"

"Maybe. I don't know, but it was up there." He sat back in his chair, ran his hand over his furrowed brow. "I heard about all of your problems with that crazy church, read the articles in the papers like everyone else. I'm sorry, Ditiro. You don't deserve all that, you and your family. It's shameful what people get up to under God's supposed banner."

Ditiro felt like his hands had been tied behind his back. So now even the police belonged to this church? Was this not Botswana, touted as one of the handful of countries in Africa where the rule of law meant something?

He felt like he'd walked into some conspiracy theory movie. He was shocked how quickly justice could be wiped away. He had depended on the foundation of the law, but now, it seemed the law was not as stable and sturdy as he'd hoped. It could be manipulated for a single person's purpose. He had always assumed that the law was the one place where equality reigned. He'd been naïve, he realised now.

"Yeah, it's all been quite rough," he said.

The big man leaned across his wide desk. "For this arson case, you must just leave it. We can't do anything. But the courts are different. I still think you can get justice there. The judiciary is still independent in this country, that I'm sure of. The judges, in my opinion, are not corruptible. There are things you can do. It's not right what this church is doing. Give up on the arson case; you're wasting your time, Ditiro. Get to the courts. You can get them in the courts. That's my opinion, anyway."

"Perhaps," he said. "But they should go to jail for what they've done. My wife could have been killed that night."

"Yes, you're right, but with people like this, a civil case might harm them even more. I understand this church is very wealthy. The head of it I hear is a millionaire some times over. If you get them in a civil court, you kill two birds with one stone. You expose them for what they've done, and you take their money. I know how these types of con artists work. Once they've lost credibility, the con is up. No more money, he'll be gone before you know it. You still have a chance in the courts."

Ditiro stood up to go. He shook Supt. Busang's hand and felt relief that there were still a few sane people left, and Supt. Busang was one of them.

"Thanks for your help. I'll keep you posted."

"Good luck, Ditiro. Anything you need and I can give, just call me."

***

Ditiro walked across the scorching parking lot. The late October summer sun was doing its job. He climbed into his car and pushed the air-con to high. He'd accepted he needed to stop wasting his time on the arson charge; nothing was ever going to stick even if he could get the police to do a proper investigation, and that was now no longer possible thanks to the President's interference.

He needed to go after the church for revealing Elizabeth's HIV status and inciting violence against her. He also could make a case for defamation, especially against Tumelo. But he had to accept he could not go the criminal route since the police would be stopped. He needed to put together a civil case. In a way, he was pleased. The court was a battleground where he had sure footing. It was a place he knew he would have the upper hand.

As he constructed the court case in his mind, he felt better. Finally, he was taking action against everything. He would show the President once and for all that he was right and Kissi was wrong. He'd be able to punish Kissi for his arrogance. He'd be able to pay Dora back for what he'd done to her. He also knew the case had everything to do with his relationship with his wife. He wanted to punish the man who'd thought he could take what was not his.

In the courtroom, Ditiro was in control. He would teach Tumelo a lesson about respect, and in doing so, maybe he would finally be able to get past the affair, forget about it forever, and forgive Elizabeth completely.

CHAPTER THIRTY

Kissi came through the door without knocking. Tumelo was sitting at his desk working on the account books.

"Good morning, Bishop."

The Bishop looked tired and stressed. He sat down in a chair opposite Tumelo without speaking.

"Can I get you something? Maybe a cup of tea?" Tumelo asked.

"Tell Joy to bring the whiskey from my office."

Tumelo called his assistant and then sat back down.

"So? Have you heard anything about Dora?" Bishop Kissi asked.

"I have someone following a reporter." Tumelo grabbed a file on his desk. "A certain John Loeto. I think he has a lead regarding Dora's whereabouts. We've been paying attention to Rre Molosiwa's calls, too, thanks to the President's men. There's been nothing yet, but we'll find her, I'm sure of it," he assured his boss. "The world is very small nowadays."

Joy came in with the whiskey, set the bottle down, and disappeared. The Bishop poured himself a drink and swallowed it in one gulp, then immediately poured another. Tumelo noticed his hands shaking. He hadn't realised the issue of Dora's disappearance had affected him so.

"She knows things, that girl. She could destroy me. We must find her. If this falls apart—" the Bishop said, pointing around the building, "—we lose everything. Even you. Are you prepared to go back to your one-roomed shack in Mochudi with your mother and two brothers?"

Tumelo had never spoken about his family to the Bishop and was surprised he knew where he was from as well as how they lived. Kissi laughed, noticing Tumelo's surprise.

"So you think I would let someone so close to me without investigating them?"

"No, I guess not."

"I also know you liked sleeping with rich women in the hopes of taking the easy road. Rich women such as Elizabeth Molosiwa." Kissi poured himself another drink.

Tumelo said nothing. He waited, knowing there was more.

"... and that you were HIV-positive long before you met that white woman. What do the Americans say, 'you can't shit a shitter.' I know a good story when I hear one. I left you to it. It's helped the church. Since your sermon, we've had a thirty-four percent increase in the collection plate."

"But it wasn't about the money. I wanted to protect people—" Tumelo started.

Kissi interrupted him. "Leave that for others. I know the truth. It's helped us with money, and it put that arrogant, self-righteous Molosiwa in his place. Two birds with one carefully aimed stone. Now the President doesn't trust him, this is good for me. It was a handy lie. It's alright as long as no one else knows it was a lie. It has served our purposes. That's all the matters."

Tumelo stood up to make tea. The problem was that Mphoentle knew it was all a lie, too. He knew the money he'd given her would not be enough; she would come again and again. She would be a constant worry. But he feared telling Bishop Kissi. He didn't want him to see that he was not completely in control of things. Up until that point, he'd been the dependable assistant, doing things before they needed to be asked for, ensuring the smooth running of the operation. He was capable. The leaky tap of Mphoentle would give the impression he was not. On the other hand, Mphoentle had to be dealt with, and the Bishop would know how.

He sat down back at the desk. "There's a small problem."

The Bishop sipped at his whiskey. "What problem?"

"Someone knows."

"Knows what?"

"Knows that I was HIV-positive before I had sex with Elizabeth Molosiwa, that I gave her the virus, not the other way around."

Kissi waved his hand. "You mean the nurse who gave you the test? She can't reveal anything. It's against the law. Nothing to worry about."

"No, not the nurse. I have a friend, a girl, who I told."

The Bishop was interested. "Where is she?"

"She's here in Gabs. She was actually here the other day. She reminded me about what she knew. I gave her some money. She'll be quiet for now, but I don't know for how long."

Kissi got to his feet. He slammed the glass on the desk. "Fuck! What were you thinking? You must make sure such problems are attended to before you start, not later. Foolish, very, very foolish. So she specifically asked for money to keep silent? Does she understand the power of what she knows?"

"Yes, she knows. But don't worry, I'll deal with it. There's nothing for you to worry about. I'll take care of her."

"If it gets out that you lied and, in fact, you infected that woman, do you know what will happen? I'll lose everything just when I'm on the verge of getting it all. Do you think I can leave this to some little boy just pulled from his mother's tit? What's her name? Where do I find this person?"

Tumelo had never seen this side of the Bishop. He was scared. He wrote Mphoentle's details down on a slip of paper and handed it to him.

"Don't talk to her again. Give her no more money. I will take care of this."

Kissi left without another word, the door closing behind him with a bang.

Tumelo didn't like that he had disappointed the Bishop. He would have to do something special to make up for it. He would have to find Dora. Finding Dora would calm him; it would alleviate a lot of his worries. He would put all of his time into that until he had something.

He gave only a passing thought to what would happen to Mphoentle. She'd been a good friend to him when he'd needed one. But still, he thought, she'd decided to push him for the money, decided to blackmail him. She'd made a mistake and now would have to accept the consequences. Now it was her problem of how to deal with the outcome of her actions. Whatever happened, at least he would be free of her.

Lauri Kubuitsile

CHAPTER THIRTY-ONE

Molosiwa and Associates was struggling to survive. In less than two months, their business had shrunk by half. Once the President's business had been withdrawn from the law firm, many of their best clients had followed suit. The firm had started with four associates, but now it was down to Ditiro and Constance Moeng, the most recently hired, just from law school, and the cheapest for him to keep. The other associates had had to be retrenched. They'd found positions in other firms almost immediately, so that helped Ditiro get past the guilt he'd felt about it. At least he had Constance to help him; he was realising she was a real asset.

"From what I've managed to get, article 3 and section 7 of the Constitution could help us. Otherwise, there is nothing but defamation," Constance said.

They were trying to come up with an approach for winning a civil case against the African Church of Spiritual Revelation and Kissi. The laws in Botswana around HIV/AIDS were vague. Unlike South Africa, there were no laws about disclosing someone's HIV status. There was also no legislation about the criminal transmission of the virus. Their only legal hook would be the Constitution. Article 3 ensured the right to privacy while Section 7 provided protection from degrading treatment, but was usually applied to the state against

217

individuals, such as beatings by police. The constitutional angle would be difficult to prove.

The right to privacy could be waived if the public was threatened. A case could be made that a person with HIV who was purposefully spreading it around, as the church alleged, would be a threat to the public and could lose their constitutional protection to the cause of public safety. Using section 7 in this instance would be a stretch, too. The problem with the laws in the country was that Botswana had never stopped to make new ones to address the world post-HIV. Because of that, it was easy for the rampant trampling of the rights of HIV-positive people and those suffering from AIDS.

"Hmmm, I thought as much. I just hoped there was a precedent somewhere," he said.

"There is a fairly recent case, I'm sure you read about it in the papers. Olorato Toteng vs Bibi Mosalagae."

Constance got up to refill her coffee cup. She sat back down and pulled out a folder with some newspaper clippings and started going though them.

"Was that the insulting case?" Ditiro asked.

"Yes, Toteng and Mosalagae were feuding over something, and on two occasions, Mosalagae insulted Toteng, referring to her HIV-positive status. The lawyers used Article 3 in their case and they won, so that's a precedent."

She handed him photocopies of the newspaper articles about the case. He paged through them. In the end, Toteng was only awarded seven-hundred Pula. If Kissi was to be taught a lesson, a judgement of seven-hundred Pula was not going to do it. Ditiro needed a big ruling.

"Yes, at least this sets a precedent, gives us a bit of hope. I think we should combine the pertinent sections of the Constitution with defamation."

"Fine, but you know what our problem is with defamation. We need to have cast-iron evidence that Tumelo was HIV-positive first, before Elizabeth. We don't have that."

"Yes, I know." He had been thinking through the case for some time and knew every weakness in it.

"Elizabeth is HIV-positive, so that's not defamation. If Tumelo truly thought she was out passing HIV around, again, defamation falls away. It becomes fair comment. He was only saying what anyone in that position might say," Constance said.

"Well, I really don't know how you jump from a person being HIV-positive and her going out and trying to kill people with it. You can't just start throwing such comments around, it's irresponsible," he snapped.

Constance held her hands in front of her as if trying to defend herself from a blow. "Hey, don't shoot the messenger. I'm just trying to point out the flaws in our case."

Ditiro knew he had no right to get annoyed. Constance was all he had, and he needed to be careful or he'd find himself all alone. It was just that he couldn't bear having Elizabeth treated or spoken about in such a way. She was a good person, the most loving, kind person he'd ever known. She didn't deserve any of this.

But he needed to try to keep his emotions out of the case or they were doomed before they started. Also, Constance was an excellent lawyer. He couldn't pay her what she deserved. He needn't add a bullying boss to the equation.

"Yeah, you're right, sorry. This case, it's doing my head in. I'll try my best to stay sensible."

Constance smiled but said nothing. She was young, only twenty-seven, but Ditiro had spotted something in her when she'd interviewed for the job. Her intelligence was razor-sharp, but it was more than that. Her insight into people was very keen. It helped her to get through a lot of the clients' issues and to the truth of the case very quickly. She knew how people worked, what motivated them, what they coveted, what they feared. Clients were calmer around her. She knew people well, which helped her to analyse cases and approaches, taking human nature always into consideration.

This was something Ditiro struggled with. For him, the law was clear. At least, that was how he'd always seen it. So much of what he'd believed now sat on very shaky ground.

Constance stood up gathering her papers. "I think we have a plan. Let me work on this. Let me see what I can get together. I think you're right, you're too close. You could harm the case."

He could see she thought he should step aside completely, that his emotions were hampering them. But that, he would not do. Not for the time being.

"Okay, but we need to get going. When do you think you can be ready to file?"

"I plan to finish by tomorrow. Most of the preliminary work is done; I just wanted to hear you out. Now I can proceed. It's going to be tricky, but we have a thin space we could get through. If we get the right judge, we could do it. If we win, this could turn out to be a very important case."

She stood up and left. Ditiro looked at the clock. It was nearly three. He had nothing pressing to attend to and could use a break, so he grabbed up his coat and headed home. He needed to see his family.

***

Elizabeth looked at the painting, now finished. Forgiveness stared back at her, but she felt none of it. After the birthday party incident, she and Ditiro had agreed that Lorato should stay home from school for a few days, maybe a week, for things to settle down.

Since then, the anger she felt simmered near to the surface. She could feel it blocking her throat; it rang in her ears. When they were after her, it was one thing, but when their words meant her daughter had to cry herself to sleep, that was something else. She would not let them do this to her, to her family. Now was not the time for forgiveness. Now was the time to fight.

She heard footsteps coming towards her studio and looked up to find Ditiro at the door. His face was drawn. He'd taken the incident at the party hard, too. Ditiro was being threatened as a husband and a father. His role as protector was being challenged. She knew it was all taking its toll on him at the worst possible time. They were both still trying to find their way back, to trust a path fraught with dangers. Everywhere she turned, all she could see was conflict and raw emotions. She found it hard to deal with everything.

"You're home early," she said, smiling up at him.

He sat on the two-seater along the back window. "Yeah, Constance thinks it's better I try to stay out of the case for now. Since it's about all we have at the moment, I thought I'd take a chance to come home."

She sat down next to him. She didn't feel quite right kissing him. They were not back to normal just yet. They were still inching along on wobbly legs as a person did after a long, debilitating illness. Their relationship had been stricken by the worst sickness a relationship could get: adultery, the destruction of trust, the life blood of a relationship. Now it needed to heal. It was on the upswing, but not strong enough to take anything for granted, even a kiss. Instead, she took his hand in hers and held it in her lap.

She wished she could scoop out all of the pain in his eyes and in his heart. Scoop it out and carry it for him. The same for Lorato. She'd tried to explain it all to her daughter, but words were so weak up against such emotions. Lorato understood it had nothing to do with her, that it was people who were afraid and acted wrong because of their fears. Elizabeth had told her she had a disease and people were afraid of catching it, but that she was fine and was not going to die. Everything would be fine. Lorato had nodded, indicating she understood, but Elizabeth could see the pain in her eyes. She was a little girl. All she wanted was to attend a birthday party and jump in a jumping castle.

"So when does Constance think she can register the case?" she asked.

"She said maybe tomorrow. We'll know fairly soon if they'll let us proceed or if they'll kick it out. I'm trying to leave things to Constance. It's hard, but I know it's for the best."

"Yes, it is," she said. "Since you have no work and Lorato is off school for a few days, maybe we could go for a quick trip together. Maybe up to the Delta for a few days. To forget about all of this."

Ditiro smiled at her. "I think that sounds like a fantastic idea. I think all of us could stand to get away from this city for a while."

CHAPTER THIRTY-TWO

The silence of the Delta when you were slowly pushing along in a mokoro was a medicine all by itself. The rhythmic whish of the pole digging in and the boat pushing though the water felt like the background music for the melody produced by the call of a fish eagle sitting high in a tree or the sudden snort of a hippo breaking through the lily pads. Nature's music, the origins of all others.

There was something about the African bush that calmed Elizabeth. It pared life down. The things that loomed large in our lives shrunk when put up against issues of survival. Human beings had moved so far way from the natural ways, tangling themselves in ropes and chains of little significance. In the bush, life and death, the basic issues, could be seen clearly. It was a relief, in a way. Yes, in a moment, you could be killed, eaten by the next one up the food chain, but at least you knew the rules; you knew how to behave. You knew what to expect from the next one. Not like the everyday life of humans.

They'd been away for four days already, and it was obvious that the trip had been the exact tonic they'd needed. The deepening lines in Ditiro's forehead had relaxed, and Lorato hadn't mentioned her friends at school and what they might be doing. Elizabeth had hardly thought of Tumelo at all. The only news they had was good news—Constance had registered the case, and they were due in court on Thursday, the day after tomorrow, to hear if the judge would let them proceed.

"Look, Mommy, elephants! Oh, there's a baby," Lorato said, pointing at the shoreline where a herd of four elephants drank, in the middle a baby protected by the adults.

"It's lovely. Look, Ditiro, it must have been just born. It hardly has any hair at all," Elizabeth said.

Ditiro looked across at the herd of elephants drinking. "Yes, they're nice."

He rubbed his hand along her thigh, and a spike of current pulsed though her body. The night before when Lorato was asleep in the room across from theirs in the small thatched house where they stayed, they'd made love. Not a quick rush to orgasm, but a slow feast of the body. Every inch stimulated and woken up. Hours spent rubbing, kissing, sucking, looking for new ways to find pleasure in each other. They were slowly healing and finding their way back. When they were finished, they lay wrapped in each other's arms, their minds still joined. Only then were they close enough to speak of the things they most feared.

"I'm trying so hard to get past this thing … the thought of you with him …" Ditiro had said, shaking his head, unable to finish the words. "I just can't understand why you did it."

Elizabeth had tried not to flinch at the pain of the words. Like always, the guilt had rushed in, and she'd tried to ignore it. Ditiro was opening up, and she'd wanted to help him. She'd known it would not be only forward movement in the healing of their relationship. It would be a progression and a regression, a step forward and then falling back, but they both needed to stand aside and let their emotions subside so that they could talk freely, without guilt and anger. He was letting her in, and she needed to give him everything he required to help him heal if they were ever going to get past this.

"At the time, I felt lonely and angry. I felt like you brought me here, to Botswana, and you'd abandoned me."

"And you thought he could fill that space?" he'd asked.

"No. Never. I never thought that. I don't know why I let it happen. I was angry. I was feeling lost and numb and didn't know where I'd gone, where Elizabeth had gone. Maybe somewhere in me, too, I was thinking I was punishing you. Not consciously thinking that, but I think that might have been it. I feel worst of all about that, so much guilt. What kind of person does that to someone they love? Sometimes, I think I'm flawed, unfixable, because of my mother. Maybe I can't love people properly. I think about that a lot, actually. And when I think about this, I just feel like a monster. Look what I've done to you, to Lorato—the people I love the most in the whole world. Look what I've done."

Ditiro had pulled her into his arms. "No one is perfect. We make mistakes. You aren't flawed, you're human. You do know how to love. Look at me. You love me so selflessly. Sometimes, I feel ashamed I don't give you enough in return. You're the best mother to Lorato. We are not chained to our past. Maybe your mother and what she did taught you all of the right ways to love. Maybe you are the champion of lovers because of your mother."

They'd laughed. Elizabeth had sat up on the bed and looked down at Ditiro. "I don't know how I can say this so that you can understand. What happened between Tumelo and me has no resemblance to what we have. Ditiro, you are the love of my life. You make me feel so special and beautiful, let me feel as if I am perfect just like this, this flawed person that I am. You take care of me and make me feel safe. You're so brilliant and interesting. When I dream of my perfect life, it is only with you. In that cottage away from you, my future stopped. I was living in a grey, cold present, moving one step after the other just to get through. I love you so much. Do you understand that? I feel sick I ever hurt you."

He'd sat up and kissed her deeply, pulling her into him, down onto the bed.

"I love you, too," he'd whispered with heated breath into her ear. He'd put on another condom and positioned her on top of his erection. She'd felt completed, whole. The night had given way to morning, and still, they were together, seamlessly.

"Giraffes! Giraffes!" Lorato said.

They'd seen many giraffes already, but they were Lorato's favourite. Elizabeth could see that missed birthday parties had faded far into the recesses of her daughter's mind and she was the happy child she'd always been.

Elizabeth hoped it could stay that way.

***

They were back in their little hut after a braai with the owners of the camp. Ditiro carried a sleeping Lorato to her bed just as Elizabeth's cellphone rang. She was surprised since they'd hardly had a signal since they'd arrived. Perhaps it was better at night. She picked up the phone but didn't recognise the number.

"Hello?"

"Hello," a hurried woman's voice said. "Are you Elizabeth Molosiwa?"

"Yes, who is this?"

"Listen, we need to talk. I have some important information about Tumelo Gabadirwe. It can help you. Where can we meet?" The woman was speaking fast but in a hushed whisper.

"Meet? Who are you? I can't meet you."

"What do you mean we can't meet? Listen, we have to meet. These people are not playing around. I know you've started a lawsuit against them. I have some information that can help you. Information you need."

"I'm sorry, you don't understand. I meant I can't meet you now," Elizabeth said. "I'm out of town. But I can meet you when I get back tomorrow evening."

"Tomorrow? Shit! These people have been following me. I think Tumelo told them I know. I don't want to talk on the phone, they may be tapping my phone. I need to tell you before they do something to me. Call me when you get in town. I'll let you know where to meet me."

"Okay, fine. At least, can I have your name, even just your first name?" Elizabeth asked.

"Mphoentle, my name is Mphoentle. I'll wait to hear from you."

Elizabeth put the phone back into her bag. She wondered what information Mphoentle had. Whatever it was, it must be important if the church was so interested that they would follow her and tap her phones.

"Who was that?" Ditiro asked.

"A woman. From what she said, she might be the person who helps us win this case."

***

They got back to Maun from the Delta in the late morning and boarded a flight to Gaborone. As soon as the plane landed and they were in their car heading home, Elizabeth called Mphoentle.

"Hello," someone said, but it didn't sound like the person she'd spoken with the previous night. The voice sounded older.

"Hi, is that Mphoentle?" she asked, thinking she might have the wrong number.

"No, I'm not Mphoentle. But this is her phone. She's in the hospital."

"Hospital? What happened? We were supposed to meet today."

"She was in an accident, a car accident. She's at Princess Marina. You can see her there."

A chill went through Elizabeth's body. The hospital? The young woman had sounded frightened on the phone. Could Tumelo be involved in putting her in the hospital? She knew now that he was greedy and a liar, but could he also be a potential killer? She doubted it.

But what a coincidence that the woman with the information they so desperately needed would suddenly have a car accident. Or was it Reverend Kissi trying to tidy up loose ends? She suspected the latter. As soon as she got a chance, she would go to the hospital, but first, they needed to get to court.

CHAPTER THIRTY-THREE

When they entered the court building, the defence team was already there. Ditiro was not pleased to see that they had employed the services of one of South Africa's best lawyers, George Bennet.

"So, Mr. Molosiwa, you decided to bring our war to the courtroom," Kissi said, walking up to Ditiro. He stood very near and spoke in a low voice only they could hear.

"Do we have a war?" Ditiro asked, trying to control his annoyance. "I just think it might be time for you to move along with your little horse and pony show is all, Kissi."

"Oh, you are the clever man, so full of advice. You know, my friend, I'd advise you to not worry about what I'm doing. Best you keep that whorish wife of yours on a tight rein; she really is causing you all types of embarrassment."

Ditiro knew what Kissi was trying to do; he wanted him emotional and upset before going into the courtroom so that his mind was not focussed on what it should be. He turned and walked away without saying anything. Kissi would not affect him, not today.

It was the first time he had ever seen Tumelo. The younger man wore an expensive suit he hadn't quite grown into. His hair was closely shaved though not bald. He looked at Ditiro straight on, but it was a forced stare.

He was playing at being a confident man, Ditiro could see. He was little more than a boy in men's clothing.

Who did this boy think he was? Sleeping with Ditiro's wife, causing such damage all around his family? He didn't care much for Kissi. Kissi was a foreigner, and if the case failed and they got a big settlement, Ditiro hoped he would skip the country. Mostly, he wanted him gone, out of the President's life so no more damage could be done to Botswana by their unholy alliance.

But Tumelo was a Motswana. It took a lot for a Motswana to leave the country. Unlike most other African countries, Batswana rarely lived as expatriates elsewhere. Within the borders, Tumelo would not be able to avoid Ditiro's wrath. If he was not punished by the court, Ditiro would ensure that Tumelo was punished. He would regret having messed with Ditiro's family.

Ditiro looked away reminding himself of the task at hand. He needed to be focused. He took two deep breaths in and two deep breaths out. He needed to make sure he didn't let his emotions force him to lose his head.

He sat at the table, but left Constance to do the talking. Elizabeth sat next to him nervously doodling on a pad of paper in front of her. He covered her hand with his, and she turned and gave him a weak smile. They'd not drawn the judge they wanted, but they hadn't gotten the worst one, either. Justice Warona was fair, but conservative. He didn't like making laws in the court room. If the law in question was not explicitly in the law books, Justice Warona had no time for the case. They would be walking a very thin line. Constance stood to speak.

"Your Honour, the first defendant acting in his capacity as a voice for the Church of Spiritual Revelations, the second defendant; and his servant, the third defendant, have violated our client's constitutional rights. In a public forum, the third defendant, Tumelo Gabadirwe, revealed our client's HIV status. This is in direct contradiction to Article 3 of the Constitution which ensures the right to privacy. In the forum in which this was done, the third defendant alleged that the plaintiff was HIV-positive and that she was using her status as a weapon to purposefully and, with evil and malicious intent, infect other people. These statements not only violated our client's constitutional rights under Article 3 but also Section 7, as all citizens of this country have the right to be protected from degrading and inhuman treatment. It is obvious that the defendant wanted and, in fact, succeeded in degrading our client."

The courtroom was full to capacity. There were plenty from the church, but Ditiro was happy to see other people he knew were on their side. He spotted Supt. Busang and Kagiso. He also saw some people he knew were members of HIV/AIDS NGOs in the country.

"Further to the point, our client has suffered grievous harm, both personally and financially, because of these utterances. She has been subjected to exclusion and ridicule because of the statements made by the defendant. Her reputation lies in shatters. Her family has also been affected because of the defendant's defamatory statements. Financially, her business has had to be closed and she has lost all income because of his slanderous and malicious statements. I must add, Your Honour, that not only did the defendant speak these untruths, he spoke them to a journalist and they were printed, so libel can also be argued.

"The facts are clear, Your Honour, all three defendants acting in collusion, not only violated our client's Constitutional rights, but have made statements so defamatory, to a large, very prominent gathering that included the President of this country, that our client's life lies in tatters and her reputation is ruined. We plead with the court to allow the case to proceed to trial."

Constance sat down. Ditiro leaned over and whispered, "Good job."

Kissi and Tumelo sat on the opposing bench with their high-powered advocate from South Africa, George Bennet. He was well-known for getting cases with a firm footing in law turned over for his big corporate clients. His most recent success saw him winning an eight-million-Rand case against the South African Competitions Board. The largest bread manufacturer in South Africa had been charged with colluding with other bakers to fix prices. They were charged and had been given that hefty fine, but Bennet got the judgement turned over on appeal. He was tough and intelligent, and Ditiro's hopes of success slipped a few notches when he saw him arrive.

Bennet stood up. "Your Honour, it is a fact that Mrs. Molosiwa is HIV-positive. She herself has revealed it in the national newspapers. What privacy was violated? She waived her right to privacy. But beyond that, even the Constitution of Botswana allows for the right of privacy to be bypassed if it is in the public good. In this case, my clients were of the opinion, based on what they observed, that Elizabeth Molosiwa was purposefully spreading the virus that causes AIDS in an attempt to harm as many people as possible. She had passed the virus on to one of my clients. He had no way of knowing if she intended to pass it on to others and, in fact, truly believed that she intended to do just that. He was doing the public a service by alerting people to what was going on.

"As for Section 7, inhuman and degrading treatment is subjective. In this case, Elizabeth Molosiwa passed the AIDS virus to my client without alerting him to the fact that she was HIV-positive. I argue if anyone has been subjected to inhuman treatment, it is indeed my client."

Murmurs moved through the crowd.

"If it is a truthful statement that was made, defamation falls away. Elizabeth Molosiwa is HIV-positive. It is a fact. As for the statement that she was spreading the virus around, my client believed it to be so, taking into consideration his experiences with Mrs. Molosiwa. In this case, it cannot be defamation since it is fair comment, a conclusion any reasonable citizen would come to given the circumstances at the time. Your Honour, I believe there is no case of defamation to answer to. Given this, we beg the court to throw out the case in its entirety."

Ditiro and Constance had gone through all of the arguments the defence team might come up with so they were not surprised. Still, George Bennet was a gifted speaker. Suddenly, Ditiro wasn't sure that they had enough to go forward with the case. The ground that had seemed almost firm was suddenly very shaky.

"I've heard your statements and have read over the file," Justice Warona said. "We will proceed with this case next week Tuesday. But I warn the prosecution to be thoroughly prepared. I have no intention of allowing rewriting of the laws of this country. You will present a case within the parameters of our legislation and the Constitution of the Republic of Botswana."

The court was adjourned. Ditiro gave Elizabeth a hug.

"Here we go, Lizzie. We're going to get them. I promise you we are going to get them for what they've done to you," he whispered in her ear.

"Great job, Constance," he said again. He knew how lucky he was to have her on their side.

"Thanks, boss. Tuesday is looking pretty near. I'm off to the office to get to work."

"I'll go with," he said, and turned to Elizabeth. "Are you alright?"

Elizabeth nodded. "Yes, I need to get to the hospital and try and find Mphoentle. Maybe she has something that will help us."

CHAPTER THIRTY-FOUR

Princess Marina, Gaborone's only government hospital, was a busy place. Besides the Gaborone patients, all complicated cases from the rest of the country were referred there, so it was crowded almost all twenty-four hours in a day.

Elizabeth asked at Reception and was told there was an Mphoentle in the women's ward. She'd come in quite battered up after a car crash. Elizabeth was sure it was the woman she was looking for and made her way through the passages, following the signs until she found the women's ward.

"I wonder if you can help me," she said to a tired nurse working at the desk.

She looked up from her paperwork. "Yes?"

"I'm looking for a woman named Mphoentle."

She said nothing, but pointed to a bed near the window and immediately went back to her paperwork.

The woman in the bed was much younger than Elizabeth had expected. She had bandages around her head, and her arm was in a plaster cast. One of her eyes was blackened, and there were scratches along the side of her face. Despite her injuries, Elizabeth could see she was a beautiful woman. She lay in bed awake, staring out the window.

"Hello. Mphoentle, I'm Elizabeth Molosiwa."

The younger woman turned. Her face couldn't hide she was in pain, but she seemed relieved to see her. "Yes, I know you ... from the papers. I wasn't sure you'd find me."

Elizabeth grabbed a nearby chair and pulled it close to the bed and sat down. "I called your phone and someone told me you were here, that you'd had a car accident."

"Yes, that was my mother. She took my phone. She didn't want me being disturbed by it. She thinks somehow, it will keep me from healing properly. Old people." She shook her head.

"So what happened? She said you had a car accident."

"Well, it certainly wasn't an accident, though no one seems to believe me. I was run off the road. I told the police, but since I'd been drinking, they think I'm just making up a story. But I know it was them. They'd been following me for days."

"Who?"

"The church, Reverend Kissi. You know, Tumelo and I are friends ... were friends, I guess I should say now. How could he do this to me?"

"But why would they want to kill you?" She didn't understand how a young woman like this could be so serious a threat to Kissi for him to take such risks.

Mphoentle used her good arm to try and position herself in the bed better. She moaned with pain as she moved. Once settled, she said, "They've told a nice story about you that fits with their plan. I heard all about it."

"Are you a member of the church? Were you there when Tumelo told them about me?"

Mphoentle chuckled. "No, I'm not a member of that church. I'm not that crazy. But I read about everything in the newspaper. A nice little scam Tumelo is running, but I know the truth."

"The truth?"

"Yes, the truth about Tumelo. He arrived at UB HIV-positive ... and that was two years ago, but he's trying to make it out that you gave it to him so that his story works. But I know the truth. I reminded him of that about a week or so ago. I guess I pushed it too far, asked for some bucks to keep quiet. It's not like he's suffering anyway. They're making piles of money at that place. I guess he didn't want to share. I was never going to tell, I'm nobody's martyr, but when they started following me, I knew I was doomed.

"I decided that the only way I could get free was to tell everyone the truth. Everyone. I talked to one reporter. I only told him I had some extra info on the case. I said I'd give him the whole story after I get out of this place. It will be out and they won't need to get rid of my anymore. Right?"

"Yeah ... sure." Elizabeth hoped that was the case. "So how did you know he was HIV-positive?"

"He told me. I'm also HIV-positive and was in a support group on campus. I don't hide my status. We had a few classes together; I guess he wanted someone to talk to. We became friends. I helped him get through those first weeks after he was told his status, it can be tough. Now he's trying to kill me, how's that? Some friend."

"Did he ever attend the support group?"

"No, he was too scared ... and angry. He didn't want people to know. He was pissed off that he got the virus, and I tried to tell him how the group really helped me to get through that, but he wasn't interested. Said he didn't want everybody knowing his business. He claimed Batswana can't keep a secret."

"So can I get someone to come and take your statement here in the hospital?"

"Yeah, sure ... as soon as possible, if you can. Like I said, as soon as I talk and everyone knows what I know, I'm safe. No reason to kill me then. I'm looking forward to a long life." She laughed. "I got plans. Big ones."

"And what about testifying in court? We just got a court date for next Tuesday. Your testimony could really help us."

"If I'm out of here, I'll be there. I don't have a problem. Why should I protect Tumelo now when he's organising shit like this?"

Elizabeth called Constance who said she would come straight over to take the deposition. She couldn't believe what a break this was. They were really going to get them, she knew it now. The one flaw in their argument was sorted.

As she was leaving the women's ward, she spotted Kagiso.

"Hello," Elizabeth said, rushing up to her.

Kagiso turned, surprised to see her at the hospital. "What are you doing here?"

Elizabeth explained everything about Mphoentle and her story. "It might be the big break we need in the case."

"I'm so glad. I was worried this morning in court. That Bennet made a good case." She looked at her watch. "Listen, I need to run, but I'll stop by tomorrow afternoon. We haven't talked properly in ages. But you look good, hey? Really good."

Elizabeth walked out to her car. The summer sun beat on her head, and she welcomed it. She loved her country, her Botswana. She felt finally peaceful. Because of the battle, she'd dug in and by accident had found a space for herself. The fight had forced her to stand firm and say "this is me."

In doing that, she realised she'd found so many of the things she'd been searching for—a family that wouldn't abandon her when things got rough and that instead closed in around her like the matriarchal elephants around their new-born calf. She'd found a friend, a true friend in Kagiso. And she'd found a home. Botswana had never been the problem, she realised now. She had pulled herself away from it, not the other way around. Now, she embraced the country, and it all made sense suddenly.

CHAPTER THIRTY-FIVE

Elizabeth decided to stay home with Lorato that morning for as long as she could. They were still keeping her home from school since the court case was drawing a lot of public attention. She was trying her best to keep her up-to-date with her schoolwork. They'd had a science experiment with magnets that morning and then a writing assignment.

Lorato's teacher had given Elizabeth the lesson plans for the last few weeks of school. They'd agreed if she finished the work, the school would let her proceed to Standard Two in January. She was a bright girl and had always done well, so they were sure she'd do fine even having missed the last bit of Standard One. They'd all agreed that it was best for Lorato to stay away from school. Talk was rampant, and the hope was by January, things would have calmed down.

Elizabeth had been sucked into believing that Lorato was back to normal, that the whole thing had been forgotten. The writing assignment the teacher had given for that morning was to write about what she wished for. Her heart broke when she read Lorato's writing.

I wish my dog Shumba would bring the ball back to me when I throw it.

I wish Refilwe would like me again.

I wish I could go back to school.

I wish Precious would cook another chocolate cake like the other one.

As she drove to the courthouse, she kept thinking of Lorato's words. Somewhere in the heat of her anger, her guilt had disappeared. Tumelo had used the circumstances to benefit himself. It was all about greed, in the end. Yes, she'd made a mistake, but what had come after that had been caused by someone else.

In the car, finally, Elizabeth stopped blaming herself for what was happening to her family. The fault lay with them: with Kissi and Tumelo. She only hoped that today, everything would be set right. She wasn't sure how they'd all survive if it didn't.

***

Elizabeth entered the courtroom and smiled. She was happy to see the room was crowded with her artist friends. Kutlo Oaitse and his wife greeted her at the door.

"Good luck," he said. "I know all will go your way."

She spotted Ludo Galani and Peter Ndlovu who waved at her from their seats.

She also saw the MmaDora in the crowd. Her bodyguards were at the back. The President's attendance would have caused too much attention, but he'd sent MmaDora to be his eyes and to act on his behalf in defence of their son-in-law.

When Elizabeth looked in her direction, she was suddenly busy in her handbag. Elizabeth wondered how much weight the First Lady's testimony in Kissi's defence would carry. She suspected once everything was revealed, any credibility the First Lady had would lie crumpled on the floor if she still chose to stand by Kissi.

Elizabeth couldn't help but be hurt by MmaDora's behaviour. At one time, she'd thought they were friends.

"Hi, Constance," she said.

Then she kissed Ditiro and sat down. She couldn't stop thinking about Lorato's words from the morning writing assignment. Her anger spiked again.

"Are we going to get these people?" she whispered in her husband's ear.

"Yes, we are," he said with confidence, and she felt immediately better.

She tried not to look over at the defence table as the case progressed. Constance explained to the court that they were asking for damages of six-point-five-million Pula which drew murmurs of dissent from the large group from the church. She went on to explain the many ways that the African Church of Spiritual Revelations had violated Elizabeth's constitutional rights and had destroyed her reputation in the community. She followed pretty much the same argument she had laid before the court previously.

"The defence will argue that since Tumelo Gabadirwe allegedly acquired HIV from the plaintiff, it was reasonable for him to think that she was passing the virus around in an attempt to infect other men. From that premise, they will argue that it was reasonable for them to warn the community through the use of the national media and in gatherings of several hundred people at their church.

"We have a witness who will testify, and I have submitted her deposition to the court that, in fact, not only did the church know that Elizabeth Molosiwa was not spreading HIV around, Tumelo Gabadirwe uttered a slanderous statement when he stated that she had infected him with the virus. He knew for a fact that long before he met the plaintiff, as much as two years previously, he had been tested and was fully aware that he himself was HIV-positive and had wilfully, and with intent, infected our client."

There were rustles in the crowd. Justice Warona warned that he would clear the room if order could not be maintained. The defence stood to give opening remarks and made no attempt to address the new information Constance had presented. They stuck to their statements given during the preliminary hearing.

Constance whispered to Ditiro. "Why do you think they're doing that? They must have seen the deposition. They know now that their clients have lied to them."

"I don't know," Ditiro said. It seemed very strange that Bennet chose to pretend that Mphoentle didn't exist, that her testimony would not topple their case. He tried to consider all sides of the argument, tried to see what Bennet was seeing that he wasn't, but he couldn't figure it out. He was sure something was there that he was not seeing.

***

The day was long. There was much court business to attend to before the prosecution presented their case. In the end, they adjourned for lunch before they could begin. They were going to start with Mphoentle's testimony. She'd sent Elizabeth an SMS that morning assuring her that she felt good enough to make it to court.

They ducked out to a takeaway across the street. When they got back to the courtroom, they found Kagiso waiting by the door.

"Hi, I didn't think you would be able to come. I thought you were on duty?" Elizabeth asked.

The court was filling up. Tumelo, George Bennet, and Reverend Kissi pushed past and ignored Elizabeth.

"Yeah, I am," Kagiso said. "I rushed down here to give you the news before you heard it somewhere else."

"News? What news?" Elizabeth asked.

Constance and Ditiro were delayed outside, discussing the case with one of the ex-associates who had a case in the courtroom opposite. They came up to Elizabeth and Kagiso and heard what the doctor had said.

"What's wrong, Kagiso?" Ditiro asked.

"It's Mphoentle."

"Mphoentle? Why? What's wrong? She said she was released yesterday. This morning, she said she was up to coming," Elizabeth said.

Kagiso looked away and then turned back. "She's not coming. Her mother found her in her apartment, dead. She'd been strangled."

Elizabeth stepped away from Kagiso. She felt her legs weaken. She looked at the backs of Tumelo's and Reverend Kissi's heads sitting at the table in front of the courtroom, and a shiver went through her body.

They had murdered Mphoentle. They'd taken the life of a young woman for money. That's all it was about, money. Power, but power only to get more money. Was Mphoentle's life not worth more than that? That's why their lawyer had been unconcerned by the surprise in their opening statement. They'd known there would be no witness to testify.

Had they told their lawyer that they planned to kill her? Surely not. Elizabeth couldn't believe that a young woman had been killed because of this, the young woman who'd had "plans for her life."

Tumelo turned just then, as if he sensed the drama that was taking place at the door. He looked Elizabeth in the eyes— and then, he smiled.

CHAPTER THIRTY-SIX

The case was adjourned for the day. The next morning, Constance and Ditiro continued without their key witness. At least, they had Mphoentle's deposition. The defence attempted to have it withdrawn since they now had no opportunity to interrogate the testimony, but Justice Warona allowed it.

The defence team took two days to present their defence. They had no surprises. It was basically a rehash of their opening statement. They called Kissi and Tumelo to the stand. MmaDora spoke as a character witness for both of the men.

It was difficult for Elizabeth to sit through it all, but she'd vowed she would be at the table every day, and she kept to her promise. Ditiro was proud of her for standing up to these men. The arguments were finished, and then the case was taken under consideration by the judge. They expected a ruling within a few weeks.

At least, Ditiro still had Professor Barnard's divorce to keep him occupied in the meanwhile. A few months ago, Professor Barnard's case had been like a weight around his neck. The wife was digging in, and the professor was an emotional basket case that Ditiro had to take care of. At times, he'd found himself going against his client's words because they were not in his client's best interest. Now, Barnard's case was welcome relief to keep him distracted from thinking about the decision in the case against the church and Kissi.

He knew that without Mphoentle's testimony, their case was weak. They had the deposition, but that wasn't good enough. They had no medical records to corroborate Mphoentle's assertion. The church's position was Mphoentle was nothing more than an opportunist. Though not saying it explicitly, they alluded to the assertion that Ditiro's team had paid her money for her testimony. They gave evidence that she had a long history of doing most anything for money. They had put some of her ex-lovers on the stand as witnesses.

Ditiro knew they had little chance of winning the case. Without irrefutable proof that Tumelo was HIV-positive before he and Elizabeth met, their case fell apart. He tried to keep his thoughts away from failure, though. When the verdict came, he would find it difficult to handle it. He needed to make Tumelo and Kissi pay for what they'd done to Elizabeth. Law was just, but if they lost the case, would he still be able to believe that?

If they lost, he would have failed at protecting his family, his most important role as husband and father using the tool he most respected—the law. He wouldn't be able to watch Kissi and Tumelo vindicated. The law would have let him down for the first time in his life at a time he needed it to hold its ground.

If Kissi won, HIV-positive people throughout the country would be scared. Their rights would be wiped clean as if they'd never existed. Then, revealing their status would be fine since a case of protecting the public could be made after the precedent set by this case. Unless the HIV-positive person could trace the exact path the virus had followed to their body with an irrefutable paper trail, they could be blamed for any number of social ills. It would be devastation for the movement forward HIV-positive people had made in the country.

He found it unbelievable that a man such as Kissi, one who used religion not to strengthen people, but to weaken them, who used their vulnerability to enrich himself, would have such an effect on the country. All along, he had thought Kissi would attack Botswana through the Office of the President, but instead, Ditiro had given him a way to change the very essence of the tolerant society Botswana had always been.

If Constance, Ditiro, and Elizabeth won the case, Tumelo would be shown his rightful place. Ditiro knew he hinged too much of his personal life on the case. Somehow, he believed if they won, the fact that Elizabeth had slept with Tumelo would be rubbed away as if it had never happened. It was not rational, but it was what he thought. The HIV which they never spoke about would somehow magically disappear since the affair would not have taken place. It was not sensible, but that's how it felt. And if they lost, the affair and the HIV would be there forever. A solid block of blackness that they would have to look around or over but which would always be in their sight line.

They'd found a way back together, but for him, it was a suspended way. It was an only-if way. The temporary way worked for a temporary time, but they had a lifetime together. He loved Elizabeth, but he was pretty sure he would never be able to forget what she'd done to him. It had torn up his core; such damage couldn't ever be healed completely. He held hope that if they won the case, if Kissi and Tumelo were punished, then there was someone legally responsible for everything. They would be held responsible, and they would be punished. If that happened, then Elizabeth, in his mind, was free in a way; there would be someone for his heart to blame.

His cellphone pulled him from his thoughts. "Hello."

"Good morning, Rre Molosiwa. It's Boitumelo ... from the President's office. He wanted to see if you had time today to see him."

What did the President want? They hadn't spoken in months, since the argument in his office and then the withdrawal of his business. Ditiro hoped the President wasn't going to try to convince him to drop the case against Kissi. He didn't fancy another confrontation with him, but despite everything, he still respected the man.

He set the appointment for later that day. He'd know soon enough what the President wanted.

***

Elizabeth sat on the high table of the consultation room. Kagiso had gone out to collect her blood samples. She'd had her blood taken the day before for her regular CD4 count, but had asked to see Kagiso specifically since she'd been feeling unwell.

When she had received her test results that had told her she was HIV-positive, the only thing she'd thought about was Ditiro and if she'd infected him. Once she'd known she hadn't, that had been all that mattered. Through it all, surprisingly, she'd never really thought of herself. Kagiso had explained everything and, since her viral load was always low and her CD4 count in the healthy range, she'd never had to accept the fact that one day, she would likely die from complications caused by this disease. She'd never thought more about the effect of the virus on her own body.

The stress from seeing Tumelo everyday and sitting through the testimony had taken its toll. Each day she entered the courtroom, she was reminded of what she had done. Each morning she saw Tumelo sitting defiantly at the defence table, she was angry again, the fury beating around inside of her.

As the days of the trial dragged on, she began to feel tired. Getting up was a Herculean effort each morning. At night, she tossed and turned, drenched in sweat, and during the day, her stomach was forever a problem. After the first few days of it, she'd realised something was wrong.

Kagiso came in carrying her file. She sat down on a nearby chair. "It's like you suspected. The stress has caused your CD4 count to drop. It's two-hundred-and-eighty-seven, it's very low. I think it's time to begin ARV treatment."

Elizabeth sat back in her chair as if she'd been hit. "But I thought you said it would be a long time before I needed to start ARVs?"

"Yes. Normally, HIV doesn't progress to AIDS for some time, years. But you've been under considerable stress with the separation, the fire, this case. The immune system responds to such things."

"So what happens if I wait to start? The trial will be over soon. Maybe without the stress, my immune system can recover."

"Maybe, but it will be tough."

"And if I don't build my immune system up again?"

"You'll get one of the opportunistic infections, TB, or pneumonia, or any of the other common diseases that take hold when a person's immunity is down. You'll get one disease after another and you'll eventually die."

Even though Kagiso was Elizabeth's friend, she didn't flinch in saying that. As a doctor, living and dying were part of her everyday life. It was about a solution to a problem. If it was successful, good. If it failed, you had to accept the consequences. Elizabeth understood this.

She had never thought it all through before. She would die. Before Lorato grew up. Before her daughter fell in love, got married, had her own children. She held the sides of the metal table. She didn't want to cry. She didn't want to upset Kagiso, so she did her best to be business-like. She tried not to think of herself; she tried to tell herself that she was thinking of someone else.

"So you think I should start ARVs?" she asked her.

"Yes, I do. There are side effects, but they're usually mild. Some people get nothing at all. If we leave your CD4 count to recover on its own, we may get down to numbers that are unable to recover from. It's the best thing, Elizabeth."

"So how long can I live on ARVs?"

"People are living longer and longer. Some a natural lifespan. You need to keep positive."

Elizabeth got the pills, and Kagiso explained the regime requiring her to take them at the exact time every day no matter what. A deviation could lead to resistance, which was something they needed to avoid. Elizabeth put the pills in her handbag.

She left the clinic and drove out of Gaborone. She needed some space to think and adjust to her new situation. She drove up the A1, past Phakalane and out to where the houses and building no longer were. She pulled down a side road and parked under a tree. She'd never get past this, past the affair, her mistake. Whenever she tried, another thing came crushing in on her to remind her that she was the one; she was the cause. She was the one who had caused all of this—the case, the separation, bringing HIV into their lives.

She'd always blamed her mother for committing suicide, for acting so recklessly when she had a daughter who depended on her, but had Elizabeth been any better? She could die because of the choice she'd made. It wouldn't be like she got in a car accident or drowned in the sea. Lorato would know she had contracted HIV from an affair and she'd died from it. It would be the second generation of betrayal. Elizabeth was no better than her mother, perhaps worse since she had the compounded betrayal of adultery.

Her tears flowed, and then her body was wracked by waves of emotion that pulsed like a living thing though her. She didn't want to die. She had Ditiro back now, and she didn't want to lose him. She wanted to see Lorato grow up to be a woman. She wanted to know her grandchildren.

Soon, the inside of the car became quiet again. She thought of the trial. Constance had admitted to her that their chance of winning was slim. Ditiro would never say that. At home, they tried not to talk about the case. If they did, he only spoke of it as successful. Though she knew he had to be aware of their chances, he never let her in on the fact that they might lose.

She needed Tumelo to be punished for what he'd done. Everything would have been different if only he had told her. If he had only admitted that he was HIV-positive, everything would have been completely different. He had to be held accountable for that, at least.

***

Boitumelo opened the door to the President's office; it was empty. "You can wait inside, Rre Molosiwa. The

President has been slightly delayed, but he just called to say he was on the way."

Ditiro sat down on the settee and waited. It seemed odd to be in here after so much time. When their relationship had been good, he had been in this office almost every other day. There were always issues that needed to be attended to. When Dora was drinking, the cases were many, and her father was always concerned with recent developments.

Now, it seemed a strange place. He was surprised how quickly perceptions changed. He noticed odd things. A new vase near the window. The carpet had been changed. He'd moved his pen stand to the other side of his desk to make room for a computer.

The door opened, and Ditiro stood up. The President held out his hand stiffly. Both men felt the distance that had grown between them.

"Ditiro, glad you could make time for me."

Ditiro shook his hand, but said nothing. The President sat down at his desk. He took the chair opposite.

"You must have wondered why I called you here after everything that's been going on."

"Yes, I did."

Ditiro found himself feeling strangely emotional towards the President. They'd been friends and colleagues for so long. The arguments over Kissi had led Ditiro to lose respect for him, but distance had allowed him to see things through more objective eyes. He shouldn't have been so judgemental. If indeed Rre Setlhoboko was his friend, he should have given him some leeway for mistakes. He could never know the pressures put on a man when he took up the leadership of a country. So much knowledge and so much responsibility could be debilitating. Perhaps he'd found relief in the church, and Kissi had taken advantage of that.

The President opened his desk drawer and removed a file which he handed to Ditiro.

"What is this?" he asked.

"The medical records. For the young man at the church. The man who gave Elizabeth HIV."

Ditiro looked through the file. Tumelo had had an HIV test in a government hospital in August 2008 where he'd tested positive. They were the official records. He was not sure of the legality of releasing them, but he knew if he could get the court to accept them as evidence, they would win the case.

"But why? Why are you giving me these?"

Rre Setlhoboko ran his hand over his eyes. They were dull and bloodshot. His complexion was grey, and Ditiro wondered if he was unwell.

"I spoke with Dora two days ago, the first time since she left. She told me a bit about what was going on out there in Phakalane." He shook his head. When he attempted to speak, his left cheek quivered. He hesitated, struggled to get his emotions under control. "I can't believe I handed her over to him."

"He's fooled many people."

"Yes ... well." He waved his hand as if trying to push all emotions away. "In any case, I did a bit of researching, research I should have done long ago when you tried to get me to see what kind of person Kissi was. Once I found these test results, it was like a house of cards. How could they lie about this? They used Elizabeth. I don't know why I couldn't see it. Now so many things seem obvious. I don't know where I'd gone to."

"I hope Justice Warona will allow this. I'm sure it's illegal for us to even have these records. But with the murder of our star witness, he might allow it. We're just about ready to hear judgement, any day now. We're just waiting to be called."

"I don't know. It will be up to him. I would think the evidence is compelling enough. In any case, the police have re-opened the arson case. I don't know what I was thinking. Kissi led me to believe that you had some vendetta against him, that you'd lost your mind and manufactured all sorts of things against him. He made me to believe that the arson investigation would bring up nothing, but instead would make the church and myself look bad. I thought I was doing the right thing, but with the death of that young woman, I can see Kissi has no problem with breaking any law to get what he wants."

Ditiro got up. "I think I should get this to Justice Warona before he makes his final decision."

"Yes," the President said. "Ditiro ... I just want to apologise. If I would have believed you earlier, much hurt would have been avoided. You were my friend, and I betrayed that friendship. I betrayed many people ...in many ways, I betrayed the country."

"Yes ... well—" Ditiro started.

The President interrupted him. "You saved my daughter from that man ... from me. I'll be indebted to you for some time."

"No," Ditiro said at the door. "I did that for Dora. I care about her, too."

He moved towards the door.

"And I got good news," the President said. "I'm going to be a grandfather."

"Yes, so I hear," Ditiro said. "Congratulations."

"Thanks. I think it may be time to retire. Time to let younger men like yourself take over. Not foolish old men. I'll retire and play with my grandson or granddaughter. Not a bad life, I think."

Ditiro knew the President was right; he needed to retire. His reputation was tarnished; his judgement would be questioned from now on.

He smiled sadly and said, "Yes, not a bad life at all."

***

Justice Warona would not look at the new evidence without opposing council present, so Ditiro and Constance had to wait at the courthouse for George Bennet to arrive. In tow were Kissi and Tumelo.

"Last kicks of the dying horse?" Kissi said, attempting to taunt Ditiro, who remained silent.

Ditiro stood to follow the group into Justice Warona's chambers. He was at the back. At first, he hadn't noticed that Tumelo had stopped and paused for the group ahead to enter while he waited for Ditiro and him to be alone.

Ditiro collected his files and looked up to see Tumelo standing looking at him. "What do you want?"

"How's Elizabeth?" Tumelo asked, smiling.

"Rubbish like you has no right to even ask that question," he snapped and pushed past him. "To even have her name in your mouth."

Tumelo grabbed him by the arm.

"I may be rubbish," he whispered, "but your wife certainly enjoyed the way I fucked her. Anyway, all Edomites are whores."

The room went black. Later, Ditiro couldn't say what happened. In seconds, he was on top of the younger man, on the floor; he was punching his already bloodied face while Constance pulled at him, begging him to stop. Court security finally pulled him off. He shook them free and stood away from Tumelo who lay sprawled on the marble floor. For a moment, he thought he'd killed him, but then he saw him move. Kissi helped Tumelo to his feet, holding a bloodied handkerchief to his nose.

"Go home," Constance ordered. She tried to contain her fury at his irresponsibility. "This doesn't help our case. You need to go home to Elizabeth. I'll call you when the judge makes a decision. I expect the boy will press charges, so be ready."

Ditiro stumbled to the car. He was embarrassed with himself. He couldn't believe he'd let Tumelo have the power to push him to act in such a way. He would go home and wait, as Constance had said. He was a liability, not an asset.

***

Lorato and Elizabeth sat at the table, their heads down over a colouring book, each colouring one side of the two-page spread. Precious was kneading bread on the counter. He could smell oxtail cooking on the stove. He stood a moment watching them.

"Daddy, look, I'm colouring Mickey Mouse." Lorato held up the colouring book for him to see.

"Yes, you certainly are. He's beautiful. I've always thought Mickey needed purple ears," he said.

"Purple's my favourite colour."

"Yes, I know, Pumpkin."

Elizabeth looked up, and when she saw the blood on his shirt, she jumped to her feet. "What happened, Ditiro?"

"Nothing, I'm fine. I'll tell you later." He set his briefcase down and took her in his arms. "Nice to come home."

"Are you sure you're okay?" She looked him up and down to check for wounds or missing parts.

"I'm fine. I'm going to take a shower."

He went to their room and got out of his dirty clothes. The shower felt great. It began to wash away his guilt at behaving so badly at the courthouse. By the time he got out from under the warm water, he felt almost happy he'd punched Tumelo. He'd deserved it; actually, he deserved much worse. But Ditiro did regret not having the opportunity to hear what the judge had to say about the submission. He hoped, too, his behaviour wouldn't affect the case in some way.

He dug out a pair of shorts and a T-shirt from the wardrobe. Just as he pulled the T-shit over his head, the cell phone rang. He quickly found it among his clothes on the floor.

"Hello, Constance? How did it go?" He listened for some time. "Okay, great. We'll talk tomorrow then. Thanks for taking care of business."

***

He could see Lorato out in the garden swinging. Precious was pushing her, and Shumba was running forward and backward, barking at Lorato's feet. Lorato's head was thrown back laughing. Elizabeth stood at the sink peeling carrots.

Ditiro took her around the waist and pushed his face into her hair.

She turned around in his arms. "So, ready to tell me what happened?"

"Okay. I punched Tumelo in the face."

"Where?"

"At the courthouse. Constance and I were there." He went on to explain how he'd been called to the Office of the President and about the test results.

"Have you spoken to Constance to find out what the judge decided?"

"Just got off the phone with her." He smiled.

"So?"

"The judge looked over the documents but felt it didn't add anything to his deliberations."

Elizabeth's face fell. "Why? I would think that would decide everything."

"No, in fact, he'd already made a decision. He decided since all parties were there, he'd read the decision right then."

She moved away from him and leaned against the counter, holding it with her hands, steeling herself for the news. "And? What did he decide?"

"He decided that yes, they had violated your Constitutional rights, both Section 7 and Article 3."

Elizabeth could feel her legs shaking. She held the counter harder to steady herself. "And defamation?"

"Yes. He also decided in our favour on defamation."

She hesitated. "And ... damages?"

He smiled. "Seven-point-eight-million Pula."

CHAPTER THIRTY-SEVEN

They'd driven back to the office in silence. Once the car stopped, Reverend Kissi jumped out. He told the driver to wait, he wouldn't be long. Tumelo watched him rush into the building and up to his office. He followed him.

Inside the office, Reverend Kissi had the safe open. On the floor were two open suitcases. Kissi dropped wrapped bundles of money—US dollars, Euros, and Pounds into the two cases.

"What's happening?" Tumelo asked.

"What's happening is you fucked up," Kissi replied while scooping the cash into the suitcases.

"So what's with the money?"

"I'm out of here. The gig is over." Kissi continued pulling piles of money from the safe and dropping them into the cases on the floor.

"What do you mean? What about the church? The conference centre?" Tumelo asked. "What about appealing the decision?"

The suitcases were full, and Kissi bent down and snapped them shut. He picked up one with each hand. "Wake up! This is over. We need to pay that woman seven-point-eight-million Pula. On top of that, I have a feeling the tide has changed ... the police may be onto things, as well."

"Onto what things?"

"The fire, that friend of yours ..."

"But you told me you weren't involved in those things."

Kissi laughed. "Yeah, okay. Listen, I'm out of here. You better make a plan for yourself. I wouldn't stick around too long. They're going to want to prosecute someone."

He unlocked a drawer in the desk and dug through it, pulling out passports. Tumelo saw a US one, EU, and Australia. He couldn't see the others, but there were seven in total.

"Okay, I'm gone. Good luck."

Kissi opened the door and rushed down the stairs. Tumelo went to the window and saw him push the suitcases into the back seat of the waiting car and climb in after them. He watched the car as it pulled out of the parking lot and onto the Western bypass.

Tumelo watched until he couldn't see anymore and then slumped onto the sofa near the window. Now what was he supposed to do?

Maybe he could stay and run the church. He wasn't involved in the fire or the murder. Kissi had said Mphoentle was drunk; that's why she'd crashed the car. When she was found dead, he'd only said, "Well, that's helpful. Must have been one of her many lovers."

He couldn't go home to Mochudi, and he was done with the university. He sat on the sofa, his hands at his sides, and could think of nothing. As young as he was, and yet, his future had come to a dead end. His bright, shiny future was no more. After all of this, could he work as a waiter at Game City? Would he cope as a security guard at some wealthy man's house?

He didn't know how long he'd been sitting when he heard the loud feet climbing the staircase to the office.

The door was still hanging open from when Kissi had left. Three police officers came through the door.

"Tumelo Gabadirwe?"

"Yes, that's me," he said, still sitting.

The police officers came forward, and he stayed sitting. They pulled him to his feet.

"Tumelo Gabadirwe, you're under arrest for aggravated assault for the knowing transmission of HIV."

He heard the click of the handcuffs as they were fitted on his hands.

"Where's Reverend Kissi?" the tall, scar-faced police officer who seemed to be the boss asked.

Tumelo thought for a moment. Where did his loyalty lie? In the end, Kissi had given him a life he had always dreamed of. It had ended, but Kissi wasn't entirely to blame for that. Tumelo should have told him that he had given Elizabeth HIV. They likely would have gone ahead with the sermon, but Kissi would have known how to stop up the leaky holes before it was too late. And even if Kissi had asked him to run with him wherever he was off to, Tumelo wouldn't have gone. Botswana was his home. He had no interest in leaving it.

"So? Where's Kissi?" the policeman asked again.

"He said he was tired. He went home to Phakalane."

He wasn't sure how much time that would buy the Bishop, but he hoped it would be enough. Enough for him to hop on a plane to Joburg with one of his many passports and then at OR Tambo pick the first outgoing flight to anywhere but Africa. By the time the police found out Kissi was not in Phakalane, he'd already be a ghost.

CHAPTER THIRTY-EIGHT

They turned all of the lights off and sat in the dark.

"Oooo ... this is nice," Lorato said.

Ditiro and Elizabeth sat on the sofa watching the coloured lights on the Christmas tree blink off and on while Lorato worked on putting a puzzle together on the floor in front of the tree.

Elizabeth thought how far away all the badness seemed. It was less than two years ago that she'd made a decision that just nearly destroyed everything, and now, they sat in the dark all together, in the glow of the Christmas lights, a family once again.

They were not fixed. It was not rubbed away; residuals still lingered. People always asked others: if you could do it all over again, would you do it differently? Elizabeth wasn't sure how she'd answer that question. It was terrible. She had to live with this virus like a time bomb in her blood, but two years ago, she'd taken all her gifts for granted. Now sitting in her house watching her daughter put a puzzle together, holding her husband's hand, there was nothing more important. Perhaps she had to learn that lesson the hardest way for her to understand it completely. For that, she was thankful.

The doorbell rang, and Ditiro got up to answer it.

Lorato held up a difficult puzzle piece. "Where does this one go, Mommy?"

Elizabeth slipped to the floor to help her daughter. Ditiro came back with Dora.

She got up to hug her. "Dora, I didn't know you were back."

"Last week. My father called and told me Kissi was gone, likely never coming back since charges waited for him. I knew it was safe to come back home."

Her stomach jutted out from the T-shirt she wore. Elizabeth expected she was about seven months pregnant now.

Dora dug about in her big handbag. "Father Christmas gave me something to deliver."

Lorato jumped to her feet. "Is it for me?"

Dora handed her the present wrapped in gold foil paper with a red ribbon. "Yes, I believe it is."

"Can I open it, Mommy?" Lorato asked, knowing presents under the tree were waiting for Christmas morning.

"Sure," Elizabeth said.

They sat down and watched Lorato open the jewellery-making set. She immediately started stringing the big plastic beads on the thick string.

"I'm going to make a necklace for you," she told Dora.

"Okay, great," Dora said, then she turned to Elizabeth and Ditiro. "So I heard the young man is in jail."

"Yes," Ditiro said. "They're charging him with aggravated assault since we don't have laws on the intentional passing of HIV. He's being investigated for the burning down of the cottage and the murder of his friend."

"And Kissi goes free ..." Dora said, shaking her head.

"Yes, well, at least he's been uncovered for who he really was. All the Gaborone big wigs are feeling a bit embarrassed handing over their hard-earned cash to a thief," Ditiro said.

"Including my parents, but they'll get over it. Did you get any of your settlement?"

"Quite a bit, actually. They sold off some of the property at the airport, and there was still money in the accounts when they froze them. But the money honestly doesn't matter. It was about trying to get justice more than anything else," Elizabeth said.

"Besides, the case didn't do the law firm any damage. We now have more work than ever. I've managed to hire back all of my associates and a few more," Ditiro said.

"So when's the baby due?" Elizabeth asked.

"February. My parents are even more excited than I am."

Lorato jumped to her feet. "Are you having a baby?"

"Yes, I am."

"Okay." She sat back down, busy again with her necklace. Then she looked up once more. "When it's born, will you bring her here so I can play with her?"

Dora laughed.

"Yes, I will certainly do that, Madam Lorato." Dora suddenly became serious. "I wanted to thank you again, Ditiro. I wouldn't have got out of there without you."

"All I did was give you a lift to the airport."

"Still, it was important. Thanks." She stood up. "I need to get going. You know my mother and the holidays; Christmas Eve is the worst. Everybody must be on time and ready to eat their weight in Christmas cookies."

Ditiro and Elizabeth walked her to the front door.

"Wait! Wait!" Lorato came running up to the door. "Dora, you forgot your necklace."

She handed her a necklace with a blue and white bead pattern.

"Thanks, Lorato. I think I'll wear it just now." She tied it on to her neck. "How does it look?"

"Great," Lorato said. "And here." She held up a shorter version of the necklace. "This is for your baby."

Everyone laughed.

"How thoughtful," Dora said.

Elizabeth and Ditiro stood on the stoop watching Dora drive away. It was a hot evening, the air still, and the cicadas cried in the trees. She felt Ditiro's arm around her waist and could hear Lorato explaining to Shumba the kind of necklace she was making for him, and, finally, Elizabeth felt that safe, beautiful circle close around her.

The End

OTHER BOOKS BY LOVE AFRICA PRESS

Fine Wine by Emem Bassey

Her Golden Eyes by Holly March

Be My Valentine: Volume Two

Love and Hiplife by Nana Prah

Bound to Liberty by Kiru Taye

CONNECT WITH US

Facebook.com/LoveAfricaPress

Twitter.com/LoveAfricaPress

Instagram.com/LoveAfricaPress

www.loveafricapress.com

LOVE AFRICA
PRESS
African Love Stories